GREAT
SEXPECTATIONS

BOOKS BY KRISTEN BAILEY

THE CALLAGHAN SISTERS SERIES

Has Anyone Seen My Sex Life?

Can I Give My Husband Back?

Did My Love Life Shrink in the Wash?

How Much Wine Will Fix My Broken Heart?

Am I Allergic to Men?

KRISTEN BAILEY

GREAT SEXPECTATIONS

bookouture

Published by Bookouture in 2022

An imprint of Storyfire Ltd.
Carmelite House
50 Victoria Embankment
London EC4Y 0DZ

www.bookouture.com

ISBN: 978-1-80314-478-8
eBook ISBN: 978-1-80314-477-1

For my little sister who gifted me my first
sex toy at the age of twenty-one.
Thank you.

ONE

'I don't get it.'

'What don't you get?' I ask my good friend, Tina, as I dip my finger in a bowl of icing. She slaps my hand away.

'Why would you sell a dildo that smells like strawberries?'

A waiter nearby stops in his tracks. I think he wants to know the answer to that question too. Yes, that's my business, I sell dildos. Yes, they smell fruity. Tina's husband, Brett, stirs a sauce, laughing to himself.

'People like scented stuff,' I reply plainly.

'Old ladies like scented stuff. I'm OK with a scent-free dildo.'

'When we were at school, kids used to get scented stickers. We used to swap them. Everyone went crazy for them!'

Tina turns her nose up to have to think that far back. 'Does the dildo taste of strawberries?'

'I'm not sure. I've not tried it.'

'Tried, as in you've not stuck one in your mouth or not tried it in other ways?'

I open my eyes widely. 'That's not my job at the company.'

'Are you telling me that *is* a job?'

'We have a testing panel at The Love Shack. We give them freebies and they tell us if they're any good.'

'How many years have I known you and your family, Josie Jewell, and you're telling me this now?' Tina jokes, shaking her head while a man that's rolling sushi next to her blanches with confusion and scuttles away to pretend to get something from the fridge. I watch as Tina opens an oven and her husband hands her a fish slice.

'You want to join a sex toy testing panel? I will pretend not to be insulted,' Brett mutters.

'We can use them together? Can we join, Josie? Is there an interview process?'

I watch the both of them. I've known Tina and Brett since school. Brett was in my year, Tina was in my brother's, and it was a wonderful convenience that they married each other so we all can continue to be friends in our mid-twenties. However, whilst I love them dearly and I'm godmother to their twin sons, I don't really want to imagine their sex life in too much detail.

'I'll see. Are those what I think they are?' I ask, trying to change the subject, leaning against the counter and commenting on what's just come out of the oven.

'Yes, they are. They are cheese straws that have been made to look like severed fingers,' Brett tells me.

'What's the nail?'

'It's a bit of ham. There are vegan versions too that we hacked off the hands of dead vegans. They go very well with the sundried tomato dip so they look like blood.'

I nibble at one curiously as they both look over for my verdict. For tonight's Halloween party, Brett and Tina have pulled out all the stops: all the food is themed and they and all their staff are dressed as werewolves, wearing orange suits like they've escaped from a high-security prison. It's a very good crossover of genres. I'd watch that film, but maybe from behind a cushion and with someone else in the room.

'These are good. Is that Parmesan?' I ask.

'The lady assumes correctly. It makes them look more gnarly,' Brett tells me.

'I am impressed at your commitment to authenticity.'

'Well, I am insulted you'd think we'd take on this gig and be complete amateurs about it, just bung out a few bowls of Monster Munch. We do this shit right,' Tina replies.

I don't doubt that for a second. I've known Brett from his Jamie Oliver fanboy days, when he idolised the shaggy-haired Essex chef, determined to follow in his footsteps. Back then, we were eighteen and he was the one who made the breakfasts as we all clambered back to my mum and dad's after a night out. He'd introduce us to chorizo in our eggs, not that we'd notice, we just needed something to soak up the cider in our systems. Now look at him, he has the matching chef wife, he's wearing a chef's bandana with his werewolf sideburns, and can chop things super-fast.

I look over the counter as people pour in and out of the kitchen with platters and Brett directs them around. There is a torso made of cheese and covered in charcuterie so it looks like flayed flesh. This worries me not as I dig into some Parma ham, a bottle of beer in my other hand.

'You should be out there with the party, Josie, not in here hoovering up my canapés,' Brett says, pointing a furry hand out the door.

I screw my face up. 'It's loud. It's all happy house music that I don't understand and people in scary masks so I don't understand what they're saying. There's a man out there who asked me to hold his glass and I thought he said arse.'

'Did you hold his arse?' asks Tina.

'There may have been light cupping.'

Tina laughs. 'Someone take out these jelly shots now before they melt,' she yells, arranging jelly worms into them. 'Go out and do party stuff or I'll tell your mum,' she orders me.

'You wouldn't,' I retort.

'I would, especially if you're going to eat all my food.'

'But... I'm like the project manager, I'm overseeing every-thing so the party runs smoothly. I have to keep an eye on the alcohol levels and the coats. Without me back here comman-deering the ship, the party would fail.'

Brett nods, not really falling for my spiel, but the truth is, I grabbed a man's arse out there and now I'm petrified his girl-friend will come after me with her razor-claw manicure.

'At least make yourself useful, pound something for me,' Brett says.

'Brett, I've known you for years, but that would be a turning point in our friendship. Plus, I know your wife. I was at your wedding. I made a speech.'

'Wise-ass. Pound the basil for our spooky pesto drizzle. It was a good speech, though.'

'It was a good wedding,' I say, picking up some pine nuts and basil.

'Less talking, more pounding.'

'You sound like porn.'

We all giggle. The man rolling the sushi doesn't get it, though.

'Excuse me, are you Josie?' a girl suddenly asks me, dressed like a bewitched doll. Unless she actually is a bewitched doll, in which case, don't kill me and take my soul. Please.

'I am.'

'Your mum is trying to call you. She called Sonny, but he's chatting to people and it's his party and he told me to come and find you. He said you'd be hiding in here.'

That's because he's my brother and he knows what I do at parties. I'm either hiding in here or in the toilet.

'Did she say what it was about? Was it an emergency?' I ask.

'It was something to do with your dad? Maybe?'

I drop my pestle. Or my mortar. I've never worked out

which is which, but even so this countertop is granite so it survives the trauma.

'Did he fall off the roof trying to put that glow-in-the-dark witch on top of the garage?'

A few people in the kitchen turn to look at me as I raise my voice. Dad was adamant that he could do it himself, but he's approaching sixty and it was windy and that thing required drilling into hooks, not the gaffer tape approach that he had in mind. He's broken his back, hasn't he?

Brett puts a hand to my shoulder to calm me down. 'Call her, Josie. Go.'

'I'll be back.'

'To commandeer the ship, yep... whatever. Ring your mum. And this is a party. Get drunk, dance, snog a stranger,' Tina tells me.

I don't take any of that in. Instead, I grab my phone from my pocket and head for the door. As I open it, I swerve around a man carrying a cauldron. Of soup? Is he ladling that into people's mouths? I stumble back as the music hits me like a wave of warm air, and I start milling through the crowd of sexy cats, sexy witches and sexy vampires, watching as a man takes out his fake fangs to take in a blini.

From a crowd of people at the door, I see my brother, Sonny, and give him a wave. He puts his hands to his face to make a phone shape and mouth the word, Mum. He doesn't seem overly panicked, so maybe Mum's lost Dad in the supermarket again, which isn't a worry as she knows to head directly to the bakery. He will be there feeling up the baguettes and complaining they're too hard for his teeth.

I head for a staircase and immediately hit dial as I climb away from the noise, waiting.

'Josie! I'm on video,' Mum finally answers.

Mum's only on video because she's being nosey and doesn't

want to feel like she's missing out tonight. I swerve my phone around to face me, jogging up the stairs as I do.

'Stop moving, you look like you're on one of those ghost-hunting shows.'

'I'm getting away from the noise. Mum, are you dressed up?'

I find a spare bedroom and close the door behind me. On screen is my mother. She's mainly boobs, corsetry and a strong red lip, but she obviously lied earlier on, telling me she was off to town to have a coffee with a mate because she's had a blow-dry and a manicure too. Still, I applaud the effort and smile broadly just hoping she's not FaceTiming me from the driveway.

'I am. It's for the kids who visit. No one likes the houses where people answer the doors in their dressing gowns and don't make a fuss. What's it like there? Is it good? Is everyone having fun?'

I was under strict instructions from Sonny not to have our parents here tonight because as much as we love them dearly, they are a distraction. Not in a terrible way, just in a way that we must babysit them because they get drunk and loud and Cossack dance without any shoes and have to be driven to A&E to get shards of a smashed shot glass removed out of their feet (Dad, Sonny's twenty-first birthday).

'It's plenty fun, just very loud. Lots of Sonny's media mates, not many people I know.'

'That's your problem, Josie... you never mingle. Anyone cute?'

'I wouldn't know, they're all in masks and make-up. Anyway, I was told to call you, something about Dad. It wasn't an emergency then?' I ask as I try to look over her shoulder.

'Oh, you know when I bought the Haribo and the lollies and you hid them so your dad wouldn't eat them all, where did you hide them?'

'In the cupboard with the muesli. He doesn't go near the thing.'

'You're so smart, my lovely girl.'

I laugh, loving that this is the purpose of this phone call.

'Where is Dad? Was everything OK with the witch on the garage?'

'Oh, all good. He called in some boys from the warehouse to help. He's just upstairs putting some touches to his hair before our curry arrives.'

Do I adore how my parents have dressed up tonight for a curry at home and to put on a show for all the kids in the neighbourhood? I do. Do I worry slightly that they will keep the costumes on for other shenanigans? Yes, I do – especially when one of them is a rental.

My eye catches something behind my mum as she stands at our front door decked out in cobwebs and LED ghost lights. 'Mum?'

'Yes, Josie.'

'Is that bowl of condoms behind you?'

'It is. Trick or Treat?'

'Mum. One... Who exactly are you expecting at the door? And two... What is the trick?'

Mum cackles, winking at me.

No, please don't tell me your sex tricks because I've had some green Halloween themed cocktail and I might be ill.

'Well, you know what it's like round here. We get the very cute kiddies in their witch dresses, and they'll get my Haribo, but occasionally you get a teen on the blag with a shopping bag so he can have a contraceptive and a telling-off from me. It's called care in the community.'

'It's called people in the community referring to our home as the condom house. What will the neighbours think?'

'I don't care. I just care about kids coming to my door asking for money, Josie. They're awful. Anyways, it's all on theme.

They're part of our Halloween merchandise. They glow in the dark.'

'I know, Mum. I ordered them in. Safety first,' I reply.

Mum cackles again. The term cackle doesn't really define it very well. It's not witchy in any way. Her laugh is full of joy, warmth yet significant volume. Dad has often said we could place her on the shore and she'd help boats find safe harbour.

'You did a very good job ordering these. I knew there was a reason we put you in charge of the business. Your father and I never thought seasonally. These are cute,' she says, holding one to the air. 'Do they do Christmas ones?'

'Yes, they have mistletoe packaging, so you can hold them over your doo-dahs for that special festive moment.'

'You can say the word penis out loud with me, you know? We run a highly successful sex toy business, JoJo. Doo-dahs is not good business lingo.'

'Well, how about you can hold them over your candy cane?' I reply in a posh advertising voice.

'Your Christmas cracker?' she retorts.

'The ultimate stocking filler...'

'Look at our marketing genius... And people say we're not alike...' she says, beaming at me. We're not, but somehow it works. 'Anyway, get back to the party. Don't mind me. Also, explain your outfit to me again?' she asks. 'I thought you were going as a cat.'

'You left me out a skin-tight PVC jumpsuit, I was thinking practically about not sweating to death and having to wee.'

'But that's also a jumpsuit,' she says, pointing to my outfit.

'But look at all the room I have to dance and high-kick and stuff.'

For some reason, I high-kick. Doing so, I knock over a lamp. Crap. I pick it up and rearrange it on the side table, hoping it's not expensive.

I hear Mum giggling. 'You look like a welder.'

'I'm a Ghostbuster, Mum. It's Halloween. Ghosts, spooky things... The man who brought the ice sculptures really liked it.'

'In that he flirted with you and poured you a drink?'

No, in that he high-fived me and knew what film I was from. I'll take that as a win.

'The party is jam-packed with sexy versions of Halloween clichés. I look original and cool.'

'And like you're about to fix a blocked drain. What's Ruby wearing?'

Ruby is my brother's girlfriend and together they are hosting tonight's Halloween party in their North London home. Both of them star in a reasonably popular soap on the television, so they have this middling level of celebrity which means they do everything to a certain level of excess – from the food, to Freddy Krueger making Halloween-themed shots and a troll-shaped ice luge serving vodka.

'Ruby's gone full Maleficent. She even has horns and some sort of prosthetic so her cheeks look chiselled.'

'Get pictures, I bet she looks stunning.'

'She looks stunning because she did a three-day cleanse to get in that dress.' I did not do a cleanse. I basically did the opposite of a cleanse because I knew I could get away with it.

'Ruby was telling me about the DJ.'

'Yes, he's very famous and dressed like Pennywise the clown. I met him on his way out of the toilet. I was so scared, I may have done a little wee.'

Mum laughs. 'You idiot. I'm going. Have a lovely night, my gorgeous JoJo. Pics please and all the goss, yeah?'

'Yes. Please don't give out those condoms to people at the door. Mum?'

She doesn't reply but blows kisses in my direction before hanging up.

Oh dear. I should perhaps ring Dad to make sure. I lower

myself to sit on the floor, backing myself against a wall next to a side table.

My parents both adore Halloween. My mother's pièce de résistance was when she dressed us as the Addams Family. She got a photographer and that portrait sits in Dad's office. I was a very authentic Wednesday. When I left the house earlier, Dad was arranging his ornately carved pumpkins down the drive, and as I got in my car, he did his best BWAHAHA at me before I reminded him that he couldn't scare me because I'd picked up his costume from the shop. He wanted full vampire. Not modern *Twilight* or *Lost Boys*, he wanted a suit with a velveteen cape and a red waistcoat and not those bargain teeth that would hurt his dentures. *I want to be classy, Josie. Sinister but alluring. Bit of leather.* I told Dad we could get leather from work; we have racks of the stuff. *Not that sort of leather, JoJo.* And he laughed. *I get enough stick from that knob-end down the road for the height of my hedges. Last thing we need is me answering the door to his kids in a gimp mask.*

That said, scouting the fancy-dress shops for vampire-wear meant I managed to find this beauty of a Ghostbusters costume. It's not hugely flattering, but it means today, I can dance freely, bundle my long brown hair on top of my head, throw on some Doc Martens and not have to totter around in heels. I also have pockets. For my keys, the odd sweet in case I get hungry, and hell, I may have nabbed a few of those Halloween condoms for myself. There have to be perks to my job. The costume even came with a proton pack so I can zap ghosts. I pick up the end of it and practise some gun-slinging moves from the corner of the room. This is a slightly sad if properly geeky wet dream moment. 'Don't cross the streams,' I whisper in my best American accent.

My moment suddenly comes to a halt as two people: sexy cat (nice tail) and sexy zombie man (where's your face?) swoop drunkenly into this spare bedroom and, well, they throw it down in a frenzied mass of limbs and saliva.

Hello? I'm here. Should I just say something? Or cough?

I back myself into the shadows, behind a heavy jacquard curtain, a little unconvincingly as my proton pack is quite bulky. I watch as they snog each other avidly and with sound effects. The sort you'd hear if someone was eating hot soup.

'Fuck me...' she purrs.

Oh dear. No. Not when I'm in the room, Sexy Cat Lady. Put your feline things away. Maybe I should laugh this off. Pretend I'm lost. Or throw them one of my Halloween-themed prophylactics. They glow in the dark. I also have one that's toffee-apple-flavoured.

'I want to eat you so bad...' replies Zombie Face.

Oh, dear. It's Halloween themed porn. Unless he's an actual zombie then this could get messy and I think those cushions are cashmere. Either way, I do not want to bear witness to any it. Just close your eyes, Josie. It's a quickie. They'll be done in mere minutes. That said, she needs to get those super-skinny wet-look leggings and thigh length boots off, and that will take a while and perhaps some talc.

'Now get on all fours like a good cat...'

That's a better line, if predictable. But I do not need to see this. And please don't get out your... Zombie phallus.

As soon as he undoes his flies, for some reason, I cover my ears. I could just curl up in a ball here and rock on the spot? Instead, I crawl towards the door in stealth Ghostbuster mode. If you snog that loudly, there will be sound effects for anything that follows that may infect my eardrums. I edge towards the door and reach up for the handle. Maybe, just maybe, I'll...

'Who the hell are you?' I suddenly hear a voice say.

Busted. Ghost-busted.

I spring to my feet. Do I turn?

I turn, which was the wrong thing to do as neither of them

seem to have any shame that they're about to have sex in a stranger's house. This could be my nan's bed. As soon as I see nipples, I clench my eyes shut and just stand here, not really knowing how to proceed.

'I'm Josie.'

'Are you leaving or joining in, Josie?' the man says, snickering.

The colour drains from my face, my legs turn to jelly and I desperately turn and pat down the door. 'Umm, not joining... I just... I was sitting in the corner of the room and you came in and...' I have no spatial awareness at all. I flick the lights on and off about four times looking for the door handle.

'We can take this somewhere else if this is your room?' the man asks.

'Oh, well... no. It's not my room. Not my house. You crack on... I am going to leave. There's an en suite there as well, should you need to use it, or...'

Suddenly, I'm also an excellent hostess. Maybe I should get them towels? Breakfast choice menus. I can hear them laughing as I finally find the handle to the door, open it into my face and get my proton pack stuck in the gap. I can actually hear their relief that I've chosen not to join in this threesome else someone gets injured.

I close the door and rest my forehead against it.

'Who the hell was she?' remarks Zombie Man, amidst inebriated, mean-spirited laughter. A part of me wishes I had the gall to march on in there and tell them to take their naked shenanigans out of my brother's house, but no, as soon as I hear more sex sounds, I stumble back and land quite elegantly on the floor. On my back. I'm really not my mother's daughter in that way, I'm not like that at all.

TWO

I should have gone into house music production. It's basically bass, three notes and a whirring noise like an airplane taking off. It rings in my ears as I lie on the floor of this corridor, spinning my body round my proton pack like an upside-down tortoise trying to roll over. This is elegance personified.

I twist over onto my knees, exhaling loudly. This is why I don't do parties. At university, I was a 'drinking in my room/quiet house party' sort of person, the occasional night out. I'm not dull per se, but I'm not the person swinging off the chandeliers in her knickers at 5 a.m. That was always my friend, Lucy. She did get caught in the chandelier once. I was the one who went in the shed to get a ladder and some wire cutters so we could release her.

'Stantz?' a voice says, while I'm still in this dark corridor, squatting on the floor. This isn't suspicious. Or sexy. Still, whoever just identified me wins points. They know I'm Dan Aykroyd from *Ghostbusters* and because of that I like them instantly.

I rise from my knees and push myself up, brushing the loose

hair away from my face. When I glance up, I look the person up and down and grin immediately.

'Wow, Spengler,' I say pointing at him.

The man in front of me has stolen my Ghostbuster look completely, though I do believe his proton pack has been made with some parcel tape, an old hoover hose and a rucksack. It's basic but adorable. He carries two bottles of beer and smiles back. Man, that's a good smile.

'You're drinking on the job?' I tell him.

'Says she who was literally crawling along the floor.'

'I could sense a supernatural disturbance in the ground, I was just... you know, connecting to it...'

He nods. 'Ghostbusting never stops. Not even for parties...'

'I mean, it's Halloween... Technically our busiest night of the year.'

'True.'

I am trying to work out if he's good-looking and why the conversation flows so nicely. Are those glasses prescription? Because they're hella cute with his blue eyes. I like the Nike Blazers, the dimples and ruffled curl to his dark hair. He looks like he belongs in Bastille – the band, as opposed to the French prison. I like his commitment to the costume, the Ghostbusters logo that's been drawn on with a Sharpie.

'While you were down there, you didn't happen to see any cats, did you? I've lost my girlfriend.'

I pause for a moment. Girlfriend totally negates anything I may have thought about him. Shame.

'She was with my mate who's dressed as a zombie. I've completely lost them.'

My gaze shifts to the door right behind me and I have no idea what to do. Obviously, it could be a different zombie and cat, they're ten for a penny round here. Or indeed, his girl-friend might be right behind that door noshing off his pal. I don't even know this guy, but I don't want him to see that, not here, at my brother's party. We Ghostbusters have to stick together.

'It's a pretty big house. Have you tried down this corridor? The mezzanine looks over the living room,' I say, leading him away from the door. Come with me, let's distract you for a moment, just in case.

He follows and hands me one of the bottles of Corona in his hands. 'Here, have this before it goes warm.'

I accept and clink the top of the bottle against his.

'I'm only Stantz at the weekends, people also call me Josie,' I say.

'Cameron, a pleasure. So how come you know your way around this house?' he asks me.

'Oh, I've been here before...'

'Do you work here?'

I giggle a little under my breath. 'You could say that...'

Yes, you could call being Sonny's little sister work. I still have to remind him to do his taxes and get his gutters cleaned, but I helped choose this house when he got his first ridiculous pay cheque for an acting gig. There was me looking at whether the roof had been insulated; he literally signed the contract based on the fact there was a gym and a toilet that could wash his butt for him.

'It's off the chain, no? A friend on the soap invited me. They're putting stuffed lychees in the drinks to make them look like eyeballs. I think I saw Idris Elba downstairs dressed as Hannibal Lecter. I was like, do I take a selfie or try to be cool and get him to be my best mate...?'

The excitement simmers off him and it's totally endearing because that is Idris – him and Sonny play in a five-a-side football team together. I don't say that out loud, though.

At the end of the corridor, we walk around the balcony and it's a perfect way to take in the party and survey the throng of people hidden in the mist of the smoke machines.

'They wasted money on the fancy DJ, though. Who has a Halloween party and doesn't play "Thriller"?' he says, scanning the room for his girlfriend and pal, who are obviously not there.

'Or indeed our very own *Ghostbusters* theme tune,' I add.

'Right? In the perfect party, you'd actually do the "Thriller" dance too.'

'Like in that film...'

'*13 Going on 30.*'

I stop for a moment, realising that he gets my film reference.

He beams. 'I guess you're silent because you think I'm sad, but I'm a film geek, I watch it all, romcoms too. I have encyclopaedic knowledge about these things.'

I hold a hand to the air. 'Fellow film geek, plus I know the "Thriller" routine too.'

'Prove it,' he challenges.

'We've literally just met...'

'You're Stantz, I'm Spengler. What do you mean? We've been friends for years.'

I look down and smirk to myself. I know I said this jumpsuit afforded me some level of dance freedom, but if he wants me to do that right here and right now, then I will not look cool. At all. I twitch my shoulder, though, and that makes him laugh, I hope with me, as opposed to at me.

A werewolf suddenly appears next to us, holding a platter of sushi shaped like little jack-o'-lanterns.

'You all right, Josie?' the werewolf asks me, animatedly.

I peek through the mask. 'Yeah, I'm cool, Charlie. That's a good look.'

Cameron watches the interaction, helping himself to a couple of pieces of sushi. I'd take more than that – it's the good stuff. I signed the order on the salmon, it was literally in the water eight hours ago.

'My mum said it was an improvement. It is mad here. Proper mad. Drink later?'

'Of course...' I fist-bump the werewolf and he moves on.

'You do work here then?' Cameron asks, assuming Charlie to be a work colleague. He is to a point. He's just left school and works at our warehouse office, he's only here as my brother offered him an evening's work. 'This is just next level. I can't even imagine this level of wealth. I still rent a flat in Streatham. Party food to me is crisps and dip.'

There is dip downstairs. It's guacamole that's being served out of a rubber severed head, which I don't think is going down too well.

Cameron looks around the mezzanine level. As mentioned, Sonny has never really known how to spend his wealth, as proven in this space that houses a real-life Stormtrooper suit, a signed football shirt in a frame and a bronze sculpture of a naked man with quite the package that people are using for photo opportunities tonight.

'And the rumour is that his parents are totally mega rich too. I didn't know this until I went on Wikipedia, but his parents own The Love Shack, that online sex shop. Apparently, they both used to be in porn.'

I take a deep breath. Not apparently. That is the truth. Our parents were huge in porn. Back when you used to get porn on DVDs from shops in Soho with blacked-out windows. In some ways, it's quite a romantic story, if you think about it like two actors who met on a film set. A closed film set with bad scripts, sturdy bedframes and fake plumbers who had no intention of fixing your fridge. But it became more than that. It became about two people who then got out of that game, got married, had kids and used all their sex knowledge to start the UK's premier online sex shop and now earn their money selling forty-five varieties of dildo.

Cameron waits for me to be surprised by this revelation. I'm in too deep now to come out with who I am. I try to slacken my jaw.

'Really? Well, sex sells, obviously.'

'I'm really in the wrong profession,' he says, examining a portrait of Sonny and Ruby, naked and on a beach, hands and legs entwined so they cover all the rude bits.

'What do you do, Cameron?' I ask, desperate to move the conversation on.

'I design video games. And you're in catering?'

'Oh, well – I do the organising, mainly sales...'

I choose the dildos, make sure we can sell them at a profit, and make sure they come from a reputable supplier who manu-factures them and ships them in at a competitive price.

'I mean, you seem pretty normal compared to most I've met tonight,' Cameron says.

I want to take that as a compliment, but I'm not sure whether to be offended at how he's semi-judging my family. Still, this isn't the first or last time anyone will do that and I've played this charade many times over the years. *Oh, Dad? He was an actor. Will he have been in anything I've seen? I really hope not.*

Our conversation is suddenly interrupted as the music comes to a halt and the famous DJ, who is still wigging me out with the authenticity of his costume, grabs a mic.

'ARE WE ALL HAVING FUN?' he roars.

The crowd howl from the smoke, drinks fly through the air, and I'm glad I advised Sonny to put a temporary floor down as a lot of the cocktails served tonight have been very green.

'I want to introduce you to the main man tonight. Mr Sonny Jewell, our spooktacular host. Big ups for Sonny...' He lets out a noise that sounds like a machine gun, and the crowd explode again as my brother walks up to the stage, standing there and busting out a dance move to go with his red Joker costume and make-up.

I chuckle and shake my head. He's the exhibitionist, the

performer – always has been. He's clueless about practical matters in life, but he's funny, generous, immensely likeable.

'Why so serious, everyone?' Sonny says, rolling out his best impression. It makes the crowd erupt, but you've quoted the wrong Joker film to go with your costume, little brother.

He keeps dancing for the rise of the crowd. It reminds me instantly of how he used to do this at Christmas to Tom Jones, entertaining our nan, who'd clap along, fuelled by Babycham.

'OK, OK, OK. So I just wanted to come up here to thank some people. I'd like to say I did all of this myself, but we had some beautiful events people involved and where's my sis? Is she about?'

I pretend to look out into the crowd, not wanting to blow my cover with the stranger I've just met but also so as not to die of embarrassment from the ridiculous amount of people in the room. I am not the exhibitionist in the family, which, given my gene pool, always confounds people.

'Well, wherever she is,' Sonny carries on, 'she was the one who made sure tonight ran smoothly and will be the reason you all go home with your coats because my plan was literally to throw them on my bed.'

The crowd laugh, hopefully not at my sad level of organisation skills.

'And seriously, this vision tonight was all Rubes. Where are you, honey? Come up here.'

You can tell where Ruby is because of the Maleficent horns. She wanders up onto the stage and they embrace, kissing.

Do I like Ruby? She's a tad extra compared to me. She needs her hair done in the same way humans need oxygen, but I like how she loves my brother. How she appreciates him for all his good traits and doesn't possess any red-flag qualities that would have me doubt her. And there've been a number of them over the years. Like the girl who tried to expense her tanning needs to our company.

'Anyway, you all know how much I love this girl and how she changed my life from day one since we started working together. You are gentle, kind and...'

...you make every day better, you make me want to be better, to do better, to be the best version of myself, I recite in my head.

'...you make stuff better.'

For an actor, you'd think he'd remember the script his big sister wrote for him.

But wait. This is happening now? He's been planning it for a while but didn't really share the details with me. Quiet restaurant? Beach at sunset? On stage with John Legend? The only reason I can think he's doing this now is that the potency of the cocktails has given him the bravado. Just don't sing, I urge silently. I do love you but the singing isn't great.

'And I just want to have lots of the best days with you in them.'

I'm not sure that grammatically made sense, but Ruby doesn't care. She's openly sobbing, the make-up has gone to shit. Make sure you carry tissues, Sonny, I told him. He reaches into his pocket. Well done, bro. She knows what's happening. So does the DJ as he's cracked on some Barry White. She's shaking her head, Sonny's tearing up. The crowd is a sea of phones and cheering.

'Ruby Reynolds. I love you so bloody much. I can't think of anything I want more than to be with you for the rest of my life.'

He gets out the ring. Yes, I helped him choose that too. Square-cut vintage with a ruby, keeping it classy and on theme. His knee is shaking and I tear up on this balcony, longing to give him the biggest of hugs.

Please bloody say yes, please. Don't give me a reason to run down there.

The wall suddenly lights up. Oh. This was not part of the plan.

WILL YOU BE MY WIF?

The E hasn't lit up. There are giggles from the crowd, but no one cares, we all know what this is. I just hope those wall sparklers don't set off the smoke alarms.

'Of course I will, you idiot. Oh my god, oh my god, oh my god...'

There's a squeal, Sonny lifts her to the air and spins her around, her horns go wonky. The crowd cheer as the DJ does a perfect fade to full volume and my worry turns to joy, my smile as wide as the moon. I didn't know about the indoor fireworks and confetti cannons, though, and I nearly crap myself as they fire out from our level. Cameron and I jump out of our skins and grab each other in fright, laughing. The world's worst Ghostbusters, perhaps.

'Wow, that was something,' Cameron says, handing me a cocktail napkin. I dab it under my eyes, shocked by the emotion that's evoked in me. Sonny is engaged? I'll have to ring Mum and Dad before people get this on social media and they get the hump. 'If this is the engagement party, can you imagine the wedding?' he adds, necking his beer.

'It'll be a little bit special, that's for sure...' I laugh through my tears, a cocktail of emotions swimming through me, all joy, pride, love. Oh, little bro. You're getting married. Please don't make me wear peach, though.

As I look into the crowd, people are queuing up to the stage to offer their congratulations and I see Sonny's eyes scan the place. He finds me, then grins, waving. I wave back. I mean, you're getting married before me and you will tease me mercilessly for this reason, but I can live with that. Seriously, though, no peach.

'I should probably tell you that I'm crying because that's my brother...' I admit sheepishly to Cameron, but when I turn around, he's not there.

Well, that was short-lived. I search the room and see he's wandered over to the corridor where we met, watching as Cat

Lady and Zombie Face emerge from one of the bedrooms. That is his girlfriend, isn't it? Damn.

I know his mate is a zombie, but his trousers aren't even zipped up. Cat Lady's hair is all ruffled, cheeks flushed. Cameron is glued to the spot as they catch sight of him. Zombie Face walks over with some speed as Cat Lady stands there engulfed by her own shame.

No, my brother has just proposed. Not now. I run over.

'You shit,' Cameron says, striking first.

A few people turn round to take in the drama.

'Mate, she came on to me. I'm so sorry. It's not been going on long, a month maybe.'

No, Zombie Face... Shush now.

Cameron's face is completely ashen. He shoves his friend and storms off, leaving Cat Lady sobbing into her whiskers. Who shags their affair at a party where their boyfriend is in attendance? That's awful but also kinda stupid.

I shuffle behind Cameron as I'm aware this will feel like a stake through the guts and part of me is worried. Don't do anything stupid. Please. He gets as far as the driveway, then just stands there, not before dropping his head and putting his hands to his knees. I watch him from the front door, the pulse of happy dance music in the background.

'Are you OK?' I call out. I open a cupboard to the left of the door and take out the first coat I find.

Cameron swings his head round to see me. 'Hey, Stantz.' He takes off his glasses and wipes tears away with the back of his hand. 'That wasn't totally embarrassing,' he exclaims, sarcasm in his tone.

'For them, not you...'

I venture out onto the gravel driveway of the house and hand him the coat. It's a fur-trimmed full-length plaid number that looks like it might belong to a pimp. I am not sure where my brother would wear this, but I put it over Cameron to protect him from the sharp autumn chill in the air. I know your heart is in pieces, but at least don't let it feel the cold. Do I say I saw them doing the do? That may be too much for his fragile soul to take.

'Is it terrible that I kinda knew?' Cameron tells me. 'They used to flirt terribly in front of me. I just thought they wouldn't be so horrible as to actually go through with it.'

Oh, Spengler. That sucks. I don't know what to tell you. You look the same age as me, mid-twenties, and my mum's only advice when it comes to love is that you have to go through some of this shite to understand what you deserve. It's what these years are for. I don't know if he needs to hear the advice of my ex-porn star mother at this moment, though.

'Do you have somewhere to go tonight?' I ask him.

'He's my housemate. I think that's the killer.'

'Oh.'

I'd offer for him to come to mine, but I live with my parents. My mum would offer him a glow-in-the-dark Halloween-themed condom.

'I might just go for a walk? Clear my head.'

This house is near a river, so this makes me worry slightly.

'Do you want company?' I ask.

He shrugs. 'You're kind, but we've just met. Please don't feel obliged to look out for me. I'll be fine. I'll find a pub and get smashed somewhere.'

Around here? We're in North London. He'll get his face smashed in wearing that costume.

'You could go back to yours and piss over all of his belongings? The smell of ammonia is particularly hard to budge,' I contribute.

This is why our rubber sheets sell so well.

This time, his breath fogs the air with laughter.

'I mean, there are other options too. The beauty of this party is that there's actual security to keep out the journalists.

His name is Kevin and he's dressed like Frankenstein's monster. I can tell him I caught them doing coke in the bathroom and get both of them thrown out? Then you can come back in, we can have a chat and you can get drunk here instead?'

'Could we get more of that sushi?' he asks.

'Yeah, there's a back door here. We could literally sit in the kitchen and take our pick. There are some damn fine Diablo chicken wings in there too.'

'I love chicken wings.' He perks up.

'Who doesn't?'

'You'd do that for me?'

'It's a Ghostbuster thing, right?' To show him how cool I really am, I then reach for my proton pack and strike a pose. I really do win at impressing people I've just met.

'Just don't cross the streams,' he says.

I pause for a moment. *Because that would be bad.*

THREE

'Then you tell him to get his arse back from Bradford? I am not wasting good money on that boy... I will drive there and get him myself...'

I have a lively Uber driver today considering it's 7 a.m. I am curious about the nature of this argument at such an early hour but also conscious that his anger is fuelling some very haphazard driving choices that make his dashboard air freshener swirl around like we're at sea. I am a big fan of Uber's commitment to passenger experiences. Today, Tamwar is offering me a mandarin and ginger scented drive. My favourites put tissues in the magazine flaps, some have phone chargers. My absolute fave was an older gentleman who had a laminated sign requesting people don't foul or have sex in the back of his car. Tamwar doesn't carry such signage but hangs up his phone and huffs and puffs, running his fingers over his chin.

'I'm sorry you had to hear that, love. It's my son. First year at uni and pissing it all away.'

'Oh, don't mind me.' Please indicate at roundabouts, though.

'Did you go to university?' he asks me.

'I did. I went to Leeds, so near Bradford.'

'You look like a smart girl. Good night? Must be if you're coming home at this hour. I like the costume.'

He has good taste in films, so this means I will leave him a five-star rating. 'Thank you, Tamwar. Busy night for you?'

'Well, with Halloween, you always get an interesting couple of days. Mostly drunk kids who've been out on the town and leave parts of their costumes behind.'

'Anyone leave anything interesting?'

'All sorts. Whole tub of sweets. A rubber severed hand, two pairs of devil horns and a hockey mask.'

I laugh. 'I'm up here on the left, the house with the hedges.'

He slows the car down and studies the place in detail, the cars to the front of the drive. 'Just what I thought. See... if my boy applies himself at university, then he can afford a house like this one day, am I right?'

I don't tell him otherwise. 'He'll get there, Tamwar. Having fun is also part of the experience.'

'Depends how you have your fun. I bet you never got so drunk that you climbed through a drive-thru window at Burger King, stole some chips and then had to be removed by firemen.'

'No. That is funny, though,' I reply, trying to stifle my giggles.

Tamwar doesn't seem to think so. 'When you get out, take a look in my boot and see if there's anything there you want... Halloween special,' he says, jokingly.

I clamber out and do as I'm told, then stand in the middle of our street cradling a severed hand as I wave Tamwar away. I hope he goes easy on his son because at least they have a family story of legend to share when he's older.

As I approach the house, it looks a little sadder in the twilight of an autumn morn. Dad's pumpkins have caved into themselves and the witch on the garage is no longer illuminated or standing, lying face down in the ivy, as if she had the most excellent night.

I do love this house and I think it may be one of the reasons I came back to live here. When my parents left their former business, they wanted so desperately to fit in to some suburban existence so they bought this huge ivy-clad detached house on the outskirts of South London's Wimbledon. It's where I grew up, had all my playdates and parties (including my eighteenth; someone threw up in the fireplace) and where my parents tried hard to carve out a safe and loving family life for my brother and me. I mean, it wasn't even in the postcode of normal. In reality, they jumped from porn into dildos. I remember boxes of them lined up as they used our dining table as a postage and packaging station. For years, Sonny and I had no idea what they were. We used to pretend they were lightsabers and fight each other on the stairs.

As I put my key into the front door, it opens and Dad stands there, a vision in some dazzling white tennis wear.

'Bleeding Jesus... you gave me a shock,' he says, jumping back in fright.

The one thing about my dad is that when he goes for a look, he commits. Last night, authentic vampire, this morning, Centre Court ready. 'As I live and breathe, aren't you Roger Federer?' I joke.

He smiles. 'I am,' he says, adopting a bad fake Euro accent and a lunge. 'I am the Swiss GOAT of tennis. You should see the swing of my serve.'

'Maybe another time, Rog. You're out early?'

'They run a special deal at the fitness club: swim, tennis, sauna and a breakfast roll. You should talk, walk of shame,' he says cheekily.

'Ha-ha-ha,' I reply slowly. 'Nothing of the sort. Thursday night party means some of us have to work the next day. I have that call with the guys in Shenzhen at 9 a.m. so I wanted to freshen up and get in the office. How's Mum? How has she taken the news?'

It's the morning after the big engagement at the party they weren't invited to.

Dad closes the door and peeks into the kitchen. 'She'd have loved to have been there, she's had a moan, but your brother was good at smoothing it over. We're all having dinner tomorrow at Brett's restaurant – you'll come, right? You have to.'

'Will I be the only singleton there?'

'Ruby's bringing her brother.'

I flare my nostrils. I've only met Ricky Reynolds once. It was at Ruby's twenty-second birthday party and he spent an hour telling me about his recent flings with veganism and a colonic he'd had at a health retreat which meant he could now get in a twenty-six-inch waist jean.

'Look, just go in and fill her in on the gossip.' He puts a hand to my cheek. It's Dad's move. He likes to hold and study my face like he's in disbelief that I'm his daughter. He's a handsome older man, a kindness in his eyes and his words, that makes you think he deals in antiques or garden design. 'I'll pop in the office later and we can have a coffee.'

'Go smash 'em, Roger.'

He salutes me as I edge through the door. The kitchen lights are on and I hear the whirr of the dishwasher in action. I breathe a sigh of relief to see that there is still a full bowl of Halloween condoms by the front door.

Mum's dog, Dave, the oldest Border terrier in the world, comes to greet me first and I pick him up to act as a shield. As I enter the kitchen, Mum is in her silk, floral dressing gown, sitting at the breakfast bar sipping from a cup of coffee. There's an effortless glamour about Mum, she looks like she should have been on one of those swish eighties soaps, like *Dynasty*, naturally pretty even without the make-up and the big hair. She shifts me a look.

'You're up early?' I say.

'Your father lost his balls so I had to help him find them.'

I snigger. She doesn't play along.

'Dad was giving me strong Federer vibes today,' I say, trying to lighten the mood.

'Roger Federer is far too nice. I met your dad when he had the mullet and the cheeky smile. More Pat Cash, Björn Borg.'

I go over and put an arm around her, resting my head on her shoulder, Dave licking her hand. Good boy, help me butter her up.

'Plus, I have meetings today and a school assembly in North London, so I've got to be out the door early.'

This is also what Mum does. She owns a charity encouraging kids to practise safe and positive sex. She speaks in assemblies, runs workshops and uses the breadth of her experience to change people's perceptions of the industry she worked in. It sounds worthy, but most of the time she goes into secondary schools, they discover what she did and then teens go and find her past work on YouTube.

I perch myself next to her, in silence, waiting for her to interrogate me about last night.

'You knew, didn't you?' she asks me.

'Maybe?' I've known for weeks, I just didn't know when it was going to go down.

'JOSIE! I AM YOUR MOTHER!'

Dave jumps down, away from the shrieking, and escapes to his bed.

'And you are awful at keeping secrets. I've known what every birthday present has been since I was five because you'd tell me beforehand.'

'How much did you know?' she asks.

'I helped choose the ring,' I admit hesitantly.

'I can't look at you right now.'

I hug her tightly so she has no choice but to hug back.

'I've seen bits on social media, but was it lovely?' she asks, getting off her stool to make me a coffee.

'It was actually. I may have shed a tear.'

'Oh, Josie. Little Sonny boy is getting wed. I'm waiting a bit longer, then I'm calling Nan.'

'Nan knows, she's on Instagram now. She's already commented on their announcement post with five dancing lady emojis.'

'Then who do I get to tell?' she says, slightly annoyed.

'The postman will be here in the hour.'

'I hate you both,' she says, not really meaning it at all. 'You're dead to me. I'm not coming to the wedding.' Of course she will.

She clatters around in a drawer looking for a teaspoon and waves it around at me like an angry witch.

'Did you and Dad have a nice evening, though?' I ask.

'Oh, it was lovely. We got a curry from the new place on the high street. Lovely big prawns in their dhansak. And it was so gorgeous to see all the kids dressed up. That mum across the way who's just had the baby, she came round with her lad. He was dressed as a pumpkin.'

Her face glows as she recounts their evening. Mum adores the littlest ones on our street and would have made a fuss. Dad would have had his teeth in and adopted his bad Euro accent again.

Many people around here don't know what we do. I guess you don't delve that far into people's lives as neighbours these days. You just wave at each other when you put the bins out, exchange pleasantries and take in their undeliverable parcels.

'I see you didn't give out your condoms,' I note.

'I went on your advice. Instead, your dad hid by the garden gate with a mask and a chainsaw and scared the shit out of the older thug kids looking for trouble.'

For a moment, she made her evening sound so wholesome. I

hope the chainsaw wasn't on and pray those kids didn't tell their parents. Or the police.

'And what about you? Did you have a good time in your welder's costume?' she says, adding milk to my coffee.

'You are so funny. I did. It was a good party.'

It's her turn to pause now, scanning my face. 'But you don't like parties?'

'I like parties where my little brother gets engaged, that's the difference.'

Remember, she can't keep secrets.

'Are you off back to bed then?' she asks me as I yawn, stretching my arms out widely.

'No, I've got to be in the office for a call. Double coffees for me.'

'Can't someone else take it?' she asks.

'No one else can speak Mandarin.'

She cradles my head and gives me a kiss on the forehead. 'You're such a diamond. Thank you for being there for your brother, I'm glad one of us was. Let me whip up some eggs while you're in the shower, JoJo. I think I've got bacon too. Were there at least party bags?'

I reach in my rucksack and pull out a severed hand. 'No, but my Uber man let me have this.'

She picks it up and slaps me round the face with it.

'Oh, Josie... Tell me everything! Were you there? Was it lovely?' Michelle squeals at me, showing me engagement photos that have crept onto Instagram.

Naturally, news of Sonny's engagement has captured the imaginations of not only this workplace but those who like to frequent the gossip columns. It hit social media first, but now news of their impending nuptials is trending and all over the glossy magazines and tabloids. What will she wear? Where will they wed? Who is the planner? I tell you who will most likely be the planner. It'll be me, because they also thought their mate, Ian, on their soap could marry them because he once played a priest on *Doctor Who*.

I take off my suit jacket that I wore on my call to China to look more official, revealing my white T-shirt and ripped jeans. I glance in a mirror on my desk, at my tired green eyes and pale freckled skin that make me look like I need a ton more sleep and caffeine – I hope I didn't scare the manufacturing team.

'I bet it was lovely. They look gorgeous together! Do you think they'll do it in the summer? I bet it'll be in the summer,' Michelle continues, taking my jacket and hanging it off the back of the office door.

Michelle is my personal assistant at The Love Shack, and most mornings, she becomes the pick-me-up that we all need. She's here because my dad gave her a job. She was also involved in my parents' previous line of work but gave it up to marry a plumber called Jeff and have four kids whose names are all London landmarks where I hope none of them were conceived as one of them is called Wembley. She now works school-run hours and keeps my biscuit supply and receipts in check.

I sip at my third coffee of the day as I overlook the comings and goings of the warehouse: the forklifts, the familiar beeping of reversing trucks, the condoms packed to the rafters. It's like a very sexy version of Costco.

'It was gorgeous and he's over the moon,' I reply, turning back to her. 'It was really lovely to see him looking so happy.'

'That is some ring. That was you, wasn't it?' she says, squinting her eyes at me.

'I'll never tell...'

'God, your mum and dad must be so excited. They love a wedding...'

'Well, I have no doubt you'll be on the guest list, so you'll be able to see for yourself.'

Michelle jumps out of her seat, dancing, spilling tea all over her cleavage. 'Oh my days, I'll have to ring Jeff. But look at me... I'm such a div.'

The one thing about Michelle is that she adheres to her own special dress code at work, which means her boobs are usually displayed in quite a fashion. You can't miss those bad boys. I lean over with a tissue and attempt to help mop her down as the office door opens.

'Crikey...' yells Charlie, pretending to look away. 'I'm sorry, I should have knocked.'

'It's all right, Charlie,' I say, laughing. 'Michelle just spilled her tea.'

He creeps his head around the door with one eye open, his face a deep blush. Charlie came to us at sixteen, keen as mustard to learn about business, slightly cocky, though, with all the sexual experiences he'd shared with a handful of girls in the backs of cars, thinking he'd seen it all. The butt plug section of our store changed that. He now often wanders around here with his hi-vis and trainers looking like he's just stepped into Narnia. I like Charlie's enthusiasm, his work ethic and excellent manners. We need to have words about his shiny Ronaldo haircut, though.

'Josie, I've been told that delivery will come in around half an hour and you said you wanted to check it when it came through, so I thought I'd give you the heads-up,' he informs me.

'Nipple clamps?'

'No, those came in last night. It's the lube consignment?'

I nod and put a thumbs up.

'Yes, last time it squirted all over the place and—'

Michelle tries hard to keep in her giggles.

Charlie sputters. 'I mean, it was summer and too warm. All the bottles shot their... I mean...'

I grin broadly. 'Charlie, I'll be down in a bit. Can you make sure we have the inventory printed out and we can go through it together?'

He nods. 'I also have those forms for that management course you told me to look up. I need some help with the bursary questions if that's OK?'

'Sure thing. Did you enjoy the party at the weekend?'

He shuffles in through the door fully, obviously keen to share his experiences. 'It were lit. I've never experienced anything like it.'

'How come he got an invite?' Michelle grumbles.

'He did some waiter work for us, dressed as a very convincing werewolf.'

'What did you and your mate come as then? I didn't get that,' he asks.

God, I'm only about six years older than this one, but his lack of filmic knowledge tells me all I need to know.

'I was a Ghostbuster.'

'Oh yeah, the film thing. That's retro. Who was your mate? He was a nice bloke.'

Michelle suddenly turns on the spot. 'She went with a date? Now this you kept quiet, spill. Charlie, you too.'

Charlie freezes on the spot as Michelle raises her voice and points a finger at him.

'It wasn't a date,' I say.

'But you had matching outfits?' Charlie adds.

'You matched! That's a moment. That's serendipity. Did you hang out? What was his name?' Michelle exclaims hurriedly.

'The costumes were a coincidence. In this country, there's a limited costume base for Halloween. There's like one of ten things people dress as, so, statistically, it's not as fate-driven as you think.' That's what I've told myself anyway.

'Was he cute?' asks Michelle.

'He looked like Timothée Chalamet,' Charlie tells her.

Michelle sits there taking in every morsel of detail. She is one of many who look out for me in this way, who wish me well in love and are eagerly waiting for me to find that special someone. She hears about my dates, my swipe-right disasters, my potential matches. I'd liken it to being in a boxing ring. Michelle and my family are the spectators: watching, wincing, cheering me on. But it's exhausting being championed like that sometimes. Having to go in that ring every time and just be suckerpunched by love. Every. Single. Time.

'His name was Cameron and if you want to know the gossip, he showed up to that party with a girlfriend and he caught her having it off with his housemate,' I tell them.

Charlie's eyes widen. 'At the party? Ouch. I didn't see that.'

'Well, I did. Sort of. And anyway, it kicked off...'

'But you two were in the kitchen, crossed legs on the sofa, doing shots and eating sushi...'

It's the turn of Michelle's eyes to widen.

'Not like that, Michelle,' I add. 'I just felt bad for him, so we hung out and I made sure he was all right.'

'In your matching costumes...' Michelle says, trying to highlight the cuteness of the situation. 'Did you rebound shag him?' she asks.

'In my brother's house? No, I did not,' I shriek back.

'Was it the jumpsuits? They're tricky, they're not really built for sexy times.'

'I did not because he was upset and we'd just met.'

'Plus, he doesn't know who she is,' Charlie adds. 'He thought she was in charge of the catering.' I glare at him. 'It's a werewolf thing, we have sharp hearing,' he jokes.

'It's because she's modest, she always does that,' Michelle tells him.

'Well, it's also because my circumstances are quite unique. I don't want to scare people off before I've even got to know them.'

'Why? This job's a hoot. Better than saying you're a civil servant or you work in HR,' Michelle remarks.

'True, but then there's the other stuff. My brother is a famous soap star, my parents were big in porn. It comes with a backstory. I like to ease people in gently...'

It's Charlie's turn to smile now. That's the problem with our line of work, the innuendo comes for free.

I narrow my eyes at him mockingly. 'Like when I introduce new boyfriends to Mum, I like to ensure they've not knocked one out to her.'

Charlie rises to a high blush again. Please no, Charlie.

Michelle looks a little sad for me, though. 'But, Josie, if they can't handle all of that stuff, that's their problem. You in yourself are one of the smartest people I know. When this company was on its knees...' She puts a hand out when Charlie starts smirking, 'You came in with your degree and your business knowledge and you saved it from going under. You took us online, we have a flagship store in Covent Garden. Our stock is through the roof because of you. That's the story you should be telling people.'

I throw her an air-kiss in thanks.

'But she's too humble to tell people that, Charlie. So, he thought you did the catering?' she asks me.

'Kinda.'

'Yeah, she even got up and chopped some carrots to make it seem legit.'

I glare at Charlie again and he shrugs. I did do that. I arranged them nicely too, so if you were trying to pick one up for dipping, you wouldn't touch all the other vegetables. And if we're being honest, I did that because I liked Cameron and I wanted to drag out the evening without my true identity getting in the way, without the five thousand questions and jokes, without him running off.

I did get Zombie Face and Cat Lady thrown out by security.

I allowed Cameron to wear that moment for a while to feel better about himself and then I let him through the back door. Not like that. Instead, we spoke for hours, huddled in a corner of that kitchen as people milled in and out with platters of food and glasses. He'd only met Imogen (Cat Lady) a couple of months ago and he'd had reservations about her because she put ketchup on everything (even a roast dinner) and had a very strange fear of pigeons, but this just confirmed that, beneath it all, she was also quite cruel. He seemed more upset by the behaviour of Russ, his housemate, who he had gone to school with, and we discussed whether this was a death knell to their friendship. There was a realisation that maybe they'd stuck together out of sheer obligation and maybe they'd grown apart. This is what hurt Cameron most of all. This is what made him down the shots that evening, the loss of another type of love in his life.

'Did you give him your number? Do you have a full name?' Michelle asks.

'Cameron Cox.'

'You both have alliteration! And his name is literally cocks. It's like you're meant to be together,' Michelle exclaims.

'C-O-X. Don't you dare cyberstalk him now.'

Don't, because I already did that this morning. I have stalked him on every social media channel. Just to check there are no surprises, like maybe he goes seal clubbing at the weekends or likes Satanic rock music. But it was as I imagined, a super cute geek who likes films, a beanie hat and bubble tea. I'm not as stupid as to approach him when he's just come out of a relationship, but the man piqued my interest and these men come along so very rarely for people like me.

'Look, I don't think it'll go anywhere. I don't want to be a rebound girlfriend. He's got to throw out a housemate and officially dump a girlfriend, so I will leave that with him to make that move. He might not even like me.'

'Was he blind?' asks Michelle.

'No. He did wear glasses, though.'

'He was into you. There was a lot of casual touching,' Charlie adds, leaning against a filing cabinet.

'You saw a lot through that mask, eh?' I tell Charlie.

'I'm just calling it how it is. There was definite flirting, that whole nudge-nudge thing you were doing and the joking, and how you guys shared those chicken wings and he wiped that bit of sauce off your nose.'

'Were you actually working at that party, Charlie, or just spying on me?'

'It's just you're single, he's single now...'

'How do you know I'm single, Charlie?'

'Because your mum's always asking me if I have friends who might be interested. She says you work too hard and you're a catch.'

I don't doubt that, as my mum once tried to get me a date with our window cleaner, but I find it quite amusing that Charlie's only been here for a few months and has already understood the lay of the land.

'I'm twenty-six years old,' I reply, 'I'm not looking for anything like that.'

Michelle and Charlie look at each other knowingly.

'But you two had the same outfit,' Michelle says, pouting. 'I'd just love for you to be happy.'

'I'm happy being single.'

'Because you work here and we sell stuff which means you don't really need a man?' Charlie asks.

Michelle's boobs can hardly contain themselves with laughter.

'Because, young Charlie, my focus is here. Yes, he was very cute and we had a lot in common, we were the same age and like chicken wings, but I don't want to get my hopes up for something that may never happen.'

Because what really happened was that we had one of those magical evenings where we talked and talked until Brett had packed up his kitchen knives and the last bottle of champagne had been drunk. We snacked and drank and we chatted about geeky film things like how we would recast the Marvel films, and the brilliant nuance of *Stranger Things* and all its nods to eighties film classics. He helped me unload a dishwasher, told me about the time he got arrested for public nudity when he was at university, and we also joked about what names we would give our obscure pets. For example, I like rhyming names, so I would call my snake, Drake or my lion, Brian. This made him guffaw so hard, a bit of cucumber flew out of his mouth.

It was one of those wonderful nights where I didn't hear the music slowly fade to nothing or even remember the house emptying of partygoers. I didn't see anyone pack the leftovers in Sonny's giant fridge or the sky glow to amber as the morning came up. I don't remember falling asleep on his shoulder. All I remember is waking up, a throw laid over me and he wasn't there. He had gone.

FOUR

Sonny and I found out our parents worked in porn when we were eleven and fourteen years old. Up to that point, we knew Mum was different to most other mums. She wasn't a cagoule and mid-denim kind of mum, she carried a bit of chic about her and when we had parties at our house, the other dads would clock that they may have seen her before somewhere, and then stand around looking nervous while we were all playing pass-the-parcel. Of course, they didn't go home and tell their wives that they'd seen little Josie's mum's vajayjay (and more), so it stayed a secret at the school gate.

Even when Mum and Dad started their business from the kitchen table, they never let on to other people what they did. I love how the word entrepreneur is such an umbrella term. You could sell organic dog food or award-winning vibrators, but essentially, you're just trying to sell things to people and hope your brand creates buzz. Well, you want a vibrator to buzz, don't you?

It wasn't until we got through the big bad gates of secondary school that our parents' past became apparent to us, via a group of lads in Sonny's year who found a clip on the internet at a sleepover one night. Someone showed their mum, who showed another mum, whose husband confirmed that my parents were part of a series of films from the late eighties. This caused friction in that couple's marriage that eventually led to divorce as it uncovered a serious addiction to porn and casual one-night stands. Anyway, it all came to a head when my parents were invited to meet the actual head to discuss how to tackle this head on. 'That's a lot of head,' my dad told us he said in Mr Jessop's office. It was probably not the best line to lead with.

That was when Mum and Dad sat down and told us about their past. I remember that conversation well because it was such a shock. When they told us they had a secret, I thought it'd be something cool. Maybe they were elite spies. Or time travellers. When they explained, I was confused. I'm not sure I knew what they meant. I looked it up on the internet, searching 'people who have sex for money'. The internet showed me a picture of Julia Roberts in *Pretty Woman*. Then Sonny found the video his friends had been swapping. We watched it together. Well, we didn't. We got through the intro of some terrible acting and a kiss and then Mum took off her bra and Sonny dropped the laptop. He started crying. We hugged. We barricaded the door and wouldn't come out for dinner.

After that, there was little the school could do. They did an assembly about porn and how no one at the school should be watching that sort of stuff anyway (I remember that assembly as the physics teacher, Mr Simmonds, blushed quite hard) and Sonny and I were told to ignore the comments, the laughter, the jokes. If we moved school, the scandal would follow us, so the best thing to do was just survive it. It's probably why Sonny and I are so close. We armed ourselves with comebacks for the playground bullies. A boy once asked me if I could work a cock like my mum. I made that boy cry by telling him I'd make his penis work by sticking it in a pencil sharpener. I was fourteen. We always felt the warm protective stance from Mum and Dad, who hated themselves for how it transformed our formative years, but we never hated them. They're hard people to hate.

These days, it's more common knowledge about who we are and what we do. It's on Sonny's Wiki page for a start, but people react to it differently. Some just want to give you *all* the details of their sex lives. They'll tell you about the time they experimented with some tea tree oil and a courgette. I've literally just met you, Ingrid, but thanks for that. Others just let it sit there so it's the elephant in the room. You can tell they don't know how to bring the conversation to the table and if I think about it properly, it's most likely because they're scared of sex and exposing themselves, in every way.

That is the feeling I get from Ruby's parents, who I'm meeting tonight for the first time.

'I get it now. Your dad is Johnny and your mum is Susie, so both your names are amalgamations of their names. JO-SIE and SO-NNY... that is bloody adorable,' coos Ruby's mum from the end of the table, a little worse for wear.

Ruby's mum is Anne and she's lovely if excitable in her chiffon scarf, smart denim and blazer combo. Take a breath, Anne. She keeps glancing over to my mum and dad like she wants to ask them everything, but it's obvious she's been told not to bring it up. Ruby's dad is in windows. Anne teaches history. She's told us stories about students and mock exams and, blimey, they've really been quite dull. Today, I ordered some sex dolls, Anne.

That said, it's been a cosier evening, a world away from Halloween. Brett and Tina have allowed us to use their chic restaurant to celebrate over bistro lamb shanks and there's still a warm, loved-up energy from recent engagement news that carries us through. Sonny and Ruby are getting married. There will be a wedding. My mother's already hired a hat maker for the day and offered to get Anne decked out. If she could, Mum would go full Carmen Miranda, feathers, fruit and all. I have a suspicion it will be my job to ensure she doesn't.

It's been an evening to chat, eat and the celebratory champagne has flowed like a river, which is down to my mum, who is one of those people who likes to refill a glass when it's half full so you never quite know how much you've drunk. I'm aware of this trick, so I know to hide my glass and watch my mother like a hawk. Anne doesn't know this, though, so Anne is very very hammered.

'And my Rubes will be Ruby Jewell. I bloody love this!' she says, pouring half her glass over her hair.

I glance over at Sonny. You'll soon be related to her, be kind and help a girl out. He offers her a napkin, a smile and does a quick switch, putting a glass of water in front of her.

'Oh my god, Mum,' Ruby mumbles, sitting next to me.

I take Ruby's hand to distract her. 'I thought the alliteration of Josie Jewell was bad. My name sounds like a bad country music star, drowning in rhinestones.'

Ruby grips my fingers. Aesthetically, everything about Ruby is perfect, it's the mask she wants to show the world, but behind the scenes, the anxiety, the insecurity shines through. Who's watching me? Is it out of place? How does it make me look? It makes me grateful for the shadows in which I'm allowed to stand and observe the world.

'She's not normally such a lightweight, it's just she was a bit nervous about meeting your parents,' she whispers to me.

I know why, but I don't say anything out loud. That said, she'll get to know them and find out they're just normal people. John Jewell and Susan Beaumont, raised in London, they're human, just like us.

Ruby puts her head on my shoulder. Ever since we've met,

she's always been very tactile with me and it's been lovely to embrace her as a little sister of sorts.

'Is this milk dairy?' the man next to me interrupts. This man I am less keen to embrace. He holds up a milk jug to the table and smells it, his face creasing with disgust. 'I think it is. Oh dear...'

The man next to me is Ricky Reynolds, Ruby's brother. Although I requested not to be sat next to Ricky, I've ended up with him to the other side of me. I try to summon up some interest in what he's just said.

'I might see if they have rice milk? Most don't. They have almond milk, but did you know that the farming of certain types of nuts is terrible for global warming... The water used to farm the nuts is ridiculous...' he continues.

Ricky has not stopped talking about his alternative lifestyle since he sat down. As my halloumi starter came out, he was telling me that he's stopped using shampoo, he's letting his natural oils do the work. I made a joke he could use those oils to dress his salad. He didn't get it.

'So, do you have a girlfriend, Ricky?' my mum asks from across the table. Whilst I am glad for the interruption, don't you bloody dare.

'I don't actually,' he replies.

I like milk. Milk from a cow. I like men who don't lecture me about milk. I don't want anything to do with his nut milk.

'My Josie is single too.'

I narrow my eyes at Mum, who knows exactly what she is doing. This interests Ruby's mum and they link arms and stare at both of us. You can see it in their eyes: a double wedding, families completely joined in union, we could have one of these photo sessions where we all wear white and light denim on a beach.

'Susie, we've spoken about this,' Dad pipes in from the other end of the table. 'Leave her be.' I send Dad a grateful smile.

Mum sticks her tongue out at him for spoiling her fun. I give her evils instead. She met Dad in her early twenties and I know she wants the same for me. To feel that magic, to find someone to share everything in life with.

'Yes... but she's been single for a long time,' Nan adds. My grandmother is also here, she's Dad's mum and when her and Mum gang up together to question me about my love life, it feels like an interrogation of the worst kind. These girls should work for MI6.

'At least a year,' Mum pipes up.

I take a large gulp of wine and let it sit in my throat. This is the adult equivalent of my mum telling the dinner table that I still wet the bed.

'That was because of Mike,' loud-whispers Sonny, drunk, from across the table. I think the whole restaurant heard that.

My dad winces, Ruby's parents sit there waiting for the story. Hell, I like how I'm taking one for the team so we can swerve all those other topics, like my parents being in porn and who's paying for the wedding.

'I went out with someone for a while, his name was Mike,' I offer vaguely.

'They went out for eighteen months,' my mum says, because the extra detail is necessary.

'He wasn't very kind to me so I decided to be single for a while, focus on my career and myself,' I explain, trying to draw a line under the topic.

'More like he was a thieving pissflap,' Nan says. I smile at Nan and her wonderful lexicon of swear words. 'I'm a nice person, Anne. I wouldn't hurt a fly, but if I saw that man again...' Nan continues, gripping on to a dessert spoon with more force than is necessary.

I see Dad put a hand to his mother's arm to tell her to turn the angry woman down a notch so the new in-laws don't think we're in crime.

'We were living together and had saved some money for a house and one day, he left me a note and told me it wasn't working. He took all our savings and moved to Venezuela to travel and expand his horizons,' I clarify.

The table goes quiet for a moment as the shame of having to retell the story to virtual strangers washes over me. However, I'm glad it at least shuts up any more lectures about milk.

Bringing it all up means the memory swoops into view. I remember that day well. I came home to the flat from work with a Chinese takeaway and the note was pinned to the fridge. I didn't see it at first. I thought it was a shopping list. So I tucked into my Singapore noodles until I spied it and the words drew me in. I then sat on the floor of our flat as the sky went dark, until I could feel my legs again, my chest. Crispy squid, sweet and sour pork, egg fried rice. *I got you your order. It's going to get cold.* I sat there for five hours. I then packed a bag and went to my parents' house. It feels like another life.

'He took all that money. He's a thief and a liar,' Mum says with the last word.

Sonny glares at Mum for bringing it up and switching the mood of the evening even though he was also party to it. They're allowed to feel anger. Mike left. He lied. I didn't even let them read the letter. That thing would have made them rage and hire hitmen. But next time I take that sort of plunge, I want to be prepared, ready. It'll have to be a sparkling warm ocean I jump into, though, not this puddle of a man sitting next to me. He's wearing a recycled waistcoat that once used to be a shopping bag.

'So as lovely as you are, Ricky, I am deeply scarred and a workaholic and I didn't even have a dress to wear out tonight. I borrowed this from my mum. I wear my mum's clothes, so I don't think I'm the girl for you.'

Dad looks over at me with sad eyes, but it is true. I would never buy a bodycon dress like this. I feel like I've been wrapped in cling film. Dad's stance is more protective than Mum's. While Mum wants me to replace my hurt with magic and fireworks, he just wants the next man to be decent, vetted. He'll hire people to work out what the next man has for dinner on Tuesdays.

My sad life story has seemed to dull the mood, so I sigh and try to summon up some humour. 'I mean, I'm sad, but has Sonny ever told you about the time he pooed himself on stage playing a camel in the nativity?'

It's like a switch has been turned on and everyone laughs. Sonny beams at me and winks. I'll let him tell that story.

'And what's this?' I ask, taking a ladle in my hand and having a smell.

'Josie, that is a pan of fat, don't sip that,' says Tina, cringing.

I put down the ladle and meander around Brett and Tina's kitchen, looking for scraps. I've done a classic Josie this evening to avoid any more speculation about my love life. Once the table had been cleared, I excused myself to the loo by way of the restaurant kitchens to hang out with my mates. Through the doors, I can see my mum looking for me. It's like grown up hide-and-seek, except she'll never find me.

'Service, Miguel,' barks Tina, ringing a bell on the counter.

I notice Brett discussing an order with his wife, a hand to her shoulder. I love the way in which these two ended up together, partners in every sense of the word.

'Was it your table with the vegan?' asks Brett.

'Ruby's brother. Sorry, was it a faff?' I reply.

'Nah, he asked me where my pineapples were from, though, and I may have made that up.'

'I hope you told him they were from your back garden. That would have made him jizz his locally grown pants. They're trying to set me up with him.'

Tina grimaces and shakes her head. At least she gets it.

'The family even brought up the Mike story,' I add.

Brett and Tina both pull the same face, that mimicry in their body language that couples have when they've been together for the longest time. Please, not the look of pity, though. I remember that look from that time I had a date with a man who took me to Five Guys and only ordered something for himself.

Do we go down that path and talk more about Mike? I vote for the swerve. 'So, a Valentine's Day wedding,' I say.

'That's like three months' time,' Brett remarks.

'They want this specific country house and a date became free. You've saved the date, right?'

'I'm best woman, apparently, and we've been told our boys are carrying the rings?' Tina tells me.

'I know because I'll be behind them making sure they don't drop them. I'm the maid of honour.'

Tina claps her hands, excitedly. 'I hope they really foof us up. I want lace on lace.'

'In mint green. With a hat and puffy sleeves.'

'Like a frilly tube of toothpaste.'

I knock my head back in laughter. I hope not, though.

A phone suddenly rings in the kitchen... one ring turns to five rings and I see Tina stare at it as she tries to flip a steak.

'Jo, be a babe and answer that. We only have three people out front today.'

I salute and do as I'm told, coughing to prepare my voice. 'Evening, you're through to Quattro, how can I help?' I say, in my best business voice.

'Oh hi! I... I... So can I check, is this the Quattro that does catering?' the person asks.

'Yes, we cater for parties, birthdays, small weddings...' I look up and Brett is pulling a zombie face. 'Oh, and wakes, for example.'

'That's great. I... Look, I'm wondering if you could help me. I was at a party a couple of nights ago and you catered at it... I've been trying to track them down...This is quite difficult to say...'

Please don't tell me you came down with food poisoning.

'But I got chatting to one of your staff. I think she was the manager, her name was Josie.'

There's a pause as I realise who's on the end of the phone.

'Spengler?' I blurt out.

'Wow, that was a stroke of luck.'

Tina glances over at me, probably confused as my complexion has gone a ruddy raspberry. 'Josie, if it's those fruit vendors again, then tell them to do one.'

I shake my head, not really being able to hide my frantic panic, instead putting a thumb to the air. I have to prepare what to say. I can't speak now. I've had champagne. He'll think I'm some habitual alcoholic who's been on the bottle all week.

'Have I caught you at work? Is it busy? I can call back if you're busy,' he says.

'NO!' I say a little too loudly. 'Ummm, this is a surprise. How are you?'

That's good, Josie. Keep it casual. Next, tackle the weather.

'Still hung-over. So, I just wanted to look you up as I wanted to say sorry for just leaving like that the other night, not even writing a note. I didn't quite know what to say to you...'

'Oh god, it's fine. You just had your heart chewed up and spat out, I wasn't expecting anything.' I think.

'You were kind.'

'I just know that chicken wings are a good way to heal a broken heart.'

Tina looks over curiously at that point, stopping what she's doing to eavesdrop.

I take the phone and wander outside behind the restaurant. 'If anything, I was more worried. Are you OK, Cameron?'

He seems surprised to hear the concern in my voice. 'I'm getting there.' I hear the crispy rustle of bags in the background. 'I was just having a clear-out. My flatmate moved out and he left a load of shite and I want it out... God, I'm sorry. I've just met you, I feel like you're really bearing the load of this drama...'

'Seriously, it's OK.' It's because I like hearing his voice again, even if it's for one short moment to thank me for feeding him and giving him a shoulder to cry on.

'Imogen and I had a huge row on the phone before. I'm glad to be rid of her toxic ways, but it still smarts...'

'It's literally just happened, it will.'

'She's tried to make out that nothing happened between them. I don't know.'

A lump forms at the back of my throat to hear him so vulnerable, confused. 'But it did,' I utter sheepishly. 'I saw them. I'm sorry. I wasn't sure whether to tell you, but I did see them in that room doing the do. Not like I'm a weird voyeur, but they did do naked things together. I was there.'

He's half-laughing, half-gasping in shock.

'I'd just met you, I didn't want to contribute to the drama and join the dots for you. But if there was any doubt, let me erase it for you. She's lying.'

I don't know how he will take that news, but at this point, it feels necessary for him to move on with all the right information.

'Then thank you for confirming it all at least. So she's a cheat *and* a liar.'

I pause. By that definition, I am also lying to him. I need to change the subject. 'Have you eaten?' I ask, sounding like his mother instead.

'I will. But for now, the fumes of solitude and heartbreak are carrying me through. I've just filled my fifth black bag. My mate was a hoarder. He liked car magazines and chutney. The fridge is filled with about twenty different jars.'

'My dad is similar. Apparently, it never goes off. Chutney.'
You really know how to engage a man, Josie, with your chutney
talk. 'Do you need any help?' I ask. I don't know why I say this.
I'm in a nice dress and I've had quite a few drinks. I'm really not
in the mood to clean someone's fridge, but there seems to be an
urge to see him again.

'That's sweet, but I'm good. I'm just trying to work out
where to dump all this stuff.'

'Well, bin the chutney. When I had to throw out my ex-
boyfriend's shit, I just put a lot of it in charity bins. Then at
least some good can come of it.'

'Or he can suffer the inconvenience of having to buy back
his own stuff when he sees it in the RSPCA shop on the high
street,' he adds.

I chuckle, grateful he didn't dig too much when I brought
up the ex.

'Look, I just called to say hi, Josie...'

I actually wave when he says that, at Miguel in the kitchen,
who is confused and waves back. Embarrassed, I step back,
attempting to negotiate the uneven concrete outside the restaurant and trip over on the wheels of a bin. 'Crap-a-doodle-
donkey.'

It's his turn to laugh now. 'Are you possibly drunk?'

'Nooo. I just had to go outside because it's pretty noisy in
the restaurant and I walked into a bin and I think I have some
old cabbage stuck to my heel.' I can hear him giggling and it's a
pleasing sound. 'But I'm also probably just a bit delirious from
lack of sleep. It's been a busy few days. You kept me up the
other night.'

Not like that. Crap. I need better words. I need to not be
standing here in November without a coat, by the bins, the
sound of my teeth chattering like horse hooves.

'I mean, you know what I mean, not like that. Urgh, I'm not

good on the phone.' Now he thinks I can't speak. 'I mean, I am but...'

He's still laughing as I turn and notice my friends gathered in the doorway, trying to get an ear into the conversation. Go, shoo. Go feed people. Let me fail at this conversation in peace. I wish I had a ladle to throw at them.

'I'm glad you're OK, Cameron. Thank you for calling and checking in. It was lovely to meet you.'

This is good. It draws a line. You can get over your heartbreak, I won't be rebound girl. I can be that nice girl you met at a party once who restored your faith in humans helping humans in times of crisis.

'I mean, if you wanted to grab a coffee...' he says.

'Really?' I reply.

'Actually, Stantz, there is something you can do for me. Are you free next weekend? I have a thing, you can come with me?'

'A thing?' I whisper.

'There'll be other people there.'

Given my line of work, I worry he's inviting me to an orgy.

'A dinner thing. I was supposed to go with Imogen. This will save me turning up alone, crying to the room and looking like a complete sad case.'

'Is it fancy dress? Sadly, I had to return my *Ghostbusters* costume today.'

He laughs. 'Come as you are. I'll send you details. It's good to hear your voice today.'

'It's good to hear yours. Hang on in there, Spengler. Things can only get better.'

'Like the song from the nineties.'

I then sing. I sing the song down the phone. What the hell am I doing?

'You're tuneful. I'm going to go. Can I have your mobile number? I'll text you about dinner.'

'Sure.' I repeat the digits carefully. '...007 at the end, like

James Bond but not, obviously, because I'm not a spy. I can't be because you found me, eh?'

He laughs. 'I'll message you, Stantz. Night.' He hangs up.

By the way, it's Josie. My actual name is Josie Jewell.

I stand here in the cold for a moment, clutching the restaurant's phone, staring into the night sky scattered with stars. In the distance, I hear the percussive bangs of fireworks going off, beating in time with my chest, rainbow colours sizzling by a nearby rooftop.

Did that go well? I sang to him. I think we arranged a date, but he didn't call it a date. He called it a thing. A dinner thing with other people. That could literally mean Wagamama where everyone shares tables. I was once sitting so close to a couple in that place that I started eating their gyoza.

I am drunk for the second day in three. I need a day off, some sleep, my bed and loungewear. Things can only get better... Mike liked that song. He had a thing for late nineties club music and I hate how he pops into my head, that he even got a mention this evening. He doesn't belong in my head, he has no right to be there, but that's the problem with exes, they live rent-free for an eternity, usually quietly but sometimes they poke their head around the door to give you a fright.

Josie,

By the time you read this, I'll be gone. Yes, I'm a coward for doing it like this, but I don't want your family to get involved and this way, it's a cleaner break. I do love you. I think you're smart, caring and amazing. I loved living with you and I really hoped we could make our life together work. The truth is, I'm embarrassed by your work, by what you do, your family. It started out as a bit of a joke, but there's only so many times you can handle people taking the piss out of your girlfriend because she's surrounded by cock and lube all day. I walked into the footie changing room the other day and one of the lads found an old video of your mum and dad going at it. My future in-laws. I just don't think I want that to be running theme my whole life. It's not normal. I don't want a wife or kids involved in all of that. Please keep the ring. I'm so sorry.

Mike

FIVE

I tell you what there's not enough of in this world. There's not enough lighting around house numbers, which means you have to get your Uber to drop you at one end of a road, and then creep into people's driveways trying to work out what number their house is without setting off security lights and freaking out their dogs. Only an idiot like me would also get dropped at No. 10 when she needs No. 42. I stand outside one home that doesn't even have a number and if I was a postman, I would signal my outrage at this by losing all their mail.

Cameron was very vague about tonight. I was given an address, which I assumed from my bad geography to be the high street, and the name of a wine bar, except it's not. That's the name of a house, Le Blanc, and this is a residential road, which I made Piotr, the Uber driver, circle four times until I was sure this was the right place. This is not typical Josie. Normal Josie would have googled the wine bar, looked through the menu, planned her order and worked out her portion of the bill before she'd even left the house, but it's been a busy week with hangovers and wedding talk, so I didn't do that this time round. I've not dressed for a residential setting either. I'm braless in a wide-leg jumpsuit, so whatever happens tonight, there will be a point where I'm tits out in someone's bathroom.

As I meander down the road, I suddenly see the house in question. The driveway is full. Maybe I should just bail. Piotr isn't very far away, I could chase his car. I see balloons at the door. This definitely does not look like the casual dinner thing that was described to me. This is a party.

'Boo!' a voice suddenly pipes up from a bush and I let out a yelp in fright, holding my keys up to the air as my mother has taught me well.

'It's only me.' Cameron emerges from the hedges that line the entrance. I smile to see him, mainly because he's in a suit with white Converse, a duffel coat and woolly hat. The Ghostbusters glasses are gone, but his eyes are blue, clear and bright like a beachy sky. Don't stare at the nice eyes.

'Why are you hiding in a bush?' I ask.

'I wasn't hiding, I was waiting. For you. I thought it best you don't have to make the walk up to the house on your own.'

'Thank you, kind sir. Though this was reported to me as a casual dinner thing.'

'It is...'

'Casual dinners for me are Pizza Express.'

'Posh. Casual dinners for me are McDonald's. You look lovely, though.'

'Again, thank you.'

He starts to walk slowly up the drive, a cheeky walk with both hands in his pockets. I follow. Do I hold his hand? Air kiss? I'm still the girl who watched his girlfriend and housemate have sex and then gave him a shoulder to cry on.

'So, do I get clues? I suppose you and your housemate don't live here.'

'No.'

'But there is food today?'

'Yes.'

'You can expand the answers, you know.'

As we approach the house, it seems very homely from the box trees in the drive and the attention they've paid to their garden.

The front door suddenly swings open. 'Camelot!'

'Moustache! Horseface!'

The ladies who stand at the door are in cocktail dresses and mid heels, with matching brown bobs. 'Moustache' doesn't have a moustache because I'm studying her upper lip a little too closely. Horseface does have a long chin and a lovely mane, though. She raises her eyebrows at me.

'Imogen?' she asks. 'You don't look like your picture.'

'That's because I'm Josie.'

She glares at Cameron, not even out of embarrassment. 'Oh. Cam, you told us your girlfriend's name was Imogen. We made a place card.'

I smile nervously. Mainly because I get the sense that he is related to these women but also because my presence has not been expected. They were expecting pretty cat girl. I am not a pretty cat girl. I am a dependable if well-groomed dog girl. They're most certainly family, aren't they? I have been ambushed.

'I texted Horseface to tell you Imogen wasn't coming anymore...' Cameron explains.

'You texted me? Who texts people anymore?' She studies my face. 'So, you're a new one?' she asks rudely.

'Yes,' he answers. 'To be fair, I bumped into her on the Tube this morning and asked her if she fancied coming to a dinner and she said yes, so...'

He's not half wrong.

'Look, Cameron,' I say, 'if me being here is a problem, then I can go. I don't want to be in the way.'

He takes my hand and shakes his head. 'No, it's not a problem. These are my extremely rude sisters, Moustache, also known as Natasha, and Horseface, also known as Heather. This is my friend Josie, who has very kindly offered to be my plus-one.'

I've been upgraded to friend. This is a level up from party acquaintance, I guess.

Heather rolls her eyes around. 'Hello, Josie. I'm an older and better sister. I guess we can write another place card. It's nice to meet you,' she says, not entirely convincing either of us. 'No gift? Wine? It is her birthday,' she says, turning to her brother.

This surprise 'dinner thing' keeps evolving into something else. I enter the hallway and look up to a banner. *Happy 60th Birthday, Mum.* Crap. Your mum? Her birthday? I haven't even brought a card. I don't even know the woman's name.

I stare at Cameron as a few more people enter the hallway, all in smart partywear, looking Cameron up and down, including a woman with a silver bob and a silk pleated dress.

'Cameron!'

'Mum, happy birthday!'

'Thank you for the case of wine, it arrived this morning – what a surprise...'

Cameron pulls a face at Natasha/Moustache.

This woman's tones are elegant and joyful, though I suspect that may be because she's seeing in her sixtieth with something sparkling. She's accompanied by a man, wearing the late sixties version of partywear, which is a suit with no tie and a casual loafer. I look at his face in panic, thinking I might know him from somewhere. Maybe he's played tennis with my dad? Maybe I've seen him locally?

'I'm Henry Cox. Delighted, Imogen!' he says, shaking my hand animatedly.

'She's not Imogen, Dad,' a sister replies from behind me.

'Is Imogen coming too? I'm confused.'

'No, everyone. This is Josie.'

An awkward silence descends as we all take a moment to take in that point. Again.

'So are you Cameron's girlfriend?' he asks. Henry's tone is brusque, short and I sense some tension in his relationship with his son. *What is this girl doing here, Cameron? Where did you find her and what is she bringing to the table this evening?* Well, not dessert as I was told this was a casual dinner thing.

Immediately, I feel protective towards Cameron and this family of wolves that circle us. I think about our evening sitting in my brother's kitchen as the party happened around us, rewinding to something he said. *I'm from a big family. I'm the runt of the litter, the youngest, the disappointment.* I didn't think it possible.

'No, I am not. Happy birthday, though, Mrs Cox.'

'Josie's a friend.' Cameron adds. 'Josie, this is my mum and dad and another sister, Arabella, but I call her Smeller.'

'Oh, grow up, Cam,' she snarls back. 'It's nice to meet you. What do you do?'

She just asked me that, didn't she? I'm still wearing my coat.

'Josie works in events,' Cameron informs them.

And just like that, the lie is already out there, hovering. If the event means sex, then yes, that is accurate. But now is not the time to clear up that little misunderstanding. Now is the time to be judged. I feel the need to spin on the spot so they can view me from all angles, to give a brief introductory monologue. Hi. I'm Josie. I like cheese, my middle name is Elizabeth and I once broke my wrist running down a slide. My birthday is in July. I got this jumpsuit in H&M.

But no, for now, she's Josie. In events. Not Imogen.

'Then why are you here?' Henry Cox asks me.

'Dad,' Cameron sighs, embarrassed.

'Well, Cameron invited me as a friend...' I push him playfully. Maybe a little too hard as he stumbles into an umbrella stand. 'And he thought it would be nice for me to come along, do some party tricks,' I explain.

'You're a magician?' Heather asks.

'No. I was just trying to be funny...' And failing.

Henry Cox still studies my face; I can tell he has questions regarding my education and salary brackets. 'Well, you are very welcome, Josie. Cameron, put her coat in the downstairs cloakroom. Let's get you a drink.'

The crowd disperse from the hallway back into the main area of the house, still grumbling about place cards, as I stand here taking off my coat, wondering whether to keep it on. What on earth am I doing? This feeling worsens as Cameron opens the door to a downstairs cloakroom. There is a vase of fake flowers, a photo of the whole family standing next to a harbour on holiday, and a cross-stitch print of some cockerels on the wall. I smile to think of the inappropriate joke my dad would make about them.

'A dinner thing,' I mumble.

'I wasn't wrong,' he replies cheekily. He laughs, taking off his hat and shaking out his curly shaggy hair. 'I'm sorry. You can leave if you want. It was bad of me to ask you to come and take them on. I forgot they'd go in like piranhas and give you the once-over. I'm an idiot.'

'You don't get on with your dad much, eh?'

'You noticed?' His body changes shape as he says that, his shoulders slump and his eyes point down and, for a moment, I want to embrace him hard and tell him it'll all be fine.

'What wine did you buy your mum?' I ask him instead.

'A case of Barolo, it's her favourite.'

'It's a good thing it's my favourite too.'

He takes my hand and squeezes it tightly, the physical contact making me sigh. Those hands fit, don't they? I may squeeze back.

. . .

The one thing I learned from my parents is that it pays to sit at a dinner party and take in the room. It gives you a chance, as a salesperson, to figure people out. Fifteen minutes with this lot and I can read them like a catalogue. It helps that they're so self-absorbed that they mostly talk about themselves, so I may as well be as invisible as the green salad that no one is touching. This is what happens when you serve people rocket. However, the confusing thing is how the very likeable Cameron is related to them all.

The conversation swerves from golf handicaps to holiday homes to Natasha regaling how her daughter is now Grade 7 in flute. She spoke for a whole five minutes about fingering. I didn't laugh. I promise.

So, who do we have at this very grown-up dinner party with matching china and calligraphy-fonted place cards? (Mine with a hastily crossed-out Imogen.)

1) Natasha has a husband with a name I've already forgotten. They both work in top-end finance. He plays rugby and I bet he's the sort that has a homoerotic fascination with striding around a changing room naked, lunging. Always lunging. I'm pretty sure his penis has a name.

2) Next is Heather and her husband, Rupert, who talk about their kids constantly, though seem physically awkward around each other, making me think it's been an age since they've had a truly intimate moment together. When they do fornicate, it's occasion sex from behind so they don't have to look each other in the eye. Sometimes with an added finger as a treat, depending on the bedsheet-changing schedule.

3) Arabella is sister three. She's married to a doctor and has sacrificed her career to be a stay-at-home mother despite a first-class degree in classics. What the doctor wants, the doctor gets. She is most definitely a submissive. You can tell by the way she serves him his meal and he puts a hand out to tell her that's

enough. Most likely, they've bought all sorts from my website. The only thing I haven't supplied are the safe words.

But, naturally, none of them talk about any of this at the dinner table. It's all a façade of normalcy, kids with very traditional names and Oxford button-down shirts. They all went to university, their lives are very centred around themselves and their success. Cameron doesn't enter into any of it, but mainly nods and smiles uneasily, occasionally side-eyeing me when someone drops something ridiculous into the conversation about the rising cost of horse-riding and artichokes so I know we're on the same page.

'Please have more of the creamed spinach!' Alicia, Cameron's mother, tells me.

Alicia and Henry are the two I still have to work out. I'd like to imagine that they are involved in some heavy kink that's steeped in shame and role play.

'Thank you,' I reply. 'So, have you lived in this house for long?' I ask, trying to find something vaguely interesting to talk about. Tonight may be awkward, but I'm still going to remember the very good manners that my parents have instilled in me.

'Well, obviously it's just myself and Henry now, but we raised the whole family here, didn't we?' she says to the table.

'Le Blanc... did you choose that name?'

'Yes, because it's a white house,' Heather explains to me like I might be stupid. I'm not so stupid that I gave my house a French name when I live in the middle of London, but still.

'I thought it might be because you're all fans of *Friends*.'

On hearing this, Cameron spits out a bit of wine and laughs hysterically. The rest of the table sit there like I've sworn in a foreign language. Come on, people. *Friends*? Your last name is Cox? It was a cultural TV event. Even my Nan knows who half those people in the show are and the only thing she watches is the horse racing, football and *Cash in the Attic*.

'Come on, guys. Matt LeBlanc?' Cameron announces to the table.

'Isn't he the lad who did *Top Gear*?' asks Natasha's husband.

'Yes,' I confirm. 'He was also in an American sitcom from the nineties. It was very popular.' Obviously not in this house. I am mortified my joke didn't go down well. That's as funny as you're going to get from me. 'Well, it's a lovely house.' With all the beige on beige and tasselled lampshades.

'Remind me what you do again? Events, is it? Like party planning?' Heather continues.

I went to school with girls like Heather, so her brand of bitch is one I deal with particularly well, especially as I spent most of secondary school with grade-A teenage frizz, braces and porn star parents.

'Catering. From parties to larger-scale conferences.'

A dry medallion of pork sits in my gullet as that lie is emitted into the air. The deceit is evolving and not particularly well. I don't even know how to follow on from this. Am I believable? Do I give an idea of menus? What napkins we use? I take a large gulp of wine as the table goes quiet so they all can get a sense of the new girl that Cameron has brought to the homestead.

'Did you go to university?' Cameron's dad asks.

Cameron glares at him at this point and he's right because it smacks of snobbery, but I don't let that faze me.

'I did actually. I went to Leeds, studied business management and spent a year abroad in Shanghai.'

This is not a lie and the flex is necessary here.

Cameron sits up in his chair as even that has come as a surprise to him, but it shuts the table up at least.

'Did you know that Cameron went to Bournemouth?' Henry says that name like it's a bad person who's done him wrong.

'Bournemouth is lovely. It's a great university,' I say defensively.

'Yes, for weekend breaks and retirement,' Rupert at the end of the table jests. 'I mean computer game design, what even is that?'

There is sniggering as someone makes shooting video game noises.

My eyes widen and I reach for Cameron's hand under the table, feeling his knee shaking. How on earth does he fit into this puzzle? He's a world away from everyone in this room.

'So, what do your parents do?' Henry Cox says, continuing his interrogation.

Oh dear, porn? 'Oh, they're enjoying retirement, volunteering, charity work. They used to own their own business.'

'Like a shop?'

'Yes.' We sell sex swings, Henry (fittings not included).

'Henry is a local MP, you know. A borough councillor,' says Alicia. And it's then I realise where I've seen his face before. On flyers shoved through our front door, harping on about his brand of right-wing politics and agendas.

I pause for a moment to let that wash over me.

'Important work, that,' I mumble, taking another gulp of wine, letting the earthiness swim around the inside of my mouth.

'Well, I like to think so. Just doing my bit for society.'

My stomach churns slightly to think of the nature of those flyers. Mum used to put them straight in the bin, occasionally using them to pick up dog faeces in the house. I get the sense that all the people around this table are similar in terms of their beliefs. And then there's Cameron. Seriously, did they adopt him?

I down half a glass of Barolo to hide my obvious discomfort. I think I need to pee, but I definitely don't want to be nipples out, sitting on the loo, facing their happy family portrait. Just grin and bear this, Josie. You've been in worse dinner-party situations. Remember that time in Shanghai when you ate a fish eyeball? I can't tell what is worse, though. Why am I here? Because about a week ago, in some drunken party haze, I thought I might have a connection with this man next to me? I'm not sure if this is worth the pain.

'But that is just scandalous. I would complain. Deffo. Go to the governors with it,' a voice projects with some volume from the other end of the table.

Cameron and I look at each other, trying to earwig about the nature of the scandal.

'What's got your knickers in a twist this time, Moustache?' Cameron asks casually.

'Sex education. In Year 3 at school. It really is ridiculous what they teach children these days, it's too much too soon.'

'Well, you only have to look at teen pregnancy statistics to know that none of it is working. It's endemic,' the doctor husband adds.

There are murmurs of agreement around the table and I put a glass to my lips.

'Too much freedom, too much knowledge,' Henry Cox proffers. 'We give young girls far too much space to roam and spread their legs.'

When the words come out of this mouth, I snort and possibly inhale a bit of potato into my lungs. As they continue to gossip, Cameron's head sinks further and further down and I lean into him.

'I'm sorry,' I whisper.

'Why are you sorry?'

'Because of what I'm going to do next...'

I shouldn't really because it's his mother's birthday, but it's either this or letting certain myths perpetuate amongst this rather vile group of people.

'Why is it the girls' problem when they get pregnant?' I suddenly ask.

The table goes quiet as I add my tuppence worth to the conversation.

'To the best of my knowledge, there is usually a young man involved in the process of baby-making too,' I explain.

Cameron's sisters glare at me. *What are you doing? You are a guest, you must nod and agree with us.*

'Babies are a joint responsibility. It's also up to the man to understand boundaries, contraception, his part in the process. I don't know where you get your statistics either, good doctor, but teenage pregnancy and STDs are actually on the decline in the UK because of sex education and greater access to support systems.'

The table is silent. Not because they've been silenced out of shame, but because I think they might be angry at me.

'Maybe this isn't something to be brought up over dinner,' Alicia mutters.

'But it was Heather who brought it up?' Cameron says. 'And Josie has a point. I don't remember talking about sex in this house growing up. It was hidden away. Where else would I have learned about these things? It'd just be misinformation from the school playground. Porn?'

As he says that word, I feel my cheeks redden.

'CAMERON!' Henry Cox shouts.

Oh, Henry. You watch your porn in the shed, don't you? With rubber gloves.

I turn to Cameron's sisters. 'Have a look at the sex education topics. It might help your daughters understand their bodies more. I just don't think you should see the word "sex" and think it a bad thing.'

'At eight, I think it is,' Natasha retorts.

'How do you tell your daughter she came into the world then?' I ask her, my frustration starting to rise.

'She grew in my tummy from a seed.'

Cameron titters under his breath.

'How is this funny, Cameron? There is a time and a place,' Heather says. 'I don't want my children knowing about these things yet.'

'Does your daughter know she has a vagina?' I ask.

'Cameron, control your friend,' Natasha interrupts. Cameron ignores her.

'My daughter has a foufou,' Heather replies.

'And that is part of the problem.'

'Excuse me?'

Oh dear, they all have foufous and winkies at this table, don't they? Except for Natasha's husband, who I really do suspect names his penis something fantasy-based like Raygar, Breaker of Chambers.

'I can go into the school and talk to them as a local councillor. I don't think this is something we should endorse,' Henry says abruptly. 'You are right, Natasha, to have your reservations.'

The way I am silenced makes me grit my teeth, clench my jaw. I inhale deeply as Natasha refolds her napkin on her lap, appearing vindicated.

'So you think a suitable course of action is to prevent sex education for all because it doesn't align with your views?' I ask.

'I speak for a community, that is my job. Sex education is a choice,' Henry preaches.

'It's a basic necessity. It's knowledge they'll carry for a lifetime. More than quadratic equations or Grade 7 flute.'

Of everything I've said this far, this seems to go down the worst. Was I supposed to be impressed by the flute? I would if she could play it like Lizzo and twerk at the same time, but I suspect she doesn't. Natasha is tapping her foot impatiently to see how else I can offend anyone else in this room. Cameron sits there quietly, though I think he may be smiling.

'We are your hosts, this is very disrespectful. I hope you don't treat your clients in catering in such a way,' Henry adds.

'If they're talking out of their backsides, then yes, I do.' And that is my parting shot. I stand up from my chair and push it back slowly. 'Alicia, happy birthday. I am so sorry that I soured the mood here...'

Henry's arms are crossed, as he glares into space. I think I may have reduced Arabella to tears. This will mean more dessert for all, no? You can hide my place card that you had to write in biro and chat about the absent Imogen, who obviously was a better match for your son. I won't have to sit through this shitshow. I can buy some chips from somewhere. I am sorry, Cameron. Whatever this was, I don't want to be here.

'Thank you for dinner. It was...'

...bloody awful.

I return to the cloakroom to get my coat, one of the cockerels in the cross-stitch staring at me with wonkily sewn eyes. Don't look at me like that, in judgement. I have sex. Maybe not regularly. My last boyfriend was a two-week Tinder fling, who was pleasant enough. It reached its peak when he considered camping in October a romantic weekend away. Romance needs an en suite as a minimum. But what I know of sex is that it's also about pleasure, self-love, connection. It's the best part of my job to have learned all those things and I wish I could tell everyone around that table. I wish I could hand Alicia a Clitmeister for her sixtieth and see her face ignite from the new sensations. Because I bet Henry in all their years of marriage has never even bothered to look for it.

As I leave, I notice the low murmur of sniping, angry language and slowly shut the front door. As I reach the end of the drive, though, I hear a voice.

'Josie?'

I turn in surprise. Cameron jogs to the end of the drive, his arms under his armpits to retain bodily warmth. I spy a sister at a bay window of the house watching over us. He takes my arm and leads me to a hedge.

'Go and put a coat on,' I say. 'It's freezing out here. I'm fine, I'm so sorry I spoiled things.'

'That was, like, the best thing ever. No one speaks to my dad like that,' he says, almost excitedly. 'Everyone's usually scared of him. But that was brilliant, it was so smart, so sparky. I'm sorry, because I should have briefed you. I asked you to be here and I was selfish about it because I needed a shield, someone to take the flak off me, because most dinners we have, it's basically me being the butt of the jokes and I couldn't take that after what happened at the party.'

This is not the Cameron I met at Halloween. He was so sweet, chatty and I've seen none of that today. I saw him climb into a shell, and it pains me to see someone put down like that.

'That wouldn't have needed a brief. I'd have needed a full-on report with footnotes. I think the doctor in there is a pervert. He just stared at my chest the whole time.'

'He sleeps around, it's known.'

'They really are not nice people. How did you grow up with that?' I ask.

'I was the rebel,' he replies.

'You mean the normal one.'

There's a pause. I feel bad for him when I compare my own upbringing. A dinner party in my family would have been full of laughs, conversation, my dad's attempts at bad magic, an eighties playlist, innuendo for days and everyone being made to feel welcome, heard, accepted.

I rub Cameron's arm to try to warm him up. 'I don't know what to say, Cameron. Look at you, you're shivering. I'll walk up to the main road and grab a cab or call an Uber, it's fine. Go back to the party.'

'I don't want to...'

'I don't blame you but—'

'I think I like you,' he blurts out.

I pause as he says that. Does he like me because I stood up to his dad or because I'm not wearing a bra? He likes me? Like is a strange word in any case. I like ham, for example. It doesn't rule my world. It's a very middling emotion. But I think I'm here because I like him too. But look at everything it's built on. My fake identity, his strange family dynamics, his cheating girlfriend...

'I like you too.' It doesn't hurt to at least say that out loud, eh? 'But...'

But I don't get to finish. Outside his parents' house, hiding in a bush under the dim street lights, he reaches in and kisses me. Woah. It's unexpected, but I don't push him away. His hand to the side of my face, the soft pressure of his lips against mine. You kiss nice. He puts a hand to my lower back and pulls me in and I grab a handful of his hair, there's a moment when our mouths are just touching, exhaling gently. And a feeling that spreads down my chest, that takes hold of my shoulders, that warms and draws me in.

Shit. I really really like you too.

SIX

'I went out with someone whose family were tossers. His dad was a casual misogynist and used to grab my bum when his son wasn't looking,' Michelle tells me as we look over the monthly reports. 'His mum was also a huge fan of The Osmonds, like she had a T-shirt with Donny's face on it, emblazoned across her tits. She used to follow them on tour.'

I stand over the conference-room desk, listening. I don't mind Donny, less enthused by the misogyny, but Cameron's family were next-level tossers. 'They were really awful, Michelle.'

She opens a box of doughnuts, taking one out and biting into it. 'But still, he kissed you on the pavement, so this thing has legs, right?' she says, chewing at the same time.

Michelle is the only person I've told about the weekend's events as I don't want to get anyone else's hopes up, least of all my own. It was just a kiss, nothing more, because the follow-up options would have been impromptu sex in a bush, sex back at my parents' house or sex in the downstairs bathroom of his family home where I'd just made a speedy exit. So after we kissed, he went back to the jaws of the worst sixtieth birthday party in history and I went to find a cab and some fried chicken that I brought back home to share with my mum's dog.

'We've had such a shaky start. He thinks I'm in catering and I pretty much despise his family. It just feels like hard work from the off.'

'But the *Ghostbusters* costumes?'

'And? I wore the same jumper as Pamela in returns last month. This doesn't mean we're destined to be together.'

Michelle laughs as the doors of the office open and people file in. It's what I do at the beginning of a week, I gather representatives from every department and we have a chat over coffee and doughnuts. Good Krispy Kremes with the toppings as I feel that's the antidote to any Monday morning.

Speaking of Pamela, she walks in with a box and places it on the table. We're not in the same pea-green jumper today for which I'm glad as Pamela is in her late fifties and last time, it gave me a severe crisis of fashion confidence. Pamela came to our company having only ever worked in biscuit factories. She said there were perks of sorting through bags of shortbread, but at least with this gig she doesn't have to wear a hairnet and a pinny and she has more interesting stories for the dinner table.

'Morning.' I smile. 'You come bearing gifts?'

'I'll say,' she mutters, her eyes wide open. 'There's a problem with the new vibes with the glitter. We're not sure if they're overheating, but they're all coming back in dribs and drabs. That was maybe the wrong turn of phrase to use...' She opens the box and pulls out a vibrator that's been returned to us in a large Ziploc bag which makes it look like evidence in a crime scene. 'They also sent a picture.'

'What the hell of?' I'm imagining an inflamed vulva, crispy burnt pubes, we really don't pay Pamela enough.

'She sent a photo of how she put it down on the bed and it left a burn mark on her sheets.'

We both examine the brown smear marks on the photo

closely. 'That could be a burn mark or it could be...' We keel over laughing.

I peer in the box, seeing an assortment of glittery vibrators suitable for a disco sex party. These are not in plastic bags, so I will assume Pamela has wiped them down or used gloves to handle them. I'll have to write an angry letter to the manufacturer. I should also think about getting Pamela a bonus.

'So, let's recall what we have sold, full refunds and vouchers issued. Does anyone have one of these?' I ask the room. This is a common line in this workplace. Please try what you want within reason. Don't take a hundred dildos home and give them to your mates, though.

'I did,' Pamela says, plainly, which surprises me, but we don't judge in this business. 'It is the vibrating element inside, it heats the glitter, which is metallic. Maurice had a look and took one apart for us. He thinks it's overheating, but it needs to be vibrating for at least fifteen minutes before it goes very hot.'

Maurice is Pamela's husband. He makes model ships from scratch. I like to think that he's got a dissected vibrator next to model replicas of some miniature ship cannons.

'That's very kind of Maurice to investigate, make sure you expense that for his time.'

She nods. 'It just depends. Like if you're having a quick session and using it on the outside of your body, then you're fine, but I don't want to think what would happen if you're going for the long haul and then suddenly it's like someone's shoved a red-hot poker up your fanny.'

She's so deadpan as she says it. I remember when she started – she walked into a wall at seeing a dildo as wide as a Pringles tube. Now it's just part of her everyday. This is definitely better than biscuits, isn't it, Pamela?

'I'll flag it, but thank you for investigating it properly so I have some detail. Keep putting the returned ones aside.'

'I will. Also, while I'm here. I think that customer is still returning things to us, pretending they don't work, but I suspect that he's used them.'

'Do I want to know why you think they're being used?'

'Can I expense a UV light to be sure?'

'I'm going to say yes, but please don't touch things without gloves.'

'Oh, I wear the thick ones, the same ones I use for cleaning my loo,' she mutters.

To my left, Pip, head of product development, sifts through the box. Pip is not shy in helping herself to goods, then coming into work and telling me about them. Such is the nature of our professional relationship that I know her husband likes a vice on his balls, amongst other things that sometimes make my morning biscuits stick in my throat.

'Thank god, I didn't take one of these. I don't see the point in prettifying a penis with glitter. They're ugly things as it is. This looks like a unicorn dong?' Pip says.

'I would feel weird putting that in me,' adds Michelle, who used to be in actual porn.

'Cosplayers, fantasy sex – there's always a market for these sorts of things,' I say, thinking about the many different people we provide for. 'But health and safety first. I don't need to hear someone's burnt their house down with a vibrator that we sold. Pip, word on the Sugar Cube range?'

Pip winces, clinging on to a folder in her hands. The Sugar Cube range is a collaboration with a YouTube influencer who uses words such as 'fleek' and 'reem' in her professional emails. 'It's like drawing blood, Josie. She's actually designed the sex toys, like a dildo thing she wants to put her name to.'

Pip reaches into the folder and retrieves something that's been drawn in biro and possibly coloured in with crayon. The few of us in the room cock our heads to the side in wonder to work out which way up it'd go.

'That looks like a Coke bottle with a bell-end?' Michelle

says. She's not half wrong, which makes me worry about the sort of things this young influencer does to get herself off.

'Why is there a plug on it?' I ask.

'Oh, it's USB chargeable. She doesn't believe in batteries.'

'So if it's dead, you need to sit by a laptop or a socket to pleasure yourself?' I ask.

The room giggles, as is the way of our Monday meetings.

'Josie, I've raised all of this with her. We hooked her up with the sex therapist for advice about ergonomics, but she ignores it all.'

'Would you like me to touch base with her management?'

Pip nods slowly.

I grin back at her. 'Anything else?'

'The scented dildo range is taking off.' I make a mental note to tell Tina, who openly mocked this. 'We are doing some surveys about the new condom range. Feedback has been healthy, some complaints about the new Durex being a little tight and over-lubed. "Like wrestling with a goldfish," said one of the comments. And people are really liking the increased vegan condom range.'

There's a little laugh of disbelief in the corner of the room. It's Charlie.

'Do you all know Charlie?' I ask the room. 'He's new, studying management part-time and rotating around departments as Christmas rolls around, so please use him while you can. He's eager to learn. Charlie, I sense you have a question about vegan condoms?'

Charlie has been standing in the shadows since he first entered the room. He still blushes to hear everyone talk so frankly about sex, but we're also a female-dominated company, so I can tell he's trying to separate his intimidation from his awe.

'Are you telling me you can get plant-based johnnies? But they're rubber?' he asks, confused.

'Traditional condoms are made of latex, which has a dairy protein in to soften the rubber,' I explain.

'So if you're lactose-intolerant, you could be allergic to johnnies?'

'Well, if you were vegan, would you actually eat cock?' Michelle adds, making the women in the room snigger. Charlie looks petrified.

'It's an evolving market, Charlie. Condoms are becoming easier to use, biodegradable, less chemicals. And vegan, so we try to expand our products range when we can.'

He stands there wide-eyed, taking it all in. There is so much to teach you, kid. I don't even know where to start.

'Anything more, Pip?' I ask her.

'I tried out the candy cane condoms and they are hilarious... and minty, which is a new feeling. All the Christmas products are taking off, even the reindeer role play stuff, which, to be fair, I thought would never sell.'

I nod. Christmas is a major sales moment for us, though I'm not entirely sure how people gift our merchandise. I don't know how you'd open a gift box (free if you spend over £40) filled with sex goodies in front of an elderly aunt. However, our sales always reach a peak, especially in naughty elf and sexy Santa lingerie. What do I want for Christmas? New socks, a roast dinner and better orgasms by the light of the Christmas tree.

'How is postage, packing and delivery doing?'

I have a team of women who head up that department, three of whom are called Martha and who all mysteriously got pregnant at the same time two years ago. They all put their thumbs up, silently munching on my Biscoff doughnuts.

'And marketing?'

My head of marketing is the wonderful Clara, who loves a sharp bob, an animated PowerPoint and a double-ended dildo with suction cups as she once told me at someone's leaving drinks.

'All going swimmingly. We got some mentions in some magazine features recently, especially in their gift recommendations articles. Ads are performing well with click-through and conversion rates up. Also, there was a production company who got in touch.'

This piques my interest as production company used to mean a lot of things in my parents' previous line of work. 'Production company?' I ask, curiously.

'For one of those mid-morning talk show things. Anyway, they're planning for the new year and they asked if we had anyone who'd go on as a panellist to chat about sex and stuff.'

Michelle claps her hands excitedly. 'Oooh, Josie – you'd be fantastic at that. You could be famous!'

I giggle under my breath, but I don't think I'm made for the screen. I can think of someone who'd be perfect, though. 'You know what, let me run that past my mum. It could tie in well with her charity work and she does a lot of public speaking along those lines.'

'Plus, she knows the ins and outs of sex better than anyone,' Michelle says.

Stifled laughter radiates through the room. I told you the innuendo came as standard. But Mum would be perfect for it, to advocate for sex and what we do. I can help her practise her spiel. It will give her something to spend her time on next to fretting over Sonny's wedding.

'Leave that with me, Clara. Look, you're all doing marvellous work. Profits are up... it's going to be a busy month, so let me know if you need my help. You know me, I'll pitch in wherever. And also, if you haven't replied yet to our New Year do invite, then let Michelle know, please. Families are very welcome.'

Everyone nods and smiles as they get up and filter out of the room. It's a good team here and you start to love all of these people like family because you get to know them perhaps more intimately than a normal boss would.

'You are such a good boss. I love being your assistant,' Michelle effuses as we stand there in the empty conference room.

'It's the doughnut bribery, isn't it? If I provided the normal glazed, you'd love me less...'

She winks at me as I move the box of disco dongs off the table and put them next to a box of crotchless knickers due to also be returned. Turns out they were crotchless but also only suitable for people with one leg.

'Circling back to Cameron,' Michelle mentions. 'If there's a spark there, you can work through all these things. Take him out for coffee, tell him who you are...'

'Then watch him howl with laughter and run out the door?' I reply.

'Or say, you've got the wrong end of the stick, I'm not in catering...'

'My end of the stick is sex toys. Fancy another latte?'

'You're just dodging it.'

I stick out my tongue at her. I'm dodging a potential bullet to my heart. When you suffer heartbreak in the humiliating way that I did, then the heart becomes a tentative, fragile thing.

I sit down, pretending to pick up a piece of paper on my desk and read it. 'It's just too complicated to navigate, Michelle. I have so much going on...'

'You don't really. You work here, you go home, you put on a hoodie and watch a lot of telly.'

'That's a burn.'

'That's the truth. You have an actual relationship with some of those hoodies.'

'Because they're warm, comforting and have never let me down.'

She comes over with one of the last doughnuts on a napkin,

shaking her head. 'I think there's a spark there. You can tell from the way your face glows when you say his name. Your parents started that way. I don't think they thought they'd find love in the way that they did. But they had spark from day one, that was undeniable. No one made your mum laugh like your dad. And it was little things, you used to see it, the way they'd smile at each other from across a room...'

I know better than to ask what was going on in the room at the time, but I get what she means. They still do that thing in the kitchen in the morning, a gaze that replaces words, that lifts them both. It's sweet, if depressingly sickening, to see as their daughter. I never delve into precisely how they met and their past canon of work – I will quite happily go to my grave not ever needing to know that detail. But was the spark felt when they were mid-shot? Or afterwards when they were getting changed and shaking hands?

'And, your mum and dad had their fair share of drama at the beginning,' Michelle tells me. 'Did they ever tell you about that?'

'I hear the romanticised version. I suspect they leave out details.'

'Your nan didn't know your dad was in porn. She thought he was an actual plumber. He kept that charade going for an age, read books about the subject. The running joke used to be he was good with pipes, leaks, massive ballcock...'

I chuckle. This I did not know. It may explain why Dad is good at fixing dripping taps, though.

'Then he got with your mum and brought her home to meet your nan and they told her your mum was an airline stewardess and they had to keep that going. The lie just grew and grew. Your mother borrowed an outfit from set and had to bulk-buy Toblerones and pretend she'd got them in duty-free.'

'How did it end?'

'Your mum got pregnant, didn't she?'

I open my eyes in shock. I did not know any of this. At all. I knew I came along before they married but wasn't wholly aware of the timeline.

Michelle senses my shock. 'Oh, you weren't an accident. They'd been together a while and were living together, but then they had to tell your nan.'

'I'm sure that was a bit lively...'

'She was the one who told them both they needed to get out of the game because you were coming. They needed to build a half-normal life for you.'

I look around the warehouse office in which I sit. Half-normal at least. Either way, they both came out the other side and they're still together, against all odds.

'I tell you what, though, there were some mighty dicks in our industry,' she continues.

'I have no doubt.'

She shakes her head at me. 'But your dad wasn't one of them. He used to look after your mum in little ways, a jacket to her shoulders, he'd switch places with her if she were traffic side on the pavement. He'd wait by the door with an umbrella if it was raining. It was kind. It was all those little things you don't see in those films we used to make.'

He still does that now twenty or more years down the line.

'It was nice to see your dad take care of your mum, to make her feel loved. Up to that point, I was consumed by the industry – seeing their relationship helped me separate love from sex and it helped me understand them as two very different things.'

'It's one of the great love stories of our time,' I say, jokingly.

'If you leave out the bit where they met because he came on—'

I put a hand up to the air again. No, Michelle. Never tell me that, ever.

She cackles and finishes the last bit of my doughnut. 'But it all started with a little spark. That's all I'm saying. Despite everything that's gone a bit wrong so far, Cameron could be your great love. Was it a good kiss?'

'Yes.'

She wrinkles her nose at me for not regaling any more detail. But it was one of those kisses you think about too much. When you're alone in bed, fantasising about what could have come next: some casual, made-up movie in my head where we jumped in a taxi that was serendipitously waiting there, back to my room (my parents not downstairs watching *Peaky Blinders*, obviously) and had the best sex. Sex which is intuitive, where you orgasm without even having to tell the other person what to do, where your boobs look pert and nice, and you laugh and hold each other like you're one and the same.

And at that precise moment, my phone rings.

Cameron. Calling.

Bloody hell. If the staff downstairs didn't know Michelle and her excitability well enough, they would think she's having an orgasm in this office with the way she's shrieking. I stare at the phone. This is just coincidence. I've had this before when I've been craving pizza and my Mum gets a margarita in without me telling her.

'Answerit, answerit, answerit,' she says, jigging on the spot. 'It's the universe. This is a sign.'

I still stare at the phone. I don't quite know what to do. How many rings before he gives up? Or leaves a voicemail? Who cold-calls someone like this? Maybe he's ringing in the workday as he knows he can leave a message, so I should leave him to it. But Michelle won't let it go.

'Good morning, this is Josie's phone,' she says, putting her finger to the green call icon.

I don't even have the chance to grab the phone off her, though I am immediately impressed by her ability to switch from screechy banshee to professional office person. She puts the phone on speaker and trots to the other side of the office.

'Oh... hi. This is Cameron. I'm a friend of Josie's...'

A friend, she mouths, impressed.

I shake my head at her, slowly. I am so going to cut your doughnut allowance after this.

'Josie is with a client right now. I'm her PA, can I maybe help?'

'Oh no, I can message her. I was just wondering if she was free for lunch? Is she busy today?'

Michelle pretends to think, a finger to her cheek. 'Let me just check her diary.' There is no diary, but Michelle pretends to flick through the imaginary pages of one. 'Actually, after this business meeting, she has a window and, between you and me, she works too hard. She needs a break.'

I hear him laugh quietly on the other end of the phone.

'Do you like Mexican food, Cameron?'

'Ummm, yes. I do.'

'Then do you know Wimbledon at all? In the village, there is a new street food restaurant called Mi Corazon. I am going to tell her to meet you there for 12 p.m. Does that work for you?'

There's a pause as he takes in this very efficient PA who books in my meals. I blush from how cringeworthy this all is.

'I need to be somewhere for 3 p.m., so that's perfect. I think I know it. Are you sure she'll be fine with this?'

'I do this all the time for her. Otherwise, she'll end up eating a Snickers and a banana at her desk.'

He laughs again. I don't because this is true and it suits me just fine. Also, I'm not dressed for a cute lunch date. I'm dressed for Monday; I haven't even accessorised.

'I'll even book a table for you guys. No worries. She will see you later, Cameron!'

'OK then, mystery PA lady.'

'My name is Michelle.'

'Nice to meet you, Michelle. Cheers! Bye!'

He hangs up and Michelle dances around the room once more. I watch as she holds my phone high into the sky.

'Seriously?' I ask her.

'I saw this place at the weekend. Mi Corazon means "my heart". That was a sign. We were literally talking about him and the phone rang. It's the sparks of your love flying into the universe and it all converging to create a brilliant romance. I can feel it in my waters, Josie.'

I sit there and shake my head, grinning to hear her enthusiasm, her excitement and, more so, her hope.

'I'm not even wearing earrings.'

'We have earrings downstairs.'

'They're shaped like penises.'

'He won't know. We'll cover them up with your hair.'

SEVEN

As mentioned, I like to be prepared for a date. I like to have perused the menu, shaved the stubble from my armpits at least and not be wearing my marketing director's stud (not penis) earrings and Michelle's very dark liquid eyeliner that I fear makes me look a little geisha.

It's just lunch. No one has full-on kisses after a date in broad daylight so we can chat over guacamole, joke over churros and then shake hands and proceed with the rest of our days. It will be lovely and civil. There will be no alcohol involved either. Unprofessional people down tequila at lunch. I will have a sparkling water, or maybe a glass of wine like the classy managing director that I am.

As I walk up to the restaurant, I can see his figure waiting by the door and immediately my body reacts, a breath I can't exhale, a warmth to my cheeks, a biting of my lip to hold back my glee. He's still wearing that duffel coat, the hair is still wild and uncontrollable, but the eyes, the smile... I'm just gawping now, trying to hold in my immense happiness at seeing him and I wave with both hands. This is not very cool at all. Stop being cute, Cameron Cox. And you, Josie Jewell, rein in the socially awkward, just swoosh in, double air kiss. How wonderful to see you, Cameron.

'Hiiiii!' I say, like I'm singing a really long note in a voice that's not my own.

He comes in for the peck on the cheek. He smells like fresh laundry and Juicy Fruit chewing gum. Urgh, don't lose it, Josie, just go in too wide so he gets a kiss of your ear and your colleague's earrings. I put an arm around him. He wasn't expecting that so we kind of hug.

He laughs in response. 'I wasn't sure if you were going to be here. I thought Michelle would tell you that you're going for lunch with me and I'd be standing here on my own.'

'Is that why you waited outside?'

'Yep. Plus, I also thought waiting was gentlemanly.'

'Like the other night at your parents' house.'

'Oh no, that was purely selfish so I could use you as a human shield.'

I laugh at this point and, quite awfully, my chewing gum falls out of my mouth. Did he see that? I hope he didn't. It catches on my coat and I pick it off as subtly as I can, stuffing it into an old tissue in my pocket.

He holds the door open and puts a hand to the small of my back. What is this? Is this a date? No, it's lunch. With tortillas and dip.

'Hi, we've booked a table for two under the name...' Shit. Did Michelle book it under my last name because that will mean letting the cat out of the bag before we've even had time to sit down and look at a menu. 'Josie?'

'Josie Stantz?' the restaurant manager asks.

Oh, Michelle and your need to romanticise this moment.

Cameron seems entertained at least.

'That's me.'

'Please follow me.'

As we walk through the restaurant, I'm reminded that eating out is actually quite a rarity for me. Such a rarity that I have long-standing friendly relationships with many of the Deliveroo drivers in my area. In fact, when I do eat Mexican, it's mainly a family pack of Tex-Mex dips and extra cheese with a sharing pack of tortillas that I share with myself. The past week has been the peak of social activity for me.

This place is also maybe not what Michelle had in mind. I think she thought it'd be small and intimate, but there's a real street food bustle element, an open kitchen and lots of memorabilia to try to recreate some sort of Mexican mercado. This is where all the sombreros are.

'Have you been here before?' the manager asks in his T-shirt with a burrito on the front.

'I haven't,' I say and Cameron shakes his head.

'It's like tapas. You order small dishes, they may not come all at once. Order food through our app. The guacamole is free. Tell us if you have allergies. Please look out for our chilli ratings. You will need to use the ladies' toilets today as someone has blocked the gents. Our apologies.'

I have a feeling the last two points may be related but don't say anything. However, I can see it's also brought a rise to Cameron's face.

The waiter scribbles something on our placemats and then wanders off into the crowd of people.

'You've not been here before then?' Cameron asks, looking over the many combinations of tortillas we can experience today.

'No, this is all Michelle.'

'Well, it's certainly lively. You have a PA?'

'I do.'

'That's fancy.'

'She's less of a PA, more there to look after me, she ensures I eat and leave the office at 6 p.m. I have a tendency to overwork.' This is where I should tell him. I overwork because I'm the MD at a company that you've assumed to be catering but really it's something else, completely. Maybe a drink first before the confession.

'So, today is on me. I feel awful after Friday,' Cameron tells me.

My body tenses a little. Kissing me was awful? I really hope not. I hope this isn't a weird lunch to dump me and let me down gently. If that is the case, *mi corazon* will literally be left out bleeding by the pavement.

'I duped you into coming with me to that dinner. I should have known things would have deteriorated like that and my family were unforgivably rude.'

'I think I felt worse for you, to be fair. There's a very good fried chicken place at the end of your road. Excellent coleslaw. I was fine.'

He scans my face. I don't know what he was expecting. For me to be angry? I was angry at his family, but none of that was ever directed at Cameron. He kissed me. It was a nice kiss. You can't get angry with nice kissing.

'I have a question, though...' I ask. He sits there waiting for me to continue. In a checked shirt, jeans and Vans like my sort of kryptonite. 'That is some messed-up family dynamics. How do you live with that?'

He half-smiles and shrugs his shoulders. 'I don't. I rarely see them, to be honest. My mum wanted me there, so I went along. I was just never the son they wanted. They wanted me to be the jock at school, playing rugby and going into a manly profession like finance or law, and it just didn't float my boat. I was a comic geek, I loved art and music and all these endeavours that are glorified hobbies really to them. I'm sorry they spoke like that about your career. That was rude and unfair.'

'I'm a big girl. I knew I wasn't quite a date and I know how to handle myself around idiots, so I was fine. I can call your family idiots, right?'

'I encourage it. So, is this a date then?'

But before I have the chance to answer, a waitress appears at the table looking like she'd rather be anywhere else than here. It may be because she has to wear a poncho.

'Hola,' she says, in not very Spanish tones. 'Drinks for you?'

'Could I get an orange juice?' I ask.

'We're out of orange juice, what about pineapple? It's kind of the same?'

I don't think it is. 'Maybe a sparkling water?'

'Or a Fanta? That's orange.'

Cameron looks like he's going to explode in hysterics.

'Or maybe a beer? Sol?' the waitress recommends.

'Two bottles of that then?' Cameron says.

I can't argue with a waitress over fruit, I'm just going to get drunk instead. Screw professional work lunch etiquette.

'And did they say the guacamole was free?' Cameron asks.

'Yes. I'll bring it over. You want tortillas or pork rinds?' she asks.

'PORK RINDS!' I almost yell, which again makes Cameron laugh out loud. Again, like my kryptonite.

I don't think the waitress writes any of it down, but I'll hope and pray something comes to our table.

'So, tell me about your family? I expect they're normal then?' Cameron says.

I pause for a moment. 'Define normal.'

'Like not uptight and conservative.'

I chuckle under my breath as I can't think of two words that describe my parents less. 'They're pretty liberal... and fun... I think the word is fun. Their mission at anyone's sixtieth birthday party would be flaming shots, half-naked carnage and dance-offs. It's like on the other end of the spectrum of your parents.'

'They sound brilliant,' Cameron comments.

'They are.' Tell him they used to be in porn. Tell him now.

'I would kill for that kind of normal. Just a nice family who don't have any secrets or issues.' Or maybe not. 'I bet you can talk to them about anything? Politics, race, sex?'

I blush because he's said the word sex in front of me. I say that word at least two hundred times a day at work, but because it's come out of his mouth, it's turning my cheeks ablaze.

'Two Sols,' the waitress says, dropping the bottles at the table before heading off.

I grab at a bottle and down at least a quarter, hoping it may cool me down.

'Or not?' Cameron says, amused by my reaction.

'Oh no, we're talking lefter than liberal with them. It was a nice way to grow up.'

And despite the lie I'm hiding behind, that is the truth. I love them dearly for how openly they raised me. Yes, they do walk around naked a little too often because they are super comfortable with nudity and their own bodies, but in terms of what they taught me about life, hard work and family goals, then I can't say anything bad about them at all.

'And siblings?'

'One brother. He's younger, a bit all over the place, but he's a good egg.' He's in a soap, he also does those annoying second-hand car commercials. Tell him.

'Free guac.' Let's blame the waitress. It's her who doesn't want me to tell him.

She plonks what I can only describe as a vat of guacamole on the table. How is this free? Avocados are expensive? This must crush their profit margins.

I can't drink any more beer without ordering proper food, so I get my phone out to download whatever food app this place is using.

'Is that your mum?' Cameron asks, glancing at my phone.

My screensaver is a selfie of the two of us. I remember that day well. We went down to Brighton, to sit by the sea, shop and eat fish and chips. Mum even dragged me on the bumper cars at the pier and this is where this picture was taken. It's not hugely flattering as my mouth is open so widely and with such happiness that you can see I've had my wisdom teeth removed.

'Yeah, that's her. She loves a bumper car.'

'She looks familiar to me.'

Oh, shit.

'Was she ever a teacher?'

'No.' Maybe in a bad film she was once in.

'She looks like my old history teacher.'

Thank god.

'She looks fun.'

'She is. You talk of your parents not really engaging in your love for animation and films. My mum camped with me outside Leicester Square once for a movie premiere. She used to help me sew costumes.'

'You're a cosplayer?'

'I was. Back in my teens. I had a whole Japanese manga thing down.' We won't mention why my mum had red knee-high boots in her wardrobe, but I made sure they were disinfected before I put them on.

'I think I'd have liked to have seen that,' he says.

Really? Oh. Blimey. Was that a bit of flirty move?

He leans over to reach for a pork rind just as I do and our hands touch. Damn. Did you feel that too? I felt that everywhere.

Say something. Talk about the menu.

'Tacos. I like tacos. Would you like to share my tacos?'

What exactly are the words that are coming out of my mouth right now?

I show him my phone so he can see the app and what tacos I

am actually talking about. They look like decent tacos, well-filled.

'I would,' he says, looking me straight in the eye.

I laugh, knocking my head back. Is this some strange sexual innuendo? Does he actually want a corn tortilla with fish, lime and sweetcorn salsa? I'll share.

'Then I will order tacos. As long as I can have a bite of your...'

'Burrito?'

I bite my lip. Everything is innuendo now, even Mexican food.

'What are your thoughts on pulled pork?' I ask.

He bites his lip. 'I like my pork pulled.'

Yep, this never happens with the Deliveroo man.

I look down at my phone, pressing random buttons and possibly ordering one of everything and three black bean enchiladas. You know that feeling when someone is looking at you but you're doing everything you can not to look back because if you look into their eyes then some strange lustful alchemy will take over your soul and you'll never be able to think straight ever again? Yeah, I look at him. Don't smile like that. Shit.

I did order three black bean enchiladas and I know because I have them in a doggy bag ready to take back to the office as we leave the restaurant. Michelle will be happy.

The flirting didn't stop. One moment he was asking if I could get my mouth around his burrito (I couldn't, it was quite large), which would send us into fits of giggles, and the next, the chat would effortlessly flow into anime, street food preferences (I love a dumpling), and everything from London to career choices. In all that time, did I tell him who I was and what I do? Of course not. Why burst this bubble? I liked being in this

bubble with him, escaping from the circus that is my life. Was it
selfish? Yes. Was it wrong? Also, yes. But the longer the date
went on, the more I couldn't extricate myself from the lie. I
reasoned with myself that this was like some sort of extended
role play. Without the costumes, of course.

'So, how are we ranking this place on Yelp?' Cameron asks,
as he buttons up his duffel coat and pulls his beanie over his
head.

'The orange juice tasted suspiciously like Fanta. Flaccid
tacos, embarrassingly large burritos.'

He chuckles, his breath fogging the air. 'Dildo-sized
burritos.'

I also smirk, knowing that I've seen bigger... much bigger.
'Solid three stars, though, for the free guac.'

'And the pork rinds, which made a lady more excited than
I've possibly ever seen.'

'They are premium snack foods.'

'That they are.'

We walk along the pavement by the village green, not really
knowing where this walk is taking us. It feels nice to be in his
company, warmed by the beer in my system and a plate full of
churros and chocolate dip.

'So, thank you for lunch. You really didn't need to do that,' I
tell him.

'Oh no, I did. You've been kind to me and I wanted to repay
that kindness. But even then, it was fun. You're a very entertaining lunch partner.'

I think he may be referring to the point where I bit into a
taco and all the filling fell out and down my front. Michelle will
see sour cream stains on this shirt now and think the date
evolved into something else.

'As were you,' I reply.

We are approaching my car and I can feel this all winding
to an end, a goodbye. There's a woman walking her spaniels

nearby, a kid on a mobile scooter, so it feels like this is not the place to kiss him again. We can hug perhaps? Maybe do a proper air kiss. Nothing sad, like shaking hands.

'Did you drive here?' I ask him. 'Can I give you a lift anywhere?' I say, stopping by my Honda Jazz, keys in hand.

'No, I took the Tube, but it's fine.'

How do I stretch this out? There's a pub there. A cheeky drink? But then I won't be able to drive at all. I'm strangely sad that this is the end of a perfect ninety minutes.

'We should bring up the kiss, eh?' he says, suddenly.

'If you want to.'

Act cool, Josie. Don't act like you didn't go home and touch yourself thinking about that kiss. Please don't say it was a mistake. Maybe it was a reaction to the evening's drama and you wanted to wind up your family. Maybe you're still rebounding and I was there. I cross my fingers in my coat pocket.

'I'm just carrying a lot of baggage at the moment. With Imogen, I've lost a best mate, you've seen the drama that comes with my family... There's other stuff. I am a lot to take on...'

I sense it coming, the let-down, the need to explain.

'So the timing of all of this, the timing feels wrong. Maybe if we'd met a couple of months down the line—'

I put a hand up to the air. 'Oh, you know what, don't explain. Essentially, we don't really know each other. We met at a party, I ruined your mum's sixtieth. We'd both had some wine, so we kissed and got carried away. I know I was a bit handsy.'

Stop talking, Josie. Seriously.

His eyes look confused, a little sad.

'Wait, you think I'm dumping you?'

'You're not dumping me?' Some strange sense of relief makes my heart leap.

'We're not really going out, so I believe I can't even do that much...'

'But you said the timing...'

'I said the timing was shit because... I can't stop thinking about you.'

Oh. I exhale slowly, my eyes wandering around the place like I'm trying to figure it all out.

'That kiss...'

So much is going through my mind right now. Mostly the fact that I'm holding this giant paper bag of enchiladas, but he feels the same. He's telling me he feels the same. I need to do something.

'Get in the car,' I tell him.

'But—'

'Get in the car.'

I go round to my side of the car and open the door, my hand shaking, enchiladas placed on the back seat. I then proceed to do up my seat belt. I start the engine. I'm not sure I completely know what I'm doing, but I indicate as I pull out, even though the road is empty. The problem is I do know what I'm doing because there's a car park around the corner from here. I head towards it and go to the furthest corner of it, away from other cars. A bland radio DJ fills the silence. I stop the engine.

'I'm going with this, but now I'm scared you're here to kill me,' he jokes.

I try to summon up a laugh, but I don't say a word. Tell him you like him, Josie. The tension in the car, the breathing, the spark. There is something here in such monumental spades, an air so humid, I can't catch a breath, but it's all a bit of a mess. Tell him now. Tell him everything. But I can't.

Instead, I reach over and kiss him and it's everything I remember. The lips, the hair, the sensation of wanting him desperately and, before I know it, I'm unbuckled. I straddle him in the passenger seat, my body pressed up against his, an urgent need to just have him.

'Here?' he whispers into my ear.

'Here...' I reply, breathily.

'But what if?'

What if someone sees? What if I'm late back to the office? What if you find out who I am and hate me for it? At this very moment, I don't think I care. I want to have sex. Now.

EIGHT

I do have sex. Contrary to what you may think about me, I'm not a prude. I like sex. I'm just not my mother. I lost my virginity when I was in college. It was like any first-time experience. His name was Paul, we didn't know what we were doing, but he aimed and hoped for the best. I brought along ten condoms because, you know, I like to be prepared. Past that, sex has varied depending on the partner and the energy. The energy is crucial. I did date a dentist once at university and, on paper, this man should have been excellent in bed because he had a six-pack and decent tackle, but the sex was mechanical, missionary, mundane – the same energy you get from a lighter that just never sparks, no matter how many times you shake it about and will it to light.

The energy between Cameron and myself is pretty seismic. We had sex in a car. I'm under no illusion we shook that car for a good six minutes or so, fogged up the windows and tested out the strength of my suspension. I tore off his beanie and I came so very hard in my passenger seat that when I think about it now, I have to bite my lip to stop myself grinning.

Girth. He had girth. And anyone will tell you, sometimes

it's just about the fit, and that it did, so very well. However, there was kindness there too. He asked what I liked, a direct look into my eyes, his hands in the small of my back to pull me in closer, a moment when the pleasure soared through my spine, up and out of my mouth, a slow whispered moan into his ear. He didn't ask why I had condoms in my glove compartment, but I've never changed – I'm still prepared.

After that, we sat there for a moment. We laughed. He really had to get somewhere for three, so I drove him to the station. He kissed me before he left. I went back to work. My only regret is that in some sort of post-sex stupor, I walked back into my office and told everyone the restaurant was excellent and that they should all go. They now have a table booked for ten at the weekend. I hope they've sorted their floppy tacos and orange juice shortage by then.

Since then, Cameron's not even tried to play it cool. We sext. Like a lot. He's unearthed some sexual version of myself that I have hidden away for a while. He makes me feel wanted, attractive. He makes me smile. We overuse emojis, we send each other pictures (with the necessary filters) and there is something illicit, naughty about it all that triggers the endorphins, that makes me crave him.

That said, in the real light of day, sometimes I panic about what this all means. We can't just keep sexting like this, one day the truth will out and the longer I leave it, the harder it will be to repair, the bigger the lie will be. Like when someone sees a crack in a wall and just pretends it's not there. Next thing you know, the whole place has come tumbling down around their ears.

Happy weekend, Miss Josie. So, last night…

Today is Saturday and the sexting has already started. It's become an all-consuming thing, not separated by night or day, work or home. He sent me a dick pic from a work toilet the other day. I may have sat at my office desk and told him I'd do things. Last night was, for want of a word, a bit of a sesh that involved twenty-two photos I've now put in my Hidden folder on my phone that I must remember to permanently delete before I ever let the IT crew at work near my Cloud.

I cradle a glass of champagne and squirm on the sofa, looking around to see who may be about.

...was pretty awesome, I reply.

Pretty? I'd say really fucking awesome...

I giggle, trying to hold in that uncontainable bliss that comes from receiving a text from someone you like. He is really good with words, saying what I want to hear and sending the sorts of texts that make me cup my hands over my mouth in shock.

Have a good day today xx

That text comes with a picture. Of him, just out of the shower, a towel tied around his waist, a garden path, a hand about to pull the towel down. I try to contain my amusement by downing the rest of my drink, at ten in the morning.

Take off the towel.

He sends a picture with the towel removed. Good morning. I tip some champagne over myself, looking over my shoulder.

Are you in bed?

No. I wish I was. I'm out in public.

I send him a selfie in return of me with my champagne glass.

Early working engagement?

You could call it that.

That is a damn shame. Enjoy, Miss Josie x

He's putting kisses at the ends of messages now. I always think that's a milestone of some description, a hint of emotion beyond all the physical stuff we've done. Here's a kiss to say I like you.

Do I put a kiss too? No, have a thumbs up back. I throw my emojis around like confetti. God bless the thumbs up for saying everything I can't and special mention to the laughing crying one too so I can reply to people's memes even when I don't get them.

A curtain suddenly gets pulled back and my brother appears from behind it.

'I'm not carrying you out of here,' Sonny says, gesturing to my glass, assuming my broad grin is champers-induced. Speaking of someone who sends me lots of unnecessary memes...

'I'd like to see you try, though,' I reply, sitting back to take a serious look at what he's wearing. 'Now tell me about this get-up...'

Today, like the helpful sister I am, I've accompanied Sonny to the tailor to help him choose his wedding suits. Yes, it's suits plural, the wedding is going to be a three-act play: one suit for the ceremony, one for the party, one for when they leave. It's Gucci loafers and personalised cufflinks, overpriced shirts and matching trousers. I have never quite bought into luxury clothing – I am high street through and through, but I make an exception for Mr Li, who makes my dad's and brother's suits. He prepares Sonny for red carpets, takes out my dad's waist-bands but also helped me alter my cosplay costumes when I was a misplaced teen trying to fit in.

'I tell him, it looks a bit shit really,' Mr Li comments in his hybrid Chinese/London accent.

Mr Li's an older gentleman, always in a waistcoat with his glasses perched on his forehead, tape measures like accessories around his neck, but always the most impeccable taste in train-ers. You go with your New Balance, Mr Li. Comfort and style personified.

'I'm a good tailor, but even I can't make this look good,' he tells us, staring Sonny up and down.

My first instinct is to laugh quite hard, but I'm also quite jealous of my brother's calves. Before me stands Sonny, in a black leather kilt with knee-high socks, a black jacket and a red bow tie.

'We're not even Scottish... is Ruby Scottish?' I ask.

'No,' Sonny replies.

'Then is that cultural appropriation? I don't even know. It looks nice if mildly ridiculous? Like you're going to take on Sparta but also serve them some canapés. Are you going to make Dad wear a kilt?'

'No. Do I really look like a waiter?'

'A respectable one. Why the leather?' I ask.

'Because it looks edgy and manly?' he says, striking a pose.

'It looks like high-end kink.'

'Is this a theme at weddings these days?' Mr Li asks.

'It is. I provided the décor for a wedding like that once.'

Handcuffs. We provided many handcuffs.

I watch as Sonny struts around the room, swishing the skirt like he's going to partake in a mean paso doble. Mr Li, mean-while, follows him, trying to take in the jacket.

'Do you get a say in any of this? It's also your wedding,' I remind Sonny.

'I know, but it's her vision. If it were me, I'd wear a bog-standard tux, but we've got magazine deals and all sorts, so she wants me to look a bit "extra". I'm wearing boxers, though, thermal ones. In February, I'll need them.'

'Are you going to wax your legs?'

'I have my limits, Josie.'

I laugh as he looks at himself in the mirror, confused.

'You like the champagne, Josie?' Mr Li asks, as he comes to sit down next to me and gives me a double air kiss. We've been patrons of this shop ever since we were kids and it's always like coming back to see a kindly uncle. I'm just glad he's replaced the lollipops he used to give us with alcohol. 'It's a big day, our Sonny boy growing up.'

'It is indeed. Thank you. This is proper luxury, Mr Li.'

'How many years have I known you? You call me Winston. And I love you guys. Sonny, I just get your next suit ready, sit down and have a drink with your big sister.'

Sonny does what he's told, grabs a glass and snuggles into me, resting a head to my shoulder. This will always be a familiar stance of ours, living off sofas as teens in the same house, confiding everything in each other. We've sat here before watching Dad get kitted out for his renewal of vows to our mother. They'd been together for ten years and they did the deed in the Chiswick registry office they married in. I wore much tulle, we went for pizza after. It was a moment for declarations of love and a brocade suit which made Dad look like wallpaper.

'Are you really wearing that, Son?' I ask, as he tries to understand the best way to sit down in a kilt. Yeah, knees together please.

He shrugs. 'I've worn worse. I did the London Marathon dressed as a carrot.'

'That you did.' It was for a foodbank charity, except he lost the green foliage to his head by the time he got to Tower Bridge so ended up looking like a big orange phallus. At least it was bang on theme for the family business.

'So that's for the ceremony? Are you going full matador for the party?' I joke.

He elbows me. 'You're funny. You wait until you see what Ruby has in store for you.'

I pull a face, thinking about Ruby's current style. There's a very pastel, beige Yeezy vibe going on and her last red-carpet outfit at the National Soap Awards looked more like a colander than clothing. I'd not be able to do either. It'd be draughty for a start.

'So, I have questions about the wedding. Ruby's put them as a note on my phone... given that you've come organised today.' He refers to the many folders I've brought along so we can stay on top of the day's sartorial decisions. 'First off, what's your fee for all this wedding planning or are you doing this for free, like a gift?' he asks sweetly, leaning further back into Mr Li's velvet sofa.

I smile back because Sonny has that sort of doe-eyed grin that means I've been helping him out my whole life. I am doing this for free, but I do have my ulterior motives. Ever since Cameron's appeared in my life, I've shoved all that nervous energy, guilt, confusion into the wedding. It's a terrible trait of mine but a coping mechanism all the same and the positive is that someone will benefit from all that hard work – that person being my dear brother here.

'I figured I was going to do it for free. The other gift idea was a ridiculously large and ornate gravy boat.'

'Ooooh, but I like gravy,' he says, weighing up the options. 'Can I have both?'

'Greedy. You celebs really are all the same.'

He shakes his head. 'Well, it's good to have you at the helm.

The call at 6 a.m. last Tuesday about flowers was really appreciated.'

I was on the phone with a flower vendor in the Netherlands, I needed answers about shades of red. My brother complains, but he knows that my attention to detail will make this whole day sing. I'll know to sit Nan away from the speakers, not have any soya in the vicinity as the bride is allergic and also have all those little things in place: a close-up magician, blister plasters in the bathroom, taxi numbers, a photo booth, a specially curated playlist so no one will be left sat twiddling their thumbs and saying that they don't know these songs. Everyone knows Sister Sledge.

'And the caterers in charge. They've sent the menus... Have you—'

'I'd recommend the blade of beef, a vegan alternative. Don't start with soup. Soup is messy when you have posh frocks on. Maybe a smoked fish/tartlet option. I'd go with something comforting for dessert. Sponge/tart and custard is old school but also helps soak up alcohol, as opposed to something like a sorbet.'

Sonny laughs. 'Spoken like someone who might be in the catering industry,' he says, cheekily.

I shift him a suspicious look. 'Brett and Tina?'

Bastards. That night after the phone call from their restaurant, I was forced to spill the beans. *You know the party? Remember that fella who I brought into the kitchen dressed as a Ghostbuster? The one who ate a fair few chicken wings? Yeah, he may call your restaurant and ask for me. Pretend I'm your boss.*

'They may have mentioned something. What's his name?' Sonny continues.

'Cameron. He was at your party. Do you know him?'

'God, I didn't know half the people there. So what of Cameron? Tell me.'

'He's nice.' I smile when I say that. The sort of uncontrollable grin that comes from talking about someone who excites you, that spreads through your face like wildfire, that you can feel creasing your eyes and warming your cheeks. That all-round glow makes Sonny smile back.

'It's nice to see you smiling for a change,' he says.

'I smile all the time.'

'Not really. You're quite serious and organised and—'

'If you say uptight, I will kick you. In the unkilted bits.'

He pulls a face at me. 'What I meant to say is that you've not smiled like that since Mike...'

I pout as he says that name.

'Tell me more,' Sonny enquires.

'He likes guacamole, he's twenty-six like me, he's the youngest of four, he has a Superman tattoo on his back.'

'Like a great big Superman face or the logo?'

'It's tiny, on his lower back, he got it done when he was drunk.'

Sonny pauses for a moment. 'So you've done the fandango?'

'Maybe. We had sex in a car.'

My brother's face quickly turns to confusion. 'OK. Jo, if that's your scene now, then go ahead, I saw the documentary on Channel 4. Just be careful. Dogging can be pretty risky.'

I push him hard this time and he laughs. 'Urrrgh, Son... It's all a bit of a mess. He's just broken up with someone. He thinks I'm someone I'm not. I met his parents, they're horrific. On paper, this should not work.'

'But it does?'

If we're talking about the sex, then yes, it works. A bit too well. I take another large swig of bubbles. I should have eaten more toast this morning.

'True love hath a sense of timing that is both a farce and a shitter,' Sonny adds.

'Is that Shakespeare?'

'Obviously. I didn't think I wanted to go out with Ruby. We

work together, I thought I wanted some freedom, I'd just broken up with that model girl...'

'The one who patented your brand and named your unborn imaginary children on Instagram?'

Sonny flares his nostrils. 'But sometimes love comes looking for you when you least expect it.'

'Spoken like a true meme...'

'With a sunset and two people holding hands on a dock?'

'The very one.' The conversation has always flowed with this one. Sonny is likeable, funny, but as is the case with siblings, there is an unspoken language between the both of us.

'Maybe just see how it goes. If it's making you this happy, then see if it has legs. I like that you're a caterer now. I once told someone our parents owned a garden centre,' Sonny recalls.

'Did we sell many varieties of bush?'

'All the bush.'

We used to do this a lot as teens. I mean, you don't make friends by opening with 'my dad won an award for his penis once'. Sometimes you lied, sometimes you waited until you knew you could trust people, sometimes you didn't tell people at all. Sonny is one of the few who gets it. As he's got older and more famous, people have dug around and things have been revealed. Sometimes with photos that blur out our parents' bits.

'Remember when that magazine asked you about Mum and Dad?' I remind him.

It was crappy tabloid journalism, someone trying to sensationalise our upbringing. Sonny denied it completely. He got quite angry actually, so Sonny pushed that journalist off his high horse. His storming out went viral.

'That was mainly to protect them, but I get it. It's not something you mention on the first date. What does he think of me?' he asks.

'He doesn't know you're my brother.'

Sonny pretends to feign sadness. 'So I don't even exist...'

'I just want to take it slowly. Maybe tell him in stages. Stage one: this is Sonny, he works in soaps. Stage two: I sell vibrators for a living. Stage three: Mum and Dad used to be in porn.'

Sonny nods hesitantly.

'Just out of curiosity,' I ask, 'how is Ruby with all of it? Mum and Dad, the family biz... How long before you told her?'

'Oh, I think she did her research and found out herself. It was a novelty to start off, a joke, but then she got to know you all and found out it was a just a sidenote, really... And, you know, without wanting to sound like a soppy bastard, those little details don't matter in the end when you love someone...'

I push him playfully to hear him talk with some depth about the girl he loves. The difference between us is that Sonny is so open, so unguarded with his heart. His has probably been broken more times than mine, in more public and savage ways, but he still never gave up looking, hoping.

'Speaking of love,' he tells me. 'I need some help with the ceremony planning. I need a good poem to read out. I've been doing my research and I can't find a thing.'

I shift him a look of annoyance. 'Sonny, I can't do that. It has to be something that's personal to you guys. Do you have a song?' I ask him.

'Maybe that Bruno Mars one?' he suggests.

'I really hope it's "Uptown Funk".'

He pushes me in jest. 'No. But we were going to have Bruno as our first dance, Rubes has someone from *Strictly* teaching us a foxtrot.'

'Dancing in public. You must be in love. Well, we can find you a poem from somewhere... I'll send you some books. Go google songs with "love" in the title.'

'"All You Need Is Love".'

'"Love Me Tender".'

'"Love on Top".'

We both smirk at each other. This feels like a game we'd

play on a long-haul car trip with our parents. It could go on for days.

'Just find a song or a poem that makes you feel all these things you feel for her.' I turn to him. 'How did you know you loved Ruby?' I ask him.

He takes a moment to think the question through. 'It's a silly thing really. We were just lying in bed on a Saturday night, all cosy and watching some Netflix crap and I realised I didn't want to be anywhere else except there. It was everything, it was enough.'

It was enough. I pause for a moment. 'Is that a line from a script?' I ask, sarcastically.

'Whatever, old maid.'

I stick my tongue out at him.

The conversation is suddenly interrupted by Mr Li walking in with a three-piece jacquard and velveteen tuxedo. I think those are feathers to the shoulders but also a breastplate to the front. I like how the theme of this wedding has suddenly moved to fancy gladiator crow.

'Sonny, I opened the box from Valentino and I thought they'd sent me a dead bird,' Mr Li says. 'There is also a mask. Is this wedding themed? I am coming to this wedding. I don't do feathers.'

'There will be a masquerade element later. Like in *Romeo and Juliet*,' Sonny explains.

'Seriously?' I say, keeling over laughing.

'She must be one special girl, eh?' Mr Li says, winking.

'She is,' Sonny replies, beaming. He stands up to go and try it on.

But suddenly a curtain swishes open and a voice, a camera charges through the changing room. 'SONNY! COULD WE GET A PHOTO? IS THAT WHAT YOU'RE WEARING? WHO IS THAT?'

Sonny doesn't flinch, but my body seems to be contorting into strange shapes as the flash of the camera glares on and off.

'OI!' Mr Li shouts. 'Piss off out of here. Shoo.' He has a large wooden ruler that he wields like a baseball bat. I cower behind the sofa.

'Is that a skirt, Sonny? Is it true you're getting married in Scotland? Are you Scottish?'

I am amazed at how calm Sonny is about everything. 'No. Get out. This is a private shop, you know the rules, as well as this being a terrible invasion of privacy.'

'Are you the wedding planner? Is it true Ruby is wearing Versace? Come on, mate. Give us some titbits. I've got a column to write.'

Staff from the front of Mr Li's shop come rushing into the area, one of whom is Mr Li's older son, Feng, who body-builds and looks like he eats his fair share of dim sum. I really wouldn't mess.

'This is a costume for a TV show I've been cast in,' says Sonny. 'I'm actually wearing bright dayglo yellow for the wedding and a fur muff made out of snow leopards.'

'Really?' the journalist replies, recording it all on his phone.

'You really are an idiot, aren't you?'

The reporter doesn't take too well to that comment, and I see male testosterone start to mist the air. I've been around these types for long enough to know that they like to get a rise, to provoke so there's a reaction worth writing about.

I get up and put an arm in front of Sonny. 'They've signed rights with another publication, you know the rules. Plus, it's a wedding, it's a private occasion. Have some respect,' I try to say with some authority.

I'd like to say I'm calming the situation here with my diplomacy, but I hate confrontation so feel a little dizzy.

'Yeah, piss off,' Mr Li adds. 'Feng, show him the back door.'

Feng puts a hand to his shoulder and the man shrugs it off aggressively before turning to me.

'It'll be a shit wedding anyway, Z-list celebs. Just column filler really. I give it a year.'

And I shouldn't. But this seems to summon up an unhealthy amount of rage in me. Sod diplomacy. I pick up the thing closest to me and throw it at him. Quite hard. Feng ducks out of the way. Sonny inhales a large sharp intake of breath. There's a scream. Thud. Shatter. Mr Li cackles with laughter. Oh. I didn't realise I had the pitch.

NINE

'It's fine, Josie love,' Mr Li tells me on the phone. 'The police accept that he trespassed and it was all in self-defence. Please do not worry...'

'I'm sorry about the glass, the damage to the wall.'

Mr Li howls over the phone. 'Oh, it was worth it to see that man's face. Next time I am in a fight, I want you on my team.'

I am not sure why and how often our family tailor gets into fights, but I laugh. You're on. It turns out whilst I have incredible pitch, my aim is a little off, though. The thing I picked up to throw at the nasty, intrusive journalist was a bottle of champagne and even though I was aiming for his head, it ended up lobbing him in the crotch area and then bouncing off the floor and shattering. Nothing really hurt except a man's pride, and possibly his ability to have sex in the next few weeks.

'This Ruby says we need to change the outfits now that they're in the papers. Did she tell you? She's now sent me designs with these stupid short trousers all the men wear. What ever happened to a nice smart tuxedo?' he asks me.

'I'll have a look at her emails, don't worry. Maybe keep the kilt for yourself?'

I love the laugh on the other end of the phone. Think of the access, Mr Li.

'You give your parents some hugs from me, yeah? I've got your dad down to come in three weeks' time for his fitting. You remind him, you know what he's like.'

'Will do.'

He hangs up the phone and I look up Ruby's new emails about the revised wedding suits. That may be a combat trouser. Sonny must really love that girl.

It's been four days since I half attacked a man in Mr Li's shop, four days since I thought I might get arrested. That reporter shouldn't have been in the shop anyway. He should have also had better reflexes.

My phone buzzing on the table gets my attention.

Is this you?

It's a message from Cameron with a photo from the shop melee attached. I love how in the photo that got to the papers, Sonny looks calm, almost stately in his wedding garb, whilst I have a look on my face like aliens have burst through the roof. However, I now realise the gig is up. Not the way I wanted to break it to him, but maybe this is for the best.

Yes.

That's a huge gig. You're planning the whole wedding? I didn't realise you did events on that scale. I'm made up for you.

When I look down at the photo, I realise that I am clutching one of my wedding folders. I hope Sonny doesn't see that photo and assume I thought it more important to save my wedding planning notes from the intruders and not him.

I don't know how to reply to this message. To be fair, I am planning this wedding, this is not a lie.

I am.

So awesome, rubbing shoulders with the slebs.

He's a really nice bloke actually. That is a terrible photo of me though, please try to erase that from memory.

I'm going to make it into a mouse mat.

I still don't know what the state of play is with Cameron. There are random nights where we strike up a conversation at bedtime and it ends up getting quite heated and kinky and suddenly, I'm sending him pictures of me in my knickers. We don't define it, we keep it light and frothy because essentially, it's an escape, it makes us both happy for one small moment of the day.

I look at my phone as another message from him appears.

Are you free today? I hope so.

I can be.

Do you know the Hilton Grand, it's in Earl's Court?

I can look it up? Why?

Meet me there, 12pm.

I'm sitting at my kitchen table and choke a little on bagel crumbs. We've had sex in a car and since then had some energetic evenings of intense sexting, but now he wants to meet? In a hotel? That's a bit naughty. And during the daytime too. I can't tell if this is turning me on or feeling a bit illicit. I mean, it might be more comfortable than car sex. But I need to get grooming. It's Saturday and I'm in post-breakfast slouchy mode. I haven't washed my hair. Is this a meet, shag and go? Do I need to pack an overnight bag? A toothbrush? Will he freak out if I bring a toothbrush?

Mysterious. Is this another dinner thing?

Haha, definitely not.

What do I wear?

Do you still have that Japanese manga outfit? ;)

My eyes widen and a bit of bagel falls out of my mouth. He wants me to wear what now?

OK. It's a date.

Oh no, I replied too quickly. It's not a date if it's just sex. That's a hook-up. A date implies food and drink and ritual. Light-hearted chat where I find out his favourite colour. He doesn't even know my favourite colour. It's green.

I run through everything very quickly in my head. Do I bring the outfit? Or wear it there? I'm not even sure where that costume is. I wore that when I was fifteen. It may be in the loft. I hate the loft. Where are we meeting? Inside the hotel, outside the hotel? In the hotel where I'm waiting at the bar like a Bond girl, sipping on something while you casually come in and go, 'Let's get out of here'? Or in the room? You haven't given me a room number. Do I need to ask in reception? Will I need a key? What if the lift has the sort of security where you need one to access the floors?

'Morning, JoJo,' my mum suddenly says, cradling Dave the dog. She goes to the kitchen counter to obtain his morning treats. 'Who is my best baby? Does my baby want yum-yums?' she says in a mummy voice. I'd have hoped I was her best baby, but we won't debate that.

I'm still sitting at the kitchen table wondering what I've just organised for midday. I've organised role-play sex. I don't think I have the hairspray.

'I see you're already up and hard at it?' my mum suddenly mutters.

I blush. Hard at what?

She glances down at the kitchen table. Oh. In front of me this morning is also my laptop, folders, highlighters, and a multi-coloured vibrator (unused, I'm not an animal). I don't really stop for the weekends, but I'm also in high-stress work mode. If my spreadsheets and folders are colour-coded and in alphabetical order, then I don't have to think about how I nearly took a man's bollocks out with a champagne bottle and am lying to a nice man who I had sex in a car with.

'You'll need a spreadsheet for your spreadsheets at this rate,' my mum says as she looks at my barely moisturised face, my frizzy hair bundled on top of my head. Mum is different to me in that she has weekend skincare routines. Today, she's in one of her charcoal cleansing face masks so looks slightly scary. Dave doesn't care. He tries to stare me out as Mum cradles him. If that dog could pout he would, he has such attitude. He won't be when he sees the tux he has to wear in a few months. Yes, Dave is a page boy, which should be interesting, given he doesn't have hands. 'Coffee?' she asks me.

'I've had three already.'

'Then maybe another bagel to soak up all that caffeine?' she says, walking over to the toaster.

'Yes, but let me just finish this email to this bloke on Etsy and I... will... eat...'

My focus is captured by my computer screen and Mum looks at me, concerned. She knows this crazed-work-obsessed Josie. She stops for no man, at the expense of her health and sanity. This is how I did coursework, wrote essays, closed business deals, through a mixture of adrenalin and manic energy. When Mike dumped me, I brokered three deals with a factory in Asia but also put on half a stone and developed an eye twitch.

'I hope we're not giving out vibes at this thing,' she comments, glancing over at my desk.

'Oh, that is something different altogether. I need to work out how to tell this client that she's designed a vibrator that looks like a rocket lolly.'

Mum picks it up. 'Why does it have a face on it?'

It's the vibrator we've been developing with the YouTube influencer. Apparently, she wanted it to look friendly. I have no words. What are you going to do? Talk to your vibrator before you put it in you? She also wanted to capitalise on tie-dye making a comeback but instead this looks a little like a lava lamp.

'I don't think I like his smile,' Mum says. Neither does Dave, who immediately attacks it, steals it off my mum and runs away to make it his own. I make a note to put this as part of the feedback.

'Did you get the invite to the hen do? It's all scheduled in from spa to afternoon tea. I've put it in your calendar so you know where you need to be and I've ordered you a tracksuit too, in a small. Is that right?'

Mum nods. Tracksuits aren't really her thing, but she'll understand when it arrives. 'Whilst we're talking calendars, block out the tenth of January for me?'

'For?' I ask.

'That TV production company, we've been chatting and it looks like I'm going to be a TV persona. That sex debate thing is set for the tenth.'

My face lights up to hear it. 'I'm glad you said yes to that. You'll be really good, you know?'

'You'll come, right? Help me practise? Make me sound clever.'

'I'll make a spreadsheet.'

She finishes preparing my bagel and brings it over, taking a bite before pushing the plate in front of me. She's always been nosey, so she sifts through my notes, admiring my mood boards. 'Are you going to be one of those wedding co-ordinators who wears a headset and barks at people on the day?' she asks, poring over my Post-it notes.

'If that's what it takes,' I say, though I suspect it may go that way. We may be able to style my hair around an AirPod, though, so it's less conspicuous.

'Am I really wearing black at this wedding?' she asks.

'You are. I'm in red, like a big tomato. It's an eclectic vibe of black and white and red and feathers. It's very cinematic.'

'I'll look like a 1940s war widow with my hat.'

'We'll class it up with fur and bows, Mum. Pity me, my job will be looking after Dave. I'll literally be accessorising with leads and poo bags.'

Mum picks up a photo of Sonny and Ruby that they want on the orders of service. It's posed and I think a wind machine may be involved.

'Can you believe little Sonny is getting married?' I say.

'Yeah, of course. He was always getting married in school, remember? He'd come home and tell us he'd wed some girl in the playground. By the time he left primary, he'd promised himself to least five different girls like some eleven-year-old polygamist.'

I laugh. I was a witness at one of those weddings. They made the rings out of daisies and he kissed her on the lips for all of three seconds. I remember a dinner lady came over and told us marriage was for fools. We later found out her husband had left her, stolen their car and moved to Hull.

'You never did that,' Mum adds. 'You never did that little girl thing of wearing a net curtain on your head and pretending to marry someone. I never knew what you thought about marriage.'

'That was because the majority of boys in my class either had nits, ringworm or their base level of humour was fart jokes. The idea of marrying any of them was abhorrent to me.'

She titters, glad that I at least had some standards as a child.

'Can I ask you something, though? You can tell me if it's none of my business, but the whole thing with Mike... It hasn't put you off marriage or anything, has it? It's just you've lived here with us for a while now. We love having you here, don't get us wrong, but we worry that he's scarred you in some way.'

I stare at my computer, not quite smiling but not quite sad either. He did leave some form of scar, but I can't quite describe it. It's not a burn or a graze. It was like he cut my chest open and punched me square in the heart and I've spent the last two years wincing, sewing myself up again, healing. One of the reasons I can sit here and plan this wedding so well is that I still had a lot of the spreadsheets on my computer from when I was going to marry Mike. Our favours were going to be personalised sweets and, at the ceremony, Sonny was going to read out an Ogden Nash poem. I had a dress. I wasn't so sad as to do a Havisham and keep the dress too, but it had laced cap sleeves and buttons all the way down the back. I sold it to someone called Lorraine on eBay, who complained about the shipping costs.

I realise I haven't spoken for a while and I'm not sure if Mum is actually tearing up. 'Mum, he was a knobhead. I feel I dodged a bullet there. I loved him, I did, but notice how I use the past tense.'

Knobhead for leaving me the way that he did but also for the reasons he left, ones I don't want to disclose at this precise moment.

'I'm a bit fussier, more guarded with who I let into my life, but one day, I may get married.'

She claps her hands excitedly.

Hold up there, madre. Because that feels a long way off, miles away. Not even on the map at the moment. I'm just sexting. No labels. He thinks I'm in catering.

'Should we maybe get you on some dating websites? I hear that's how people do things these days? If you ever want the house to yourself, then Dad and I can go out and make ourselves scarce. You could have someone over for dinner. You make a lovely carbonara.'

I put an arm around her. 'Maybe?'

'Just as long as I know you're happy, JoJo. You know that?'

I do. I think that's all Mum's ever wanted for her kids. She wasn't loved in her own family growing up and has no relationship with her own parents, so she works doubly hard to compensate for that. To know that whatever happened, we would always be loved.

'I could try to get you a date with Dad's tennis coach. He's not got much hair and has an electric car, but he has nice legs.'

'Or not,' I say, laughing, as she gets up to clear up the kitchen, knowing for all her good, her role as matchmaker is sometimes a little too enthusiastic.

She kisses me on the forehead. 'Well, if you're free later, I was thinking of having a shopping afternoon in Selfridges? Look at potential outfits? Your dad is out, doing his Federer thing. I could treat you to one of those salt beef sandwiches you like?'

I smile. My mum knows how salt beef and giant pickles have a special place in my heart.

'Oh no, I have a thing, later,' I reply, maybe a bit too nervously. It's a sex thing and thinking about it again makes my stomach flutter in waves.

'That's fine – don't worry about me. I'll ring your nan and see if she wants to come. You doing anything nice?' she asks.

I nod, in some panicked train of thought. I can just keep it vague. *I'm going into town. I'm having a me day. I'm running an errand.* But, at present, it's just lies on lies and I'm loath to hold in all these secrets.

'Well, I hope it's not just wedding stuff or work. Do take some time out for you. I don't want you being ill, JoJo.'

Plus, she's expressing concern for me, about my love life, my health. My really sweet and lovely mum.

I look up at her, still in her face mask, loading the dishwasher. 'Mum, if I tell you something, promise you will not freak out.'

'Is it something wedding based? Is it dress related? Is Ruby flapping and going to make me wear flats so I'm not taller than her?'

I take a deep breath. 'I'm going out with someone later.'

She inhales sharply, throws her hands into the air and does a strange flamenco tap in her slippers.

'Don't get too excited. I don't think it's got legs. He's just come out of a relationship. He thinks I'm someone I'm not. I'm a little worried about where it's headed.'

She stares at me for a moment. 'Rewind there, sparky. Why does he think you're someone you're not?'

'I met him at Sonny's engagement party. He thought I was the caterer. I didn't tell him otherwise.'

'But why?'

I can't tell her, can I?

'It's just a strange mistaken identity thing.'

'Have you shagged him?'

This isn't a typical question a mother might ask her daughter, but I guess she's not a typical mum.

'Yes,' I say through clenched teeth. She can't quite read my reaction. 'The sex seems to be the motivating factor here. We're both very attracted to each other, maybe too much. I think it detracts from us speaking in more depth about what's happening.'

'Is it good sex?'

Mum is excellent at talking about these things with her kids. No shame, my children. Sex is what gave us this house, this life, it's how I met your father, it's the reason you're both sitting here.

'What we have done is pretty decent.'

She wrinkles her nose. 'Josie, decent is a word you use to describe a hamburger. It's on par with "passable".'

'It was very good.' I don't want to say too much, but I basically came so hard, I gave myself a sex migraine.

'Well, maybe you just have some good sex with a nice man for a while. Don't overthink it. If it gives you both pleasure, then that can only be a good thing? He is nice, right?'

'He's really nice. His name is Cameron, he designs video games. We're kinda into the same things.'

'Does he share your scarily geeky knowledge of films?'

'He does.'

She does that happy jiggy movement again.

'I really like him. But all these emotions that come with it... The lies. I just see the future and in the plain light of day, I think it may end badly,' I admit.

She studies my face. 'JoJo...'

'Mum...'

'It's sex. It's not a risk assessment.'

I laugh as she says that. I am also queen of those. No one in my company should ever fear the health and safety aspects of their job.

'So why all the panic? The white face? I'll take it this isn't some caffeine overload.'

'He wants to meet at a hotel...'

'Oh,' she says, worried. 'Like a nice one or one of those guest houses on the Great West Road?'

'The Hilton Grand in Earl's Court.'

'Fancy. Your dad used to take me to hotels for a bit of fun sometimes, when you were little. A change of scenery, a bit of room service. Maybe he just wants to treat you?'

'But what do I wear?'

'Clothes?'

I giggle. 'But it's like occasion sex? I should whip out the nice underwear, right? If he's paid for a room.'

'Don't go feeling you have to put out or put on a show. This needs to be on your terms too, not because you feel bad he's spent money on a room.'

I nod, nervously.

'Go classic. Lingerie, big coat on top. He opens the door and boom.'

He explodes? I don't want that.

'I've never done that before,' I say, sheepishly.

The look on Mum's face tells me she has. Many times.

'I have a very cute three-quarter trench you can use. Do you have nice underwear? The Love Shack had that super cute line last year with the tassels. I'm sure you brought home samples.'

I did. I never used them. Tassels feel like super occasion sex that has a soundtrack and a pole and a lithe rhythmic bendiness that I'm lacking.

'I have some things you can—'

I shake my head. I'll take your coat, but no way am I sharing anything else with you, Mum.

'He's mentioned a bit of role play, I think?' I am blushing, hard, but perhaps out of all the people in the world I could discuss this with, my mum is the most qualified.

'Is it a film geek thing?'

Again, I nod.

'Well, don't wear those sorts of costumes out. I remember a time when your dad and I did that in a hotel and there was a fire drill and we had to stand outside in hotel-issued dressing gowns over some pretty outlandish...'

The panic in my eyes means she doesn't finish that sentence.

'I do have lingerie, I guess?' I suddenly remember. It's see-through in all the correct places – I may need to dig it out from the back of my drawers and dust it off, but it could be useful.

'There you go. What time has he asked to meet?'

'12 p.m.'

'Then put all this work stuff aside and go get ready, have a bath, sort out this,' she says, pointing to my hair. 'Have a day for you.'

'Can you maybe not tell Dad I'm seeing someone? I mean, you're awful with secrets, but do this? For me? Until I work out what it is?'

She nods. This could go either way with Mum, but as long as I don't tell her his last name, then she'll never be able to find him on social media and stalk the hell out of him.

'Please, Mum...' I hope she can read the desperate panic in my eyes.

'I will try. I mean, Dave knows now too.' The dog sits by the door of the kitchen looking up at me, his multicoloured vibrator in his mouth. 'But if this man hurts you, Josie, know I will take him out, me and Dave and a crowbar.'

I don't doubt it. Mum does have strength in her upper arms, but her fierce maternal energy is everything. I hug her and she holds me close for a second.

'And could you help me with my eyeliner? Make me look all sultry and sexy...'

I say that in the most unsexy tone I could summon up,

rolling my shoulders around. This is just not in my bloodstream and it should be deeply engrained in my genes.

Mum nods but looks unsure, tucking strands of hair behind my ear. 'I will but, Josie, don't go as someone you're not either, yeah?'

I smile. I think it may be too late for that.

TEN

Let's talk about *Sailor Moon* for a moment. When I was a teen, it was hard to find female role models that appealed. I had just found out my parents were in porn and to hide all my distressed confusion, I threw myself into two things: schoolwork and anime. *Sailor Moon* was shojo manga specifically meant for teen girls of my age, and it exposed me to all those amazingly bold female characters who were powerful, brave and colourful. I became obsessed, I collected magazines and figurines and my walls were lined with posters. We won't talk about the bad hair dye jobs, it's a wonder I have any hair left. I had the one costume. Dad was sceptical about it because the skirt was less a skirt and more a pelmet, but I used to wear it and feel like a warrior.

I don't feel like a warrior today because I found the costume in the back of my wardrobe and it's no surprise that my shape has certainly changed since I was fifteen years old. So I made a quick diversion to our warehouse as we do stock sexy sailor outfits (they sell very well in the summer). It would have to do. Underneath that is a thong that is perhaps more low cut and high cut than I anticipated, so I'm also super sexy

Sailor Moon with a wedgie, my nipples on show, my hair in buns on the top of my head, all covered up by my mum's trench coat. And knee-high boots. Platform boots. Yes, also my mother's. If I had my way, I'd have worn Converse to this rendezvous, but Mum nearly blocked the door when I tried to leave in them.

'Sorry about the traffic, love,' my taxi driver tells me.

It's the weeks leading up to Christmas so the streets are adorned with twinkly lights, mistletoe and shoppers, headed into the big smoke. My nerves become more unsettled as I spy the glow of brake lights ahead of us, a warbling Mariah Carey coming through the radio. I also should have just driven myself. They have a car park at the hotel. It's extortionate but it would have saved the embarrassment of sitting in this car wondering if when I bend over, people will be able to see my foof.

'It's fine.'

It just gives me more time to sweat into my costume and work out a get-out plan. It was ridiculous to think I could do this. I am not this person. The seductive, overtly sexy, strutting down the street, Josie. However, maybe this is a good way to get the truth out there. *And guess what? Funny story... You think I'm awkward at this? I sell this stuff for a living and you should hear what my parents once did.* And then I can walk away and be done with it.

I suddenly hear the taxi driver laughing, please don't be at me.

'What are people like, eh?'

I assume he's talking about the traffic, a terrible driver, a cyclist who doesn't know the rules of the road, but I look out the window and suddenly see a lot of Stormtroopers. Like a group of them. Is there a collective noun for Stormtroopers? An empire? It's not just them, though. Hey, Boba Fett. Hey, Hobbits. Have I been fretting so much that we've driven into another dimension?

I gaze out the window at the lines of people walking along the pavements. 'Where is everyone going?' I ask.

He pulls a face in the rear-view mirror. 'Same place you're going, love. It's some sort of sci-fi convention, innit? If you wanted to walk from here, maybe you can ask Superman there for a lift?'

My face freezes. What in the holy Dickens? Superman strolls past. Some men should really not go near tights.

'Are you that bird from *The Matrix*? I thought with the sunglasses you might be?' he asks, confused.

I'm wearing the sunglasses because I wanted to hide behind them. I take them off and put them in my rucksack. In the bag is a change of underwear and clothes, a sex toy and a lot of condoms that I'm realising I won't need. Plus, if there is a security bag check, I may die of embarrassment. 'My costume is underneath, I'm Sailor Moon. It's a cartoon. Anime–manga thing?'

He smiles with wide eyes to let me know he doesn't need to know any more. I'm one of them. Cameron invited me to a Comic Con-style event. This makes perfect sense. He knows we like films and sci-fi and this is the sort of thing I would most certainly be into and I am a bloody idiot for thinking anything more. We're not here to have sex. I could have worn normal underwear. I shouldn't have packed a toothbrush.

'Look, it's all good. I probably will walk. Thank you so much.'

I open the door and head out, behind a set of Avengers where you can tell Hulk has pulled the short straw because it's early December and he's only in torn purple jogging bottoms. I don't quite know what I'm doing, but at least my eyeliner is nice, and yes, my mum did that for me too.

As I head up to the hotel, this place seems to be rammed, there's no theme, no order, but just a lot of excitable comic geeks like myself because we have found our north, found our people.

I bet none of them are in thongs, though. Is there time to change my underwear? I am such a donkey.

'Hello, hello,' a voice suddenly says from behind me.

I hold my breath and turn around, smiling. Too late.

'You're either Hopper or Rick Grimes,' I say.

He's a sheriff. He's a hot American sheriff. There's a hat. I now know that I'm turned on by hats, which is new. Yep, permission to arrest me and give me a body search. I don't know how to say this, but I see his eyes glance down to the boots and he smiles. 'You look amazing by the way. Is this Sailor Moon or... Do I get to see your costume?'

Oh dear, if I open this coat and flash you, then you will see nipples. It would be indecent.

'I'm pretty cold. It can wait?' I say, trying to wink but not really succeeding. 'So this is the thing?' I ask.

'Yeah, were you expecting something else? I thought it was a good-quality date idea. We can stand in a line and get Stanley Tucci's autograph. We can also pose with the actual Ghostbusters car. Too cheesy?' he says, oblivious to how this invitation could have been misconstrued. It's very pure and innocent, given what we were talking about a few nights ago. In bed. Naked.

I grin back at him. 'No, this is perfect.'

'I'm Rick Grimes from *The Walking Dead*, by the way.'

'It suits. Do you have a Colt Python?' I ask.

He widens his eyes at me. Are we doing the sexy flirting now?

'It's the gun he carries in the show,' I say, explaining myself. 'Colt Python .357 Magnum revolver.'

He stops for a moment in his tracks to hear me say that out loud. 'You knew that?'

'I do. I remember things like that.' Please don't think that's weird, please don't think that's weird.

Instead, he grins and takes my hand. OK, Rick. Let's go get our geek on.

I've been to a few Comic Cons in my time, more so as a teen who was excited about minor celebrities and found security and community in this world, but there is something so brilliant about them. Everyone is so invested in being here. You see it in the costumes, in the way people are on a mission to track down their favourite supporting cast members, in the way they marvel at some piece of rare memorabilia, pick it up and try to work out if it's worth the money and the shelf space. Case in point as two Jedi next to me are trying to figure out if they can afford an actual lightsaber once held by Samuel L. Jackson. It's certainly different to the sales exhibitions I attend for work. These include SEXPO, where people come at me with lube, harnesses and strange sex inventions where I enquire about their patents and Kitemarks.

'Do you think Samuel L. Jackson actually touched it? How can they prove that?' asks Cameron.

Cameron is more excitable than me today. You get the sense he wasn't allowed to attend such events as a child so everything is amazing and wondrous, in the way he literally whips his head around, taking everything in like an excitable dog. Together, we've posed with the *Ghostbusters* car from five different angles, had cocktails in a replica *Star Wars* cantina (and danced to the band), did a fake photo shoot for our own film poster, and I'll admit, this is a cute date, a diversion from the very intense sexual nature of our relationship so far. We walk through the exhibition, not quite holding hands, not quite apart, but every time I point at something and reveal more of my inner geek to him, he moves in a little closer, his eyes smiling, nudging me jokingly, unfazed by the fact I'm very into prequels, and have very in-depth knowledge of filming locations and statistics from awards seasons.

'No way! Come here, little dude!'

I laugh as Cameron erupts with happiness to see a kid coming towards us dressed in exactly the same outfit as him. My heart smiles, but you can't be older than ten, I really hope you haven't seen that show, kid, there's a lot of exploding heads.

Cameron squats down to his level to chat to him. Such is the joy of Comic Con that we're all friends here.

'We've got to get a picture of this, Josie. Serious face, like we're about to kill a zombie.'

I get out my phone and oblige, biting my lip at the adorability of it all. He stands and high-fives the kid before he scampers away.

'Did you see that?' Cameron marvels.

'I did.'

'Isn't this place the best? Would you think it really really sad if we go back to the *Star Trek* bit? I think I might get that T-shirt? That's sad, isn't it?'

I shake my head. It's not sad because I have a *Star Trek* onesie. I wear it to bed.

'And did you see *Guardians of the Galaxy*'s Groot before? We need to get pics of that.'

That we can do. I did see Groot. He was like a walking fence panel. I wince to think of the splinters but applaud the dedication to his craft. That said, I think he might be the only other person in here as uncomfortable as me. The problem is that I'm still wearing my trench coat and it turns out it's fleece lined, which is perfect for the winter months but less so in a hotel conference hall full of people in costumes. It means I'm now sweaty Sailor Moon and I have a feeling it's also ruined Mum's eye make-up. I feel the discomfort most in my bottom half, where these knickers are cutting into the creases of my thighs.

'We can do whatever you want,' I say, wiping a trickle of sweat from my upper lip.

'Are you sure you don't want to take off your coat?' Cameron asks, watching the perspiration forming around my hairline.

'I'm just... I'm a little shy.'

He gives me a quizzical look. 'Really?' I guess the girl he's been sexting has been less shy. 'Then allow me to buy you a drink. You cool hanging here while I join the queue? Coke? Sprite?'

'I will take anything...' Especially if it helps replace the bodily fluid I'm losing.

'Don't go anywhere.'

'I won't.'

He leans in and kisses me on the cheek. I want to say it's driven by an uncontainable attraction, but it's because there's a youthful Peter Parker excitement that just simmers off him. He's like me. I don't meet many people like that. The energy is contagious, attractive and the way we're bonding over these geeky shared endeavours makes me want to jump on the spot and erupt with joy. You get me. I can't, though. Mainly because I'm bloody boiling.

I watch him disappear into the crowd. You're such an idiot, Josie. This rucksack is also strangely heavy as not only does it contain condoms but also a necklace and headband that I was going to put on later if and when this went full role play. In my hands is also a photograph that we paid to take with Stanley Tucci, who was brilliant in real life, except I look incredibly nervous because of all the sweating, so I think he thought me a tad strange. How do I make this work? Do I run and go get changed? I have jeans in my bag, but that won't work. I'd still be half naked on top. Facing a wall, I undo the trench coat, fanning myself like I'm flashing the bricks. I don't even have nipples anymore, they've kind of melted into my body. A man dressed like Wolverine makes eyes at me. Don't you even dare.

I glance at the exhibit opposite. A clothes stall: *Got T-shirts?* I hope you do.

'Can I help?' a heavily bearded man suddenly asks me as I step inside his sales space. He wears a T-shirt that says I AM THE GOD OF TITS AND WINE and I realise the GOT refers to *Game of Thrones.* I've seen that show. I can do this. It doesn't quite match, but it's better than what's underneath this coat. I can style it out.

'I am looking for a T-shirt, any colour, about a size 10.'

He holds up a black one that says MOTHER OF CATS.

'I don't have cats.'

He nods and puts it back on the rail. 'Do you have a favourite *Game of Thrones* character?'

'The Hound?'

'Who likes The Hound?' he asks, confused.

'He's funny and he has all that trauma with his brother who burned his face.' I spin around, trying to work out where Cameron is. I don't know why I'm having this discussion with this man.

'I don't have any T-shirts with The Hound. What about this?'

It's Littlefinger and underneath a cartoon drawing of him are the words FANCY A LITTLE FINGER?

'NO.'

'That's my bestseller.'

'Just give me that one with Jon Snow's face on... Is that a small changing room? Can I put it on?'

'I guess... Do you want—'

'I can pay you cash and if you could cut out the tags that would be awesome and very kind of you.'

As I get out my wallet, he shrugs and I grab at the T-shirt and disappear, pulling a curtain behind me, taking off the coat and standing here for a moment to allow myself to cool off, using my hands to wipe my face down. I look at myself in a skinny full-length mirror and don't know whether to laugh or cry. What am I doing? This is fun. Being here is fun, but crossed wires seem to be at the forefront of this relationship and I'm not sure if it's worth all this panic.

I pull the T-shirt over my head. With the mini skirt of my sailor dress, stupid knee-high boots and melted mascara, I look like a very confused, grungy student from the nineties. I roll up the trench, put it in my bag and open the curtain.

'Nice,' the exhibit vendor tells me. 'Good fit. Everyone loves Jon Snow,' he says, winking, and I shuffle away cautiously.

It's the skirt. It is too short. Case in point as a budget Cyborg walks past me, nodding and smiling. I'm good, thanks. I'm looking for a sheriff. I see Cameron's face through the crowd, hoping and praying he doesn't think I look like a hot mess.

'Iced tea?' he says, stretching an arm out.

I take the bottle from Cameron and literally down it in one, burping a little under my breath.

He laughs, furrowing his brow at me. 'You took the coat off. No Sailor Moon?'

'No, *Game of Thrones* instead,' I say, doing a mini curtsey. 'The look is a bit all over the place, I'm sorry, I look ridiculous. This is not my usual style.'

'You look great. Don't be silly. I'm dressed like a sheriff and don't have a change of clothes. It's likely I am going to get a lot of abuse on the train later.'

'Everyone likes Rick Grimes, though.'

'Do you like Rick Grimes?'

'Of course. The whole show, if you think about it, revolves around Rick's journey from waking up to reconnecting with—'

He stops for a moment. He wasn't asking about the show's storyline development, was he? He was talking about himself, in that costume. I like the costume very much. To be blunt, I'd do him in the costume, for sure. As a character, he's growing on me.

'I like Rick Grimes very much.'

He reaches over and kisses me, gently on the lips. This still is my new favourite thing, kissing him and having him close. I pull him in to make the moment last and as I do, the lights suddenly dim. That would be because we've taken all the electricity out of the place. It's right here, in this kiss, his hand barely touching my face, his lips grazing mine.

We're suddenly surrounded by some crazed strobe lighting from a *Star Wars* event just about to start in the next room, the bass of the theme tune pulsating through the floors. Damn. I mean, if you're going to share a kiss, then that's the music you want to raise the cinematic quality of the moment. We both laugh.

'Come,' I say, breaking away. 'I need to get some merch for two little boys I know.'

He seems willing, but as I walk away, I hear Cameron choke on his drink and then explode with laughter.

'OK then. Maybe that outfit was kinkier than I thought,' he says.

I swivel around. Is my skirt stuck in the thong part of my outfit? Am I showing bum cleavage? But Cameron comes up to me and moves my rucksack aside, seeming to read the back of my T-shirt and then giggling.

'That's a fun T-shirt.'

'There are words on the back?' I ask, trying to crane my head over my shoulder awkwardly like I'm a dog chasing its own tail.

'You didn't know there were words on the back?' he says, bent over in hysterics. He takes his phone and takes a picture, then shows it to me.

GIVE ME 6-8 INCHES OF SNOW

'For the love of... What the...'

I immediately drop to my feet in some sort of mushroom shape, hoping it might make me less visible. I'm going to go back to that vendor and throw this tee in his face. If I duped my buyers like this, then Trading Standards would kick my arse.

Cameron bends down to meet me as I rifle through my bag. The coat is going back on, and I don't care if I sweat myself to death. But as I pull it out of my bag, other stuff falls out. Namely a string of condoms, about twenty of them. Josie Jewell, still ever prepared.

'Here, try me, I never miss.'

I'm sitting on the steps outside this hotel in my weird sexy goth-geek get-up with the sheriff as I aim popcorn into his mouth. I shoot, I score. We both cheer. After my literal condom explosion when Cameron's eyes nearly popped out of his head, I watched the realisation wash over him about how I'd completely misread this situation. Was it awkward? Oh, I wanted the ground to swallow me up, I wanted to run away from the shame, but as he helped me re-pack my bag and put on my coat, there was also a sweetness in his eyes. He didn't think me some sex-crazed woman obsessed with Jon Snow's length, but it was clear we had stuff to talk about. It started with a bit of fresh air and a bag of stale popcorn from a concessions stand.

'So are you a salty or sweet person?' I ask him.

'I mix it up. Half and half at the cinema.'

'Same. I sometimes pour in a box of Maltesers too.'

'That's genius,' he says in genuine admiration.

'It has been said.'

Outside this hotel, there's a massive twinkling Christmas tree in the courtyard as a backdrop, a line of festive soldiers with handlebar moustaches looking over us, Mariah still warbling in from somewhere. The winter air is still biting so Cameron huddles in closer to me, smiling.

'So. I am very sorry. I guess I thought this would be a nice date?' he explains. 'Maybe I should have been clearer about what we were doing.'

'I should have asked. I just jumped to the conclusion that this was some sort of...'

'Sex liaison?'

I chuckle. 'You make it sound vaguely romantic and respectable. There's me looking like some sort of nympho. First, I accost you in my car, now I'm showing up to hotels in lingerie and a trench coat.'

He widens his eyes. 'Is that all you had on under there?'

'I had a sailor outfit on, but it's a little brief... There are nipples on show.'

He shifts me a look. It's what I will now call the burrito look.

'I mean, if you want to... I wouldn't be opposed to the idea of seeing that costume in more detail.'

His leg brushes against mine. I look at him, he looks at me, we pretend to look away, blush hard and then catch eyes again, some comedy flirtation that makes us descend into giggles. God, I'd very easily straddle you now and give you a preview, but there's a Mandalorian vaping next to us who'd see the whole thing.

'You know, this whole week has been fun,' Cameron proceeds. 'That's understating it – it's been like truly... amazing,' he stutters nervously. 'But unexpected too. And I didn't want you to feel like that's all I'm here for. That bit is crazy fun, but you're kind and nice. If this is something, then maybe we need to do something more than...'

'Have very animated phone sex.'

We both laugh. It was two nights ago and so animated, he dropped his phone twice.

I feel his hand fall to my knee. And I feel all that spark, all that warmth flood through me every time he's been around me, the sort of spark that you're begging to ignite, to see where the fire will take you.

Tell him. Tell him now. *Hey, Cameron. While we're on the subject of rebuilding this very vague relationship, it's important that I tell you something. You know that the party where we met? That was my brother's house and I don't work in catering. I'm actually a below-average cook. The sort who burns toast. That evening, you know you alluded to his parents who both used to work in porn? Well, they're my parents too. And that sex empire they own, I run that too.* Let's start this again, maybe shake hands.

'You're really lovely, Cameron. Maybe you're right. Maybe we need to start from the beginning without all the drama, the misunderstandings.'

He nods, earnestly. 'I'm Cameron.'

'Josie.'

'And you're vibrating.'

For some reason, I think he's making a sex joke, but then realise he's talking about my phone. With a big sigh, I reach into my pocket. Mum. Oh my life, you choose your moments. I reject the call.

'Like I was saying, let's be upfront. Start afresh,' I say.

The phone goes again. Reject.

'She's keen,' Cameron says, peering over.

'She's my mum.' She should also assume I might be naked and not to be disturbed.

The phone rings. Again. I glance as messages pop up and my phone chimes like church bells.

Call me.

Now.

This is very very important. I'm so sorry.

'I'm sorry, Cameron. This is so rude but let me handle this and then you can have my full attention.'

He nods and beams, understanding the will and persistence of mothers.

'Mum, seriously,' I whisper.

But the sound I get on the other end of the phone makes my face drop. Why is she crying?

'Mum?'

'Josie, darling.'

'What's up? Are you OK?' Fear rages through my veins.

'I'm at Kingston Hospital, it's your dad, my lovely. He's not well.'

ELEVEN

My dad handed the company over to me when I was twenty-three. I had just returned from a year in Shanghai where I'd been finishing my degree and I came back ready to take on the world. I had veered away from the family business and Sonny's chosen path of minor celebrity, figuring I'd get on the payroll for a big finance company and live a nine-to-five existence in a range of well-fitting suits with interesting salads and gym breaks at lunch. When I came back from Shanghai, I remember sitting at a kitchen table whilst Mum and Dad were trying to brainstorm ideas for their business.

I think we should be going after the gay community.

Not with pitchforks, obviously, but they were keen to expand their client base and wanted to provide fun and frivolity for all. They used to write their ideas down on bits of paper. Dad wrote the word LGBT down in big letters.

'I think it's different now, Dad,' I said. 'It's LGBTQIA.'

'How do you know this?' he asked.

'I'm worldly now. I've been around Asia. I've been to Thailand and I've seen things. I went to Sydney Pride last year too.'

'Are you trying to tell us you're gay?' Dad asked very calmly.

'No. I'm saying research your market. We should get you a proper website.'

'What's wrong with our website?' Dad questioned, slightly offended.

'It was made by Roger. Most of the websites he creates can't get past firewalls.' This was not a lie. 'How about parties?'

'*Sex parties?*' Mum asked.

'No, like not pyramid schemes, but target the people who need better sex in their lives. The gay community know what they're doing and what they like, but take Linda who's forty-five who doesn't have a clue about what gets her off. Send Linda a gift pack and have her host a party with ten of her mates where they can have some wine, nibbles and a laugh over sex toys. If everyone buys something, then they tell their mates and... it's called the power of referral, word of mouth. It's the best sales tool in the industry.'

Up to that point, Mum and Dad hadn't really known much about my life, my degree and my knowledge. But they shouted from the rooftops that they had a daughter at university. They'd have put that on the side of buses if they could. But I remember that morning around the kitchen table, the moment they gave me a marker pen and invited me to share that piece of paper.

I think about that now as I sit in a taxi heading for a South London hospital, Cameron sitting closely beside me. The sky of a winter's night is dark and bitter, the roads shiny and bleak from the drizzle. We stop outside a shop, where a happy Santa dances for me. It's not the time for dancing, Mr Claus. Cameron and I don't say a word, but every so often he puts a hand to my knee to let me know he's there. He's been there since the colour drained from my face and my panic made me keel over. He caught me, he hailed a taxi. 'It was Halloween three weeks ago,' the taxi driver commented as he saw our costumes and we both laughed, even though I could hardly breathe after hearing what Mum just told me.

Dad collapsed during a tennis match apparently. Shortness of breath, tight chest, pale as a ghost. Please be OK. Please.

I get my phone out again and try Sonny and Ruby, but I know they're filming and all phones are prohibited on set. Maybe I should try his manager. I send him the forty-ninth text I've sent him today.

'How old is your dad?' Cameron asks, trying to break the tension in the cab.

'Late fifties. He's normally quite fit, so this doesn't quite register,' I stutter, my eyes shifting from side to side. He's not even on medication. He has the odd steak and bottle of red, but I never worry about him in that way.

'He'll be fine. We're nearly there,' he reassures me.

I am crying. I've been crying since Mum told me. Never mind goth-geek chic, my eye make-up has melted in rivulets down my face, so I'm a fully fledged member of KISS now and have made my way through two packs of tissues.

The taxi rolls to a stop and I jump out, noticing Cameron paying, as I sprint through the sliding doors and try to make out the labyrinth of signs. A&E, A&E, A&E. I race into the waiting area and run to a reception desk, but before I have a chance to speak, a hand goes to my shoulder.

'Josie...'

It's Mum. Hair scraped back from her face, no make-up, wearing a hoodie, leggings, with fluffy socks and slippers on her feet. She'd have found out about Dad and not cared about anything else; she'd have run out of that house to be with her Johnny. I throw my arms around her and sob on her shoulder.

'Calm down, he's OK. He's all right,' she says gently.

'Where is he? What happened?'

'They think he overdid it. He had his flu jab yesterday and

then went to play tennis today and his body was just trying to tell him to stop.'

'So not his heart?'

'They've wired him up to a machine to monitor him, given him some drugs... and... I'm sorry, is there a problem?' she says all of a sudden, looking over my shoulder. 'I know I spoke to your colleague. I'm parked terribly, I am so sorry.'

I turn around to see Cameron standing there. Mum thinks he's hospital security? I laugh through tears of relief and ridiculousness.

'No, I'm Cameron. I'm with...'

As soon as he introduces himself, my mum stops in her tracks. This is the hotel sex man. You can tell she doesn't know what to do with her eyes.

'Oh my... I called you away when you were—'

'Mid-date,' I intervene a little too loudly. 'We were at a sci-fi convention...'

'I'm so sorry,' she says, cupping her hands to her mouth, looking immensely confused.

I try to signal that she shouldn't delve any more.

'Don't be sorry... this is important,' Cameron says. 'It's nice to meet you. Sorry, what is your name?'

'Susie.'

Mum being Mum grabs him and goes in for the hug and you can tell the physical proximity is something he's not entirely used to.

'Well, it's very sweet of you to be here, Cameron.'

Mum, again being Mum, mouths the word 'CUTE' over his shoulder, recent drama doing nothing to quell her need to matchmake her daughter.

'It *was* sweet. I'm sorry I am such a mess,' I explain, trying to re-correct my eye make-up by swiping my fingers over the curve of my cheeks.

'You know what, it just showed me how close you are to your parents, that's a nice thing.'

He comes over and gives me a hug and I feel my body relent against his, warm and comforting, still smelling like sweet buttered popcorn. My mum grins. I also now realise how ridiculous we both must look to those in the waiting room. A man who seems to have put a nail through his hand keeps eyeing my boots.

'You don't have to stay, you know?' I tell him. 'You've gone out of your way already. I can pay you back for the taxi.'

'Oh god, don't be stupid. Look, I'm here. Let me be useful. I can move your car, get you vending-machine hot drinks. Let me be here.'

My mum watches him curiously. This is more than a sex date, this is a nice kid, Josie. She reaches in her handbag and gets her keys out. 'It's a black Mini Cooper. I literally parked it in front of other cars, car park 1. I didn't know what I was doing. I was so panicked,' she says, flustered.

'I'll have a walk around and find it. Go be with your dad, Josie.'

He touches my arm and leaves as Mum links her hand into mine.

'You're into policemen? That's some specific kink,' she whispers.

'Shush now. Take me to Dad.'

'Josie. Christ alive, that's a get-up.'

I run over to my dad, sitting upright in his hospital bed, chuckling at me. I approach the bed and punch him in the arm.

'Owww! There are needles in that arm. Isn't that your mum's coat?' he asks. I punch him again.

'You scared the monkeys out of us. Why aren't you taking better care of yourself?'

My mum grins smugly, as in these situations I am always the bad cop and this is perhaps a bit of what he needed to hear.

'Who were you playing tennis with?' I ask.

'These two young finance upstarts down the club. Jumped-up little things thought they could take me and Clive on.'

'How old?'

'Early twenties.'

'Idiot.'

'I nearly died.'

'But you didn't.'

'I threw up on the tennis court, though. There will be a fouling charge, I think. Teaches me to eat pie and mash before I take on two kids at doubles.'

'And combine that with your super tight eighties tennis shorts, then it's just a recipe for disaster,' my mum adds, going over to the bed to kiss him on the forehead.

I scan his body, he still has his socks and tennis shoes on, a paper gown over his body. I sit on the edge of his bed and put a hand to his arm.

'I'm sorry, Josie,' he whispers and I lean over and rest my head on his chest, reassured to feel the echo of his heartbeat, the way it rises and falls like it should. He puts a hand to my cheek. You stupid big lump. Thank god it was nothing more.

'You also interrupted her date,' Mum adds.

I glare at Mum.

'Oooooh, a date? We love to hear it. What's the tea?' he asks.

'Stop talking in youth speak, Dad.'

My parents both wait expectantly for details. They won't get them from me, mainly because it's not the priority right now and I'm too much of a mess of emotions to deal with the interrogation.

'His name is Cameron. He looks like a young Tom Hanks,' Mum says, trying to tease more detail out of me.

'He really doesn't. Remind me to book you in for that eye appointment.'

Mum smiles sarcastically back at me.

'You know. I had quite the scare, JoJo,' Dad says, trying to act poorly and withered. 'And it's been quite the day. To hear you've met someone and get some morsels of gossip would be quite medicinal.'

I shake my head at him. I don't think any father needs to hear the details of his daughter's sex life.

'He's dressed like Rick Grimes today from *The Walking Dead*. You watched that with me.'

'The zombie show?'

I nod. We binged it over three weeks, a proper father-daughter activity, and then we plotted how we'd ever cope in an apocalypse. Most likely using golf clubs, tennis racquets and giant sex toys from the warehouse.

'So you have a comic book friend. Finally, your mother and I don't have to pretend to be interested in all of that.'

They both grin at each other.

'It's not serious, we're just seeing where it goes...'

'He thinks she's someone else, though,' Mum adds.

My dad sits there for a moment, slightly confused.

'Like an alter ego? Is that why you're wearing the costume?'

'He doesn't think I'm Batman, if that's what you mean.'

Mum can't stop giggling.

'It's just he doesn't know I'm related to Sonny or anything about the family business. He thinks I'm in catering, it's a bit of a mess.'

'He thinks you're in catering. But your cooking is awful? Have you cooked for him? He'd surely find out that way.'

It's Mum's turn to hit Dad now. 'Don't be mean, it's just a case of mistaken identity. Did you manage to have a moment to clear it up?' Mum asks. I shake my head. 'So what does he think about us?'

'He thinks you're both retired. You do charity work and volunteer. This is not a lie.'

'But retired from what?' Mum asks.

'You used to own a shop, also not a lie.'

Dad sits there, looking puzzled. I guess it's because he's trying to work out why I'm keeping this pretence up.

'Well, as long as you're happy. Maybe it will sort itself in the end?' he says.

There is doubt in his tones. Since Mike, he has become protective of me, a constant fatherly wing hovering over me, hoping I'll never get hurt like that again. It pained him to see me when I first got cruelly dumped, to see me crawl back to their home and just survive for days off air and little sleep. On the third day, I said I thought I might be hungry, I fancied a biscuit and Dad went to the supermarket and bought one of everything – party rings, giant cookies, even those lemon puff biscuits that nobody really likes. He fanned them all out on a tray. *Are we having a party?* I said through my laughter. *No. But it's worth it to see a smile on your face.*

'Hello, hi, sorry... there's no door, only a curtain, so I didn't know how to knock...'

Cameron. He stands there adjusting his sheriff hat.

My dad takes a glance over the costume. There are strong beige and taupe notes going on.

'Dad, this is Cameron. Cameron, this is my dad...'

'Fabio,' my dad says, sitting up in bed.

Mum cocks her head to the side as he says that. Thank you for playing along, Dad, but of all the bloody names to choose.

'Hi, it's good to meet you. Just sorry about the outfit. This is not usually me. That said...' he continues, giving my mum back her keys, '...when I was moving your car, I think this outfit got you out of a fine.'

Mum beams at him, her eyes glancing to the plastic bag in his hands.

'Oh... And there was a shop by the entrance so I just did a dash and grab. That sounds like I stole it all, I didn't.'

'Well, you are a sheriff,' Mum says.

'Yes, howdy,' he replies, making his hand like a gun.

I chuckle because it's insanely cute, but Mum bites her lip to hold in the giggles as Cameron goes a little beetroot at how awkward this first interaction with my parents is going. It could be worse; I told his dad he was talking out of his backside the first time I met him.

'Well, I will judge you now by what's in that bag,' my dad says coolly. 'Come at me with what you have, Cameron.'

Cameron opens the bag gingerly. 'Well, I guess I just thought, go safe and KitKats all round, right? No Snickers as you may be allergic to nuts and nothing chewy like Skittles that could get stuck in your teeth. So I went with the light snack option. Have a break, have a KitKat and all that. I also got some juice and water and fizzy stuff. Crisps, I went plain because I find flavours really divide a room. And I'm rambling...'

'You are, but it's bloody hysterical,' replies Dad. 'I will take a KitKat. I bloody love a KitKat. And maybe some juice.'

Cameron digs around in the bag and hands it over.

'Eat it slowly, I know how you are with Kit Kats. You inhale them,' my mum adds.

She puts a hand to Dad's brow and I see Cameron observe the tactile nature of their relationship. You really have no idea.

Mum's phone rings. 'Oh my days, it's your brother. I'm just going to take this outside so the nurse doesn't shout at me again.' Before she goes, she dips her hand in Cameron's bag and takes out some crisps for herself, then winks at him. Yes, my parents are big winkers, get used to that.

'Thank you for being here, Cameron. For looking out for Josie,' Dad says, scanning the length of his body again, trying to assess what this lad is about. 'I need to ask you a dad question now, don't I? What are your intentions towards my daughter, young man?' he says, his tone changing.

'They're totally honourable, sir.'

Dad glances over to me. I like him, Dad. Give this a chance, whatever it is.

'Well then, it's really good to have you here.'

'Thanks, Fabio. Is that Italian?'

'It is,' my dad says, nodding, flattening out his bottom lip. 'My family are from Milan.'

'I like your football club... and your salami,' Cameron says.

Dad and I stop in silence, trying not to erupt in hysterics. Please don't talk about my dad's salami.

TWELVE

'Hold up, you're where now?' I ask Cameron on the phone, standing in Brett and Tina's flat.

'I'm at your house.'

The colour drains from my face. Cameron and I haven't done this yet, the houses thing. We meet for dates, we snog in bushes and do carnal things on phones, but this is where I live. We've not invaded each other's space in that way. Yet. For one, you'll find out that like some sad case, I live at home and there is far too much there that might give the game away: the photos of Sonny, the yoni sculpture in the living room, the cupboard under the stairs where I'm currently storing a box of multi-coloured vibrators that need to be posted out. I feel the panic envelop me.

'Your mum invited me round for a coffee. We got talking at the hospital and she said they had problems with their Wi-Fi and I said it was a really easy fix.'

I pause. If you have problems with the Wi-Fi, you call Roger, who's the IT man at The Love Shack, you don't call my potential love interest. This is her being nosey.

'Your parents love Christmas, eh?' he tells me.

He has no idea. With the big day in a fortnight's time, they've gone for broke, in the same way they did at Halloween. An animatronic reindeer on the garage, an eight-foot tree, a lights display that is likely to be reported by air-traffic control for interfering with flight patterns in the Greater London area.

'That they do. Is my dad there too?' I ask.

'Propping up the sofa, it's good to see him better.'

'How many questions have they asked you?'

'It's going into the hundreds. They're very sweet questions, though.'

'Like?'

'She asked me my shoe size.'

I blush. Hard. 'She did what? Is she buying you shoes?'

'I hope so. Christmas *is* around the corner. She got out some baby photos too. That naked one of you on the potty is a winner. Your graduation pictures. I liked the fringe.'

I can't speak. Please, no.

'I'm so sorry. I should be there... To at least throw myself in the way of that car crash...'

'Well, it would have been good to see you. You're babysitting?'

'My godsons. They're five.'

He pauses. 'That's very cool. And a good age.'

'Well, kids generally like me because I know Marvel and I'll sing the Baby Yoda song with them.'

He doesn't reply immediately. I don't know if that's because I've mentioned kids or the fact I know the Baby Yoda song. Don't sing the song, I tell myself.

'Well, they're lucky to be spending time with you. I think I miss you, Miss Josie. I'm busy tonight, but maybe the cinema in the week?'

I grin to myself. He misses me? I am familiar with that feeling. Since the Comic Con mix-up and Cameron coming to the hospital, I've seen a new side to him that's warm, considerate, the buds of a new relationship coming to blossom. We haven't met up since the hospital, but we're at a juncture now where he's held me at a low point and he continues to check in to see how we're all doing. He does, however, think my father's name is Fabio.

'Well, I think I miss you too,' I reply.

'I miss just being next to you. Is that weird? Is that soppy? I just like hanging out with you. You're fun and I like kissing you. God, I sound like a teenager. I also miss the other more grown-up things we've done,' he rambles.

'Same,' I whisper in reply, biting my lip. 'I mean, I think we could have really explored the potential of those costumes, right?'

'We could do that at the cinema... It might get us thrown out the multiplex, though.'

My face is a few different shades of blush. 'It's a date, Sheriff.'

'You're on, Miss Josie.'

'Now, is my mum there?' I ask him.

'Shall I hand you over?'

'Yeah. I'll catch up with you later.'

I hear a muffled exchange of words, the radio in the background.

'Hello?'

'Mum! What the actual... You're killing me here,' I shriek at her. 'Did you wait until I was out of the house to invite him round? Why are you asking him his shoe size?'

'He had big feet.'

'Please tell me you didn't ask him whether that meant he had a big—'

'No. Anyway, that's an urban myth. I knew someone with feet like flippers who had a tiny one like a lipstick...'

'Can he still hear you?' I cry painfully.

'I've dipped into the hallway. I've also been really clever and hidden all our family photos and I'm wearing a polo-neck dress, and a cross around my neck.'

'Why?'

'To look more Catholic Italian, so me and Fabio match.'

I don't know what to say. I hope she's not dressed as a bloody nun and cooking him spaghetti.

'JoJo, he brought a box of KitKats for your dad. He's got such a lovely energy. He's polite and he smells nice. I like this one.'

Why are you smelling him? She makes him sound like a puppy in a shop that she wants to keep.

'He's going to find out, isn't he? And I'm not even there,' I say, staring into space.

'You forget, your father and I are actors. We are very good at what we do.'

'I wouldn't call what you did acting, Mum.'

'Rude.'

'Just stop asking him questions. There is nothing wrong with your Wi-Fi and I am mortified you have done this,' I say, pretty much snarling.

'Oh, love... you're breaking up. I can't quite hear you...'

'Don't you dare—'

'Kiss those boys for me...'

She hangs up and I stand in Brett and Tina's kitchen staring at the kettle. It's over, isn't it? She's done the photos, next she'll reel out embarrassing souvenirs from my past. She still keeps our baby teeth in a jar, a video of me playing Villager #3 in a school play, in the loft there's a shrine I once built in homage to Robert Pattinson. It was nice while it lasted.

'Aunty JoJo. You're missing the best part of the film,' a little voice says, his head peeking around the corner.

'Just a minute, Vinnie,' I say, reaching for drinks and sweets, trying to hide my panic.

'Who was on the phone?'

'Aunty Susie.'

'Is she coming round?' he asks excitedly.

'No... She's been very naughty.'

'So Father Christmas might not visit her?' he says, aghast.

I'd put her on the naughty list but I don't want to ruin this kid's vision of the festive season. 'Oh, he will. She might just get a sprinkling of reindeer poop over her gifts.'

This makes little Vinnie crease over with laughter.

I hand him the sweet packet, ruffling his blond hair as we head over to the living room so I can re-engage with *Ant-Man*.

'WHERE WERE YOU?' his brother, Xander, asks me.

'On the phone. Now where were we?'

'He's just put on the costume and turned really small and then he got stuck in the bath,' Xander tells me. 'And met a GIANT RAT,' he shouts, jumping up on the sofa, waving his arms around to demonstrate the size of the rat.

'Off the sofa, kiddo. It's an awesome film, right?' I say.

They nod in unison and pull my arms to get me to nestle in between them. How much do I love these kids? Too bloody much. Their story starts when Brett and Tina were barely out of their teens, just graduating from catering college and Tina got pregnant. It was a shock to everyone, not least Tina's parents, who threw her out and told her she'd have to fend for herself. Brett had only lived with his dad his whole life and suddenly they were young, alone and expecting twins. Twin boys.

When my parents found out, I never saw two people react to a situation in the way that they did. As Brett was working long hours, Mum went with Tina to all her appointments, every single one. Dad bought them a small flat and told them it'd be rent-free for a year, giving them time to settle in and save up. He would do little things like show up with cots – saying he knew someone who was getting rid of them, that they'd cost him nothing, but I knew differently. It was Mum and Dad all over, it was philanthropy but for no other reason than to help two kids out who were once them.

And five years later, we now have Vinnie and Xander, who we all love like our own. Don't get me wrong, they come with a unique little-boy-based energy that is both super loud and super draining, but they're ours and Sonny and I are their proud godparents. I also am a godmother who comes with her own superpowers, though, because these little boys are very into Marvel and Godmother Josie knows that shizz, so they think I'm very very cool. They're the only people in the world who think that.

As Ant-Man does his thing, Xander climbs on top of me to twist my hair around in his fingers and I lean into him. With Christmas nearly upon us, the anticipation runs through the veins of these kids like electricity. I wish I could remember that feeling. For now, Christmas feels like checklists and last-minute shopping trips and Mum fretting because everywhere is out of chipolatas. I made a joke about that. It didn't go down well.

'I'm going to miss you boys at Christmas,' I tell them glumly. Since they were little, the four of them have always camped around ours on Christmas Day, but this year they're off for a well-deserved weekend away.

'Same. We'll miss Uncle Johnny dressing up pretending he's slid down the chimney.'

I have a feeling he might miss it too.

'Have you guys seen Santa yet?' I ask.

'Yeah, kinda. He was at the garden centre, but I don't think it was him,' Vinnie tells me.

'Why would you think that?' I ask.

'Because his beard fell off.'

'Oh.' I don't know how to parent this situation and realise I have to think on my feet.

'Maybe he was a stand-in? A representative of the company.'

'Santa works for a company?'

'It would make sense for him to be part of a limited company for tax reasons.' They both look at me blankly. Change of subject needed. 'So, Uncle Sonny's wedding is coming up, that's exciting?'

'Are you going to be there?' asks Xander curiously.

'Well, I hope so. I am his sister.'

Vinnie giggles. 'Do you have to wear a suit?'

I rest my arm on their sofa as we forget *Ant-Man* is on the television.

'I forgot, you had your fittings the other day. What were they like?'

They scrunch their little faces up at me. Vinnie has the best brown curly hair that may or may not remind me of someone I know. How can I miss his hair? Would our kids have his hair? Don't even go there.

'They were itchy and we have to wear ties and I couldn't breathe.'

'I doubt that.'

'We all matched Daddy's suit and Mummy saw it and she cried. I don't know why,' Xander adds.

'It's probably because you all looked amazing. I'm not wearing a suit. I'm wearing a red dress.'

'Like Mummy?'

I nod.

'Are you bringing your boyfriend?'

I giggle, shaking my head at them both. Good news travels fast obviously and even more so when it's being wielded by my mother.

'He's not really my boyfriend. That's who I was just

speaking to on the phone actually,' I tell them, the anxiety of Cameron being in my family home shooting through me again.

'Mummy said we have to cross everything that's he a nice guy because some of your past boyfriends have been bad news.' They both come at me with crossed fingers. I'm glad their parents put it more politely than others would.

'Well, we will see what happens there. Have you heard what you're doing at the wedding?'

'We're carrying the rings. And giving them to Mum at the end of the island,' Xander erupts with excitement.

'The aisle. It's an important job. I'll be there, though, so I can help, you won't be on your own. I'll have Dave with me too. Have you practised your walking?' I ask them.

They both stare at me. Aunty JoJo, we've been walking since we were one. Do we seriously need a tutorial on how to do that?

'Come, stand up. It's a special slow walk.'

The boys rise to their feet, Xander pretending that he's on the moon. I giggle and move some toys out of the way, so we have a stretch of carpet to glide along.

'It's one together, two together, next step together... Try to go in time to the music.'

'What's the music?' Vinnie asks.

'Rick Astley.'

'We don't know what that is.'

'Neither do I.'

But every person is entitled to their own wedding song choices. There are rumours there may be a routine for us to learn. With the dog. Good luck with that, guys, because we have trouble telling Dave not to eat out of the bin.

'Come practise with me.' I grab two cushions and place some Haribo gummy rings on them. 'One for you and one for you, the trick is to hold the cushion super super straight. If we lose the rings, the wedding will be ruined.' Their eyes widen to hear of such responsibility being placed on their tiny shoulders. 'I mean, it wouldn't be ruined-ruined, but it's an important job, and Sonny gave it to you guys because he knows you'll be awesome.'

They high-five each other and walk down the stretch of their living room, maybe a bit too slowly like they're on a tightrope, but it makes me grin from ear to ear to see them looking so earnest. As they reach a bookshelf at the end of the room, the sound of a key goes in the door and Brett and Tina walk in, the boys rushing over to their parents, cushions and jelly rings falling on the floor. Let's hope the actual day doesn't end like that.

'DUDES! How's it going?' Brett says. 'What are we doing?'

'We're learning how to carry rings, it's the most important job of the day,' Vinnie tells his dad.

'That it is,' his mum says, kissing him on the cheek. 'Have you been good for Aunty JoJo?'

'They've been the best,' I say.

'Aunty JoJo watched *Ant-Man* with us,' says Xander.

'She does that so we don't have to sit through it, this is why we love Aunty JoJo,' Tina replies. 'Come, I have leftover treats. Help me with these bags, lads.' The boys do as they're told, and head on through the flat as I follow. 'Thank you so much for babysitting, you are a lifesaver,' she says to me.

'How was it?' I ask.

'They were just super grateful we could step in at the last minute, it was easy – little christening buffet and the baby was super cute,' she says, pouting. 'Boys, there are some sausage rolls, help yourself but use a plate.'

It is always a joy to see Tina as a mum. Back in the day, she was a rebel who wore a lot of camo, accessorised with military boots and goggles, and once burned down a sports equipment storage shed as she was that opposed to track and field athletics.

She opens up a container of pink iced cupcakes and puts the kettle on.

'Brett! You want tea?' she shouts into the hallway.

'Always!' he echoes in response.

'Help yourself, I also have finger sandwiches,' she says, getting some mugs out of the cupboard. 'We also need a catch-up – I feel I haven't seen you in an age. What's new?'

I give her a look as she leans against the countertops. 'You mean, how's my new boyfriend? The one you've told your sons about?'

Vinnie and Xander, mouths full of sausage rolls, suddenly look sheepish and go and find their dad.

'Keep using those plates, boys!' their mum shouts before returning to me.

'Did Mum tell you?' I ask Tina.

'Who else? She wanted to know if I had gossip. They like him. He came to the hospital, that's like huge brownie points. Who is he?'

'His name's Cameron. I met him at Sonny's party.'

'THE GHOSTBUSTER!' Brett suddenly says from the hallway.

Tina's jaw drops. 'That became a thing-thing? Josie, shame on you for not telling us.'

'I generally don't broadcast these moments, you know me well enough for that. After he rang the restaurant that night, we went out for a few dates.'

Both of their eyes widen, large and hopeful. Josie's back in the ring, how many rounds will she last this time?

'You know, Brett and I were in the kitchen that night watching the both of you. We left you to it because we were working and professionals, but even we could see a spark. Tell us more.'

'He designs video games...'

'Could he get us a PS5?' little Xander pipes in from the hall.

Their mum points them away from the adult conversation and back to *Ant-Man*, getting Brett to follow them.

'So, how much do you like him?' she asks, turning back to me.

'A bit. I like him a bit,' I say, unconvincingly.

'Josie Jewell,' Tina whispers, 'tell me.'

'Tina, I'm really falling for him,' I cry out, exasperated. 'He's just perfect for me and it all just fits: he kisses nice, we like the same stuff and I'm at that stage now where I'm thinking about him too much.'

'That's not a thing.'

'It is. It's distracting. I can't concentrate because I'm looking at my phone, wondering what to text, daydreaming about his laugh, wondering what we'd look like on holiday together.'

'That's what you fantasise about?'

'Yep, we're on a catamaran, day drinking, eating good calamari and his eyes are the same colour as the sea.'

'Colour?'

'Blue, slightly paler towards the pupils.'

Tina grins broadly and I throw a tea towel at her.

'Look at you all loved up.'

'It's not love, not yet.'

'It's the beginnings of something and we like that.'

'What else have Mum and Dad told you?' I ask curiously.

'Well, they like him. They think he's very polite and has nice hair. But hold up, are you keeping that charade going with him?'

'The charade where he thinks I'm still in catering? Yeah...' I reply hesitantly. 'He believes Dad's name is also Fabio. Dad even adopts an accent around him like he's advertising pizza.'

Knowing my dad, Tina chuckles, but also looks slightly worried on my behalf. She hands me my cup of tea. 'OK then... Josie, it's nice to see this, you finding someone and all these initial butterflies, but none of us want to see you hurt if this doesn't work out. We all love you too much. Where is this all going if he doesn't really know who you are?'

'But do we ever know who anyone is really?' I say, trying to fob it off with some crackpot cliché philosophy.

'He should get to know you and all your family. You're the best. He'll fall in love with you, it should make no difference.' She comes to put her arms around me. Tina never let my bizarre family history affect our friendship. I think as a teen it made me more interesting to her than all the bitchy know-it-alls in our year and even now, she gets that it's more of a sideshow affair than something which really defines me and my family.

'Maybe you can tell him at Christmas?' Tina suggests.

'What? Wrap it up in a box?' I ask.

''Tis the season, new year coming, new start. You've not been going out long, just don't drag it out.'

I smile. But now my parents are involved and my mum is inviting him around for random coffees, I worry that we're in too deep now. What would I tell him? We all duped him? He'd think we're a family of conmen. He'd get us arrested.

'Can you tell him?' I ask Tina.

'I love you but no.'

'I just babysat your sons.'

'Still no.'

'I gave your boys Thanos gloves for Christmas, they're under your tree.'

'You did? I didn't even know what they were going on about.'

'Well, someone's got to remain cool and relevant in their lives.'

A voice suddenly drifts in from the hallway. 'Cool and relevant are the last words I'd use to describe you, Josie,' Brett jokes, putting his hands to my shoulders and helping himself to a cupcake.

'Bastards, both of you.'

'Well, at least a new boyfriend will take your mind off everything else,' Brett suddenly mumbles through cupcake crumbs. 'How are you taking all of that? You do seem very calm.'

I scan both of their faces as the words come out of Brett's mouth and I try to recount what he might be talking about. Tina grits her teeth and shakes her head at her husband.

'Taking what? Wedding stuff? Well, you know me. I'm very good at organising, I don't exude stress when I'm in planning mode,' I jest.

Tina looks down to the floor, Brett realises he may have put his foot in it.

'Or were you talking about something else? Is everyone OK? Please don't worry me.'

Dad's not ill, is he? Have my parents hidden that from me? Is Sonny OK?

Tina throws her arms up in the air in resignation. 'You bloody spanner. You'd better tell her now.'

Brett looks hesitant but takes his phone and opens up a Facebook page. 'It appeared last week. Someone forwarded it to me to let me know, I told your mum, but she said not to tell you. I thought that meant *she* was telling you.'

'Tell me what?'

He shows me the page. It's Mike's profile. Michael Dolman. My ex. I inhale sharply to see it. It's a picture of him in a suit next to a woman with a white dress. They've just got married. He looks happy, so does she, but the telling part is that the photo has been taken against a London skyline. He's not in Venezuela anymore. He's back.

As I drive home that evening, the news still reverbing through my bones, I think about what that whole experience with Mike meant. We're supposed to have our hearts broken so that they can mend and are thus stronger from the experience. We learn the different ways to be loved, what we really deserve in life, what makes us better people. Why is it then so mind-numbingly awful to experience those broken feelings? Why does it feel like time wasted? Energy poured into something that came to no good? That's how I always feel about Mike.

At the time he disappeared, he also withdrew £18,000 that we'd saved together in a joint account, ready to put a deposit on a house together. You'll survive without it, was the message he sent me after I tried to track him down. You have Mummy and Daddy. So never mind me totally misjudging someone I was going to marry, he was cruel. Really terribly cruel. And when I think back to him, I just feel like a complete idiot for having imbued all that trust, for letting him have any piece of my heart at all.

Mum knew about Mike, which means Dad knows. I wonder if it was that news which made him keel over on the tennis court and throw up his guts? I know why they kept it from me. Why dredge it all up when Cameron is in the picture? Protect me. But there are questions. Did Mike really go to Venezuela? I bet he didn't. He was not an exotic man of travel. He didn't even eat kebabs. I bet he just moved down to the coast. What did he do with all that money? Secretly, I hope he spent it on a penis-lengthening operation that went really badly. That made his penis shrivel up so now he can't pee without pain or irritation. Or maybe a house that had bad foundations, termites even, that ate his face in the night. This is what I think about when I think about Mike and I don't think that level of rage is healthy.

'Is that you, Josie?' I hear my mum's voice sing across the hallway as I enter the house.

This was the house I came back to that evening he left and I spy my parents' heads in the living room in exactly the same position they were on that day; watching some true-crime documentary, eating a takeaway off the coffee table, Dave nibbling on the end of a spring roll.

'Have you eaten? How are the boys? You not seeing Cameron tonight?' she asks.

I pop my head through the door, shaking my head.

'How's the Wi-Fi working now?'

'Like a dream,' Mum replies, winking.

'Cameron's busy tonight. The boys are fine. I'm not feeling great, so I'm going to get an early night,' I say wearily.

'You OK?' she asks, studying my face, I guess expecting more of a charged exchange after our phone call before. I don't want to know what happened. I don't think my brain can process much more.

'I just need to sleep.'

'Maybe it's the beginnings of a cold? I have some lemons in if you need a hot toddy.'

Ask them why they didn't tell you about Mike. Go on. But that seems to be what life is built on these days – secrets, fragile little secrets. I don't want to bring it up now.

'I'm good. We can chat tomorrow.'

Mum puts a hand out and I reach for it before heading up the stairs to my room. Inside, I strip down to vest top and knickers and get under my covers with my phone.

Search: Laila Dolman.

That's his wife's name.

Like some awful exercise in masochism, I find her easily. Her new wedding photo is her profile picture. I click. Everything is public. She's got a link to the wedding pictures and she also likes a make-up tutorial about cut creases. I shouldn't. I really shouldn't, but I click on the photos link.

They got married in a big hotel in London, funded by more than just our house money, looking at the size of the ballroom hosting their reception. It's a classy affair, his suit is Prada, there are fire-eaters to entertain the guests, a band with a singer that looks like Adele. Shit, that *is* Adele. She is glamorous beyond belief (Laila, though Adele also looks flawless) and there's a Kardashian flair to her, an hourglass to her shape.

What I can't get over, though, is Mike, or Michael, as she likes to call him. He's got fake tan, a more sculpted hairstyle and eyebrows, but there's a look in his eyes, like he adores her. And I shouldn't. I *really* shouldn't, but I shed a tear because that's not a man I know. I couldn't have done a wedding like that with all its opulence and spectacle. I'd have hated the extravagance. Maybe this is what he wanted and I couldn't provide.

I can't help it – I go through her photos. She's from Manchester. It doesn't look like she works, she spends a lot of time shopping and on exotic trips abroad. She had a lovely time in Dubai in 2012 and she knows her angles to create the ultimate thirst traps. She's everything I'm not and I think I'm fine with that, even if my tears tell a different story. It's only when I come across a picture with a date tag that I hold my breath a little. It's a picture of her and Mike. In London. Two months after he left me. Wow. So much for broadening your horizons. The tears flow fully now as my bedroom door opens. I pull the duvet over my head.

'Oh lordy, you're not naked and sexting, are you?' my mum yelps. 'I thought you were asleep, I made you that hot toddy and brought up some cold meds.'

I pull the duvet back. Mum's face drops as soon as she sees mine.

'Oh, Josie. What on earth's the matter?'

'It's just a tension headache, I think. I've been burning the candle at both ends.'

She comes over and sits on the edge of my bed, putting the mug and medicine boxes down. 'I'm sorry I invited Cameron around and didn't tell you.'

I shrug my shoulders.

'Do you want a compress or anything?' she asks, visibly concerned.

'I'll take a hug.' My tears still roll down my face. She comes and wraps her arms around me. She hugged me like this the day he left, the day he told me that he hated everything about my life, about my parents, about me. 'I'm OK, Mum. I'll be fine.'

'Are you sure?'

No. Not at all.

THIRTEEN

In my family, there are people of legend. Yes, there's Mum and Dad, who had their own following in the late eighties/early nineties and who, and I hate to say this, actually have a small Facebook group of fans who collect their canon of work. Yes, they chat about it and all its artisan filmmaking quality. You then have my brother, who started acting when he was six years old. He was a charming son-of-a-bitch even back then, so Mum signed him up for drama, which led to an agent, which led to things like pantomimes and parts on hospital dramas. As he had these big green kitten eyes, he was excellent at looking very convincingly sad when he had to stand there and cry about the death of his fake mother because she'd fallen off a cliff in the mist walking the dog (we still have that episode taped). Anyway, he then went into a soap and he's still there. His latest storyline is a complete doozy: he's gone into partnership with a conman who's sleeping with his girlfriend AND his sister AND his mother. The tumultuous love pentagon will come to a head at Christmas, where there will be a gas explosion and much shouty confrontation. Apparently, it's some of his best work, but he will survive (apologies for the spoiler).

And then there is Nan.

Nan has always been a part of our lives, always there with advice and a packet of whatever biscuits she's bought in for the day. When we were children, she'd occasionally do the school run when Mum and Dad were busy trying to build their kitchen-table sex toy business. She'd pick Sonny and I up and do the little things that would sear themselves into memory. She'd stop at the chippy to get us hot chips and bottles of fluoro pop, she'd take us on the buses and occasionally to bingo, where the caller would tell her off. *Barbara, this is gambling, they're not allowed to be here.* But then she'd come at him. *Whatever, Trevor. Get your balls out of your arse like you're the bingo police.* Nan says it was exposing me to all those numbers at such a young age that made me such a whizz at maths. She was a single mother so she's always exuded resilience, fight, fire.

'Remind me why your tool of a brother isn't here today?' she says in her London tones, sipping at a tumbler of Baileys. It's Christmas Day. Nan is as much a part of Christmas Day as baby Jesus and the turkey, and she has no problem knocking the alcohol back at 9.45 a.m. I picked her up early so she could have some breakfast with us and I love that when I got to hers, she was already waiting in the car park, in a Christmas jumper with a rude snowman on the front.

'It's because he's alternating now. One year with us, one year with Ruby,' I reply, clinking her glass. I mean, it'd be rude to let her drink alone.

'That's a shit rule.'

'Nan,' I tell her. 'We'll see him between now and New Year. It means two roast dinners in a week.'

'All them brussels sprouts. That's not good for anyone's digestion.'

I laugh and give her a hug. We've nestled ourselves into one of the big sofas in the front room, slippers on, the multi-coloured lights of Mum's tree hypnotising us into a trance. My parents' attention to holiday detail in here is winning. For the past month, it's been like living inside a sparkly festive disco. There are rules. Christmas jumpers all round. Bublé for weeks. Eat and drink without regret. Don't put the empty sweet wrappers back in the box. There's no colour scheme when it comes to Christmas, it's bright and rainbow-coloured and, more often than not, if it sparkles, it is bought and hung off some empty part of the ceiling. You call it tacky, they call it joy.

'Right,' my dad says, entering the room, clapping his hands together. 'Let's get these presents open, eh?'

'About sodding time,' Nan mumbles.

I think about my two godsons and wonder when Christmas became a restrained affair, when you stop running down the stairs to rip the paper off your gifts and become more obsessed by the drinking element of the day.

Mum canters into the room to hear Dad clapping.

'How's that turkey looking, Suse?' Nan asks her.

'Not bad, I think,' she says, grabbing her hand. They've always been close, the two of them, allies and friends. Nan will always be the one person who welcomed Mum into a family when she had none. 'Here, this one's for you, Babs,' she says, handing over a gift basket.

Nan shrugs her shoulders and does a little dance sitting down. 'Is this what I think it is?' she asks.

Mum and Dad nod. I do love that for all the money the company brings us, Nan always asks for the same thing. It's a hamper from Fortnum & Mason so she can be like the Queen. Jams, tea and shortbread. It's all she ever wants. I smile to see her so overjoyed.

'Earl Grey? You going posh on me?' she tells my dad.

'You were always posh, Mum.'

'Never. Thank you, darlings. What's that you got, Suse?' she asks as Mum unwraps her presents.

Mum beams up at me. I've bought her some antique pearl drop earrings in a little box.

'Josie, these are lovely,' Mum tells me.

'I thought they'd look good for that TV debate thing you're doing?'

'They are perfect.' She blows me a kiss and moves on to a small gift wrapped in tissue paper. She opens it, a grin creeping across her face. 'It's a tea towel.'

Dad and I look at each other curiously. He'd better not have got Mum a tea towel, she'll object to the underlying message of that. And whereas Nan doesn't mind getting tea bags for Christmas, Mum likes to be spoilt. A bit of jewellery, a city break, a pair of nice Jimmy Choos. I hope there's something that goes with the tea towel, Dad.

Mum is smiling, though. She holds it up. 'It's Prince. A Prince tea towel.'

'You love Prince,' I tell Mum. 'Well done, Dad.'

'It's from Cameron.'

I pause for a moment. That's great, but how does he know that Mum likes Prince?

'When he was here to fix the Wi-Fi that time, Prince came on the radio and we had a conversation and a dance.'

'You danced with Cameron?' I ask, mystified.

'Just a little disco moment,' she replies.

'I was there too. He knew all the words,' Dad says. 'That's a sweet gift.'

'Hold up,' Nan suddenly says. 'Who in the tits is Cameron?'

I laugh to hear her swearing, sitting there watching us all.

'He's Josie's new friend.'

'Ooooooh,' she says mockingly. 'This is new information, why haven't I heard about this yet?' she asks, punching me in the arm.

I shake my head. I know why. It's because even though I like him – I like him a lot – it's still built on lies. Is it a relationship? A friendship? A love affair? I have no idea and given what I've recently heard about Mike, it just feels too tumultuous to sort in my own head. 'He's a nice guy I've met recently.'

'He's like Josie, but a fella,' Dad contributes. 'They're into the same stuff, I like him. He's a good guy.'

'Well, that's not enough information for me. Is he on Instagram, can I follow him?' Nan asks.

'No,' I say and she sticks her tongue out at me. 'It's just... complicated.'

'Do you want to see what he looks like?' Mum says. 'We could give him a FaceTime? I could thank him for the gift?'

'No,' I say, shaking my head. 'It's Christmas. Leave him alone. Why don't we open more gifts? What about your turkey, Mum? I'm sure there are vegetables we need to peel?'

But before I have the chance to toss a present in her direction, she's dialled. She has his number saved? Where the hell did she learn these skills? I have to help her send emails most days. Terror sears through me. Nan doesn't know. She could totally blow this. What are you doing?

Brrring, brrring. Dad's laughing as I sit here panicked, half worried about how my hair looks.

Brrring brrring.

'Hello, Susie? Heyyyy!'

I hear his voice and I smile. I saw him a week ago. We went to watch a Christmas showing of *Die Hard*. We didn't opt for costumes, but there was no chance to tell him anything in the cinema because there was a film on and we were too busy snogging and giving each other hand jobs in the back row. But aside from the hot sex stuff, it was also another evening of being with him, getting to know those little things about a person that make you fall deeper for them. The care and attention he takes in choosing his sweets, the way his whole face lights up when he laughs, the way he slipped his hand over my waistband, pushed my knickers to one side and knew exactly what would make me lean forward and grab the seat in front of me. All I'll say is I'm glad that seat was empty.

'Merry Christmas!' my mum squeals, high off her Christmas spirit.

I don't dare get into frame yet. This can just be a quick call for Nan to satisfy her curiosities and for Mum to say thank you. *What a wonderful gift, Cameron. How kind. Do you have a favourite Prince song? 'Raspberry Beret'? Fabulous choice! Greetings of the season to you!* Hang up.

'Cameron, I just opened your present – you sweetheart!' she continues.

'You are most welcome. I saw it and I thought of you – please share it with Fabio, though.'

Nan looks at me. You can tell she's staring at Mum's dog, trying to work out his name. I thought we called the dog Dave. Who the hell?

'I will. I'm sorry we didn't get you anything, I feel awful,' Mum says.

'It's fine, please.'

Dad gets into frame and waves at the screen. 'Merry Christmas, Cameron. You having a good day?'

'Oh, yeah. Just chilling.'

They both freeze as he says it, as do I. I'd sent him a Merry Christmas message this morning, but I thought he'd be with his family today and he would need all his nerve and energy to face them. I tentatively move into focus.

'Hey. Chilling?' I ask. I see a figure in pyjama bottoms and a hoodie, the hood pulled up over his head with his scruffy hair framing his face.

Nan feels the need to budge in at this rate. 'I'm the nan. Hello?'

Our four faces peer in at him and he laughs. 'Hi, Nan. I'm Cameron.'

I see her inspecting him and she glances over at my mum and gives a thumbs up.

'You're in your pyjamas,' I tell him. 'What's the deal?'

'There's chickenpox in my family. My nephews gave it to Mum, who's really poorly, one very scabby sister, it's all a bit of a mess. We decided to cancel today.'

'So you're on your own?' Mum exclaims in horror, like it may be the worst thing she's ever heard.

'It's fine. I was just going to watch some Christmas films and lounge all day.'

'What are you going to eat?' Dad asks.

'Baked beans?'

Mum and Dad shake their heads simultaneously, in slow motion.

'Come over here, it's only the four of us. I've made a whole turkey,' Mum says.

As soon as she says it, I pause, feeling my body stiffen. Today? It's Christmas, that's pretty big in terms of relationship milestones. And we're not even in a proper relationship. I can't keep this up for a whole day especially as I wanted to spend most of it drunk.

'That's too much, it's a time for family, don't mind me,' Cameron replies.

'That's such bullshit,' Nan says. Cameron tries to stifle his giggles. 'It's a time to welcome people into your fold when they've got nowhere to go. Like Mary and Joseph and the whole innkeeper thing. We've got plenty of room. Come on over and I can inspect you properly. I hope you've got a Christmas jumper.'

'Only if you're sure...' Cameron mumbles, looking at me. I'm not going to have much choice in this matter, am I? I shrug. 'I do have a jumper. It's got Santa on it.'

'Well, my jumper's got a snowman with a carrot for a knob,' replies Nan.

He chuckles heartily this time. 'Well, count me in. Let me have a shower, be there in about an hour?'

Mum claps her hands excitedly. 'Yay!'

'Are you really sure? Susie? Fabio? I won't be intruding in any way?'

Nan furrows her brow again.

'It'll be our pleasure,' Dad says. 'We'll see you in a bit.'

The screen goes blank and Nan looks over at all of us, her Nan cogs whirring. We all avoid her enquiring gaze.

'Johnny,' she says to Dad.

'Mum?'

'Are you back in porn again?' she asks.

'WHAT?' he squeals back.

'You were in hospital a few weeks ago, did you overdo it sexing someone?'

Mum erupts into hysterics. 'No, Barbara.'

'Then what sort of rubbish, Eurotrash name is Fabio? I thought you'd got back into the game and it's one of your personas.'

Dad looks mortified, if very, very confused. 'I haven't done porn in years, Mum. This is not related to that?'

'Then is it a nickname?' she asks.

'Also, no. He thinks my name is Fabio.'

'Doesn't sound anything like Johnny.'

Mum and Dad look over to me. 'You'd better prep your nan before he comes over?'

'Prep me for what?' she asks, her tone stern, slightly serious.

'Well, Nan... It's kind of a funny story.'

FOURTEEN

'Well, after I had my run in Vegas, I then went to live on a commune in San Francisco and that was where I met Fabio's father. Lovely fella, his name was Gianni, but terrible with the drink and there came a moment when I knew I had to leave and get out of there, so I came back to London.'

I can literally feel a roast potato lodge in my throat as Nan recounts the very made-up story of her life, a purple paper hat rested on her silver curls. It's all utter crap. After we FaceTimed Cameron, I told her the whole complicated story. *So if he's coming here, Nan, just go with it. You can be whoever you want. Just play along for today. Don't talk about Sonny. I'm going to tell him who I am eventually, but it needs to come from me.*

I thought Nan's story would at least have come with a touch of normal. She was born in London, raised in London, my grandfather left her when she was six months pregnant and she's lived here ever since.

'So you were a showgirl in Vegas?' Cameron asks. 'You must have some stories.'

He seems to be falling for it completely, which makes me worry how gullible he actually is. I guess the story my nan is spinning is far removed from the boring, self-involved boasting fest that he'd normally be subjected to by his family. He seems mesmerised by Nan and her tall tales.

'Well, I actually met Sinatra once...'

'MUM, more gravy?' Dad intervenes, knowing there is a point where her stories are going to carry great big plot holes.

'SINATRA? FRANK SINATRA?' Cameron cries out.

'I served him a drink and he told me I had nice legs, and you know what I told him? I told him, you're married and I don't do that sort of thing, Frank.'

Dad flares his nostrils and takes a large sip of wine so he doesn't laugh.

I look over the table at Mum. Please make her stop, I beg of you.

'Good for you, Estella.'

Yes, Nan's name has also been changed. If you want to know where Dad gets his playful streak from, then look no further.

I shake my head and stuff another potato in my mouth. Mainly to hold down my complete panic but also to try to soak up all the alcohol in my system. Since I knew Cameron was coming round, I've hit the booze supplies quite hard. From Buck's Fizz to Baileys to red wine to white, waves of festive drinking swim around my stomach uneasily.

'What's up, Josie? You usually love your old nan's stories,' she says, winking at me.

I like the stories about how she beat up a milkman once for offering her milk for sexual favours, how she used to pour weed-killer in the noisy neighbour's hanging baskets, how she still does open-water swimming and was once so cold, she thought she'd lost a toe.

'Oh, I love them. Why don't you tell Cameron about the time you auditioned to be a back-up singer for Cher? You're still mates with her, aren't you?'

The way I say this makes my dear grandmother narrow her eyes. Nan, I am slaughtered. If I can't stop you, I may as well play along.

'Oh, Cher and I fell out of touch. Sweet bird, though. Loved a buffet.'

I start to laugh at this point. She loved a what now? I'm beginning to wonder how and when this got so ridiculous. Everyone at the table looks over at me as I snort so attractively that a bit of carrot flies out my nose. Cameron can't quite tell what's happening. Look at you with your Christmas jumper with the detachable Santa legs. You showed up with flowers and a selection of chocolates and wine that I suspect you bought from a local petrol station but you're here. In my house. At Christmas. And I want to snog your face off.

Mum tops my wine glass up again.

'Why do you do that?' I ask her. 'It's one of your worst habits.'

'It's called being a good hostess,' she says, smiling at me.

'It's called being a sneaky bitch. It's why I spend most Christmases under the table.'

Mum pauses for a moment to hear me swear as it's unlike me. She looks to Dad, who does a good job of distracting Cameron by loading up his plate with ham.

'The ham is all me. I cook it in ginger beer,' Dad says, eyeballing me.

'It's amazing, Fabio – thanks.'

I giggle again to hear that name. He could have been Keith or Richard, but then he would have been Dick and that would have been super super funny. Mum glares at me as if to say stop it or this fella will dump you for thinking you're some sort of cackling loon.

'Anyone want stuffing?' Cameron asks me, passing the bowl round.

It's Nan's turn to laugh now. Keep it together, Nan, if only to keep your teeth in.

'So, tell us about your family, Cameron? Bet you're missing them today?' Nan says.

Cameron takes pause as he chews through my mum's turkey. 'Actually, this is far more refreshing. My family are a bit old-school, a bit traditional. Christmas is a bit of a stuck-up affair.'

'Oh, how so?' Nan asks.

'There's church in the morning. I have a sister obsessed with co-ordinating her whole family in tartan, my mother's drier than dry turkey and there's usually an epic fight by the time the pudding has come out. Normally involving me and my life choices.'

Mum pouts in her seat to hear this. I mean, she's still topping up his glass, but I know she'll hear that and some sense of maternal concern will come pouring out to look after him, to make things better for him.

'But you seem a lovely lad. Any parent would be proud to have you as a son,' Nan says, grabbing his hand.

Cameron looks visibly moved to hear this and squeezes her hand back.

'You should hear what my Fabio got up to back in the day,' Nan says. We all glare at her.

'I'll take some stuffing. Mum, Dad? Stuffing?' I gabble.

'He left school, did all sorts. I thought he was training to be a plumber. Turns out he went to work for some sort of TV company. Sneaky little thing...'

'NAN! SPROUTS! PASS THE SPROUTS!'

Cameron looks at me strangely. I like sprouts. They are an underrated vegetable.

'...was working in porn.'

Oh my shit. I can't breathe. Nan? What are you doing? Not like this. I needed this to be a sincere conversation over coffee, not when I'm drunk out of my skin wearing a jumper with a robin on the front that says CHRISTMAS BIRD. This man is the best thing that's come into my life for an age and now he's going to walk out of that door. On Christmas. Now that's a story for the ages. I think I'm going to throw up. Mum is crimson with the embarrassment, Dad stares Nan out. You had one job, Nan.

But before any of us can backtrack, there's laughter.

'That funny, is it?' Nan asks Cameron.

It would seem it's hysterical as he's the same colour as the cranberry jelly.

'Well, I thought you were on the wind-up with the Cher story, but that's bloody brilliant,' says Cameron. I think he might be crying. Dad and Mum don't know whether to be relieved or offended. 'Fabio in porn? I mean, he has the name to go with it, but don't be silly...'

Dad shifts his eyes from side to side. Mate, I was known in the business. Reliable, staying power, an everyman quality that appealed to the masses.

I snigger awkwardly to try to mask my panic.

'You are funny,' he says, elbowing my nan.

'It is known. You heard that, Josie. I am hilarious. Come on, Cam... let's get you absolutely bladdered tonight. I can call you Cam, darling, right?'

'Well, that was pretty...'

'Intense?'

'I thought it was nice. Best Christmas I've had in a while. Your nan is a cheating cow when it comes to Scrabble, though,' Cameron jokes.

We're outside in the winter cold, the inky sky above us clear and dotted with stars, these driveway meet-ups becoming all too familiar, except we won't be diving into any hedges for a fumble. Mainly because I can't really stand straight and I know for a fact that even though my nan told me she was going upstairs to get ready for bed, she's really in Sonny's old bedroom spying on us. I can see her old-lady hands from behind the curtain. Nan does cheat in Scrabble. She feels up all the letters and puts them back if she has too many vowels.

'I got you a gift. I was too embarrassed to give it to you in the house.' Cameron reaches into his duffel coat pocket and pulls out a small box, unwrapped. 'Don't panic, it's not a ring. It's silly, really. I just thought, I know we're not quite going out. I don't know what we are, but this felt right.'

I open the box and beam as I open it. It's a Ghostbusters proton pack keyring, nothing flashy or gaudy, but the sentiment makes me smile, especially when I think what's in my pocket. I kiss him on the cheek, then place my gift in his hands.

'Similarly, I also have something for you. Nothing huge.'

He opens the package and his jaw drops. 'Are these...'

'Ghostbusters socks. They're a bit silly, but I liked the Stay Puft Marshmallow Man's face on them.'

He takes a moment to think that we both went out and bought similarly themed gifts, what that all means.

'It's fricking adorable is what it is. You're adorable, your whole family are.'

I blush to hear him call me adorable. Is that a good word? Babies in animal hats and kittens are adorable. I hope I'm more than that.

'We're all right. You just have a low benchmark when it comes to comparing these things. Thank you for dancing with Nan too. That's normally my brother's job.'

Yes, Nan was that drunk, she asked Cameron for a twirl around the living room in the space between mince pies and the cheeseboard. He obliged. He was surprisingly debonair. I'm glad Nan didn't reach down for the ass grab.

'I'd love to meet your brother. Where is he today?'

'He works... abroad, so we don't see him so much. His name

is...' Crap, why can't I think of a name? The alcohol and the cold slow my brain down. I see Father Christmas waving at me from the window. 'Nick. Little Nicky. Nicholas.'

He laughs under his breath at me repeating my brother's fake name three times.

'Thank you for letting me be a part of this today. I really needed it.'

'I'm glad. I'm really sorry about the cheese?' I tell him.

'The actual cheese or all the decorations?'

One of my father's greatest festive achievements is being able to source the smelliest and largest wedges of blue cheese in the land, the sort that make the dog look over his shoulder to check where that smell's coming from.

'All of it,' I reply. 'Also, my mum likes to play songs on repeat. You'll have Bublé in your head until February now.'

'I don't think I'll mind.'

As he speaks, he gets closer to me and there's that warm, familiar feeling of his proximity, an arm touching mine, but also his breath getting perilously near to my skin. He smells sweet and minty like a candy cane. I'm drunk and I could very well lick him at this moment. Oh, Cameron. What the hell is this? Also, what the hell are my family doing, because not only is Nan behind an upstairs curtain but I can see Mum peeking out from behind the Christmas tree and Dad waving from the kitchen.

'We have an audience, I'm afraid,' I whisper.

'Oh, I'd be disappointed if we didn't. Can I call you tomorrow? Maybe the next day?'

'Any time.'

'Are we doing this then? For the people in the front row?' he asks.

'Doing what?'

But before I have time to approve, he grabs me, dipping me to one side and giving me a drunken Christmas kiss, backlit by chasing icicle lights and a disco snowman. I hear clapping. I bet that's Nan. Am I swooning? Of course I am. I swing my neck back, laughing, but I'm also glad I don't fall over. He returns me upright and kisses me on the forehead. Stay. Don't leave. I want to unwrap you. To fall asleep next to you.

'Merry Christmas,' he whispers into my ear, before walking over to his car, waving as he goes but also laden with at least two weeks' worth of leftovers that Mum packed for him in Tupperware.

As I re-enter the house, I lean back onto the door to relive the moment, to have had him near, inhaling deeply.

'I like him, Josie,' a voice says, coming down the stairs. Nan comes over and hooks her arm into mine. 'Did I overdo it at lunch?'

'Yes. A showgirl, seriously? You know what showgirls do, right? Have you not seen the film from the nineties?'

Nan laughs, so hard that I can see that her teeth are a bit loose. 'Oooh, you naughty thing. No, I was the respectable sort. I'd wear feathers out my backside and just stand near magicians and stuff,' she says, striking a pose.

I giggle as we make our way into the living room to find Mum with a box of chocolates open, rifling through to bagsy her favourite strawberry creams.

'Look at you two, having a little kissy on the doorstep,' Mum jokes, a tad too much sherry in her veins.

'Thanks, everyone, for looking by the way,' I announce to the room.

'It's our right, this is our house, you are our girl,' Dad says, carrying in yet another tray of mince pies and teas. 'He is a nice kid, Josie. I like him a lot.'

Mum nods and reaches for my hand.

'I have a question then,' Nan says, taking a large noisy sip on her tea before settling into an armchair. 'Why all the lies and deception? I like being a showgirl of some notoriety, but there's only so far we can take this, right? This can't be fair on the lad.'

I sit there in silence. I've kept this going for two months now and the truth is, she's right. The longer we leave this, the weirder it will be, the guiltier I will feel, the stranger we will look. But there just doesn't seem to be a right moment. Every time I try to, fate intervenes. My dad collapses at the tennis club, I have sex with him in a car, I dodge it and talk about something else.

'I'll tell him in the new year. It's just a hard subject to talk about, that's all.'

Nan looks over at me, confused.

'How's that?' she asks.

Dad and Mum sit with the television on, scanning through all the Christmas specials. Nan senses me looking at them.

'It's a good icebreaker, you know. I had this horrible woman in my bridge club who used to always brag about her son, who went to Oxford and became a doctor. "Oh, he's so clever, he was top of his class..." Never mind you only see him once a year and he's completely nasty to you. I was sick of hearing it, so one day, I told them all my son was in porn. Your son is a big dick, mine has a big dick.'

'How did that go down?' I say, laughing loudly, watching as Dad bows his head at Nan's choice of words.

'Shut her up. I know it's not the easiest thing to bring up, but no shame, Josie. There's no shame in how you came to be, how you were raised... Remember that.'

Our conversation stirs Dad's interest. 'Is that why you haven't said anything to him yet, Josie? You're ashamed?' He appears surprised by that. Shame is not a word we use in this house and, aside from this situation with Cameron, it's something I've never felt in everyday life and work especially – I do carry a level of pride in what I do.

'Not that at all. But you saw what he was like when Nan cracked her joke... A terrible joke by the way,' I tell her.

'I was just testing the water,' she teases.

'He laughed. He couldn't believe it. It is a bit out there, you know?' I add.

Mum and Dad watch me for a moment as I squirm awkwardly in my seat, half drunk, half confused.

'All your boyfriends you've brought home, you've never hidden things from them before, so why now?' Mum asks.

'I just... Maybe I just don't want to bombard him, all at once. This is not normal, what we do, what you used to be...'

'Define normal?' Dad asks, pulling a silly face to lighten the mood.

'Normal is not having a sideboard full of dildos, or wondering if your boyfriend has seen your mum naked?'

'JOSIE!' Mum shrieks, as she senses my tone changing.

'I'm sorry, Mum. He's a nice guy and I just want him to get to know me, for him to get to know our family for who we are rather than what we are. I don't want to feel judged or that I'm not good enough.'

Everyone stops for a moment to hear the words fall out of my mouth, fuelled by the alcohol in my bloodstream. I've never wanted to project any of this onto anyone as I didn't want anyone to feel sad, to feel as low as I felt. My eyes start to well up and I blink super quickly to stop the tears falling. Damn Christmas, damn all that cheese I ate. This a Brie-induced moment.

Nan comes over and puts her arm around me. 'Don't be daft, you ninny. Any man should be bloody proud to have you on his arm. You're the catch of the bloody century,' she tells me, cupping my face with her wrinkly hands to let me know she means business.

'I'm sorry. Don't mind me. It's Christmas, just whack *Love Actually* on and forget I ever said anything,' I say.

Whatever day it may be, it's too late to backtrack now. 'Nah, where has this come from?' Mum asks. 'Is this from him? Does he have opinions on this stuff? If so, then maybe he's not the one for you? You shouldn't change who you are to be with someone. He should like you for you.'

I run my tongue over my teeth, trying to keep my words from leaving my mouth. 'Well, it's easy for you two. You found each other. You literally slipped her one before you even knew her.'

'JOSIE!' Mum shrieks again, shocked but saddened to hear me so confrontational, callous even. 'Don't talk like that... You've never had a problem with all of this before?'

'Mum, it's always been there... The bullying in school? The time the papers found out and gave Sonny hell in the media?'

'And we've always just batted it away, we're better than all that gossip, all those folk who trash-talk us.'

'Well, what about that time my fiancé dumped me?' I utter.

Silence cloaks the room as I realise I've let the cat out of the bag. The words hit Mum the hardest and I see her eyes well up immediately.

'Josie,' Dad mumbles. 'You told us he left you to go travelling.'

I sigh loudly, sadly. 'Oh, he did that. But with some pharmacist's daughter. They got married two weeks ago.'

'You found out?' Mum says.

'Not from you,' I say, anger in my tones. 'And if you want to know the real truth, the reason he went off with her is that he couldn't stand what I did. He didn't want to be married into it, to expose his future children to it. He made me feel ashamed about who we were...' The tears flow at that very moment. It feels good to say it out loud, to not have it pent up anymore, but I don't think I can take the hurt etched in everyone's faces.

'I'll kill him. He took all that money and said that to you?' says Nan, the fumes literally making her hands shake.

'He wrote it in a note.'

'Oh, Josie,' Mum cries.

Dad sits there, silently.

'So forgive me if I need to tell some white lies to cover up everything. I know I've lost control and the whole situation is a farce, but I'm scared now. I'm scared because I think I'm falling for him and if I tell him everything and he leaves, then it will break me all over again...'

Dad starts crying. He does this. He does it watching wedding scenes in films or charity commercials about sad donkeys. I feel awful sharing this with them, but the alcohol has made it flow so easily.

'Oh, Josie... You never told us. Why?' Mum asks, patting her cheeks with the end of her sleeve.

'Because... Because...' I whisper.

'She blamed you for it,' Nan mutters, filling in my words. 'If she was just a normal girl, if you were both accountants and she was an accountant too, then maybe Mike would still be here, am I right?' She says it softly, gripping on to my hand. It is an awful thing to say, this horrible dichotomy of emotion to feel, but she is right. Even though I ran back to my parents, back to the safety of our home and family, a part of me always wondered how things would have been different had I been a part of a different family.

'Nan's right,' I whisper. 'Because for one small moment, I thought why does my future have to be about this? About something both of you started that I got dragged into. How is this my life?'

Mum can't bear to hear any more and stands up and leaves the room, sobbing. This makes me sob, which makes Dad sob, which confuses Dave the dog more than anything. It's only Nan who quietly takes in all of the drama.

'Susie,' Dad intones, his hand missing Mum's back as she

runs out of the room. He turns to look at me. 'That was cruel. You're not cruel, Josie,' he says, standing up.

This makes my bottom lip quiver, and I can't make out anything through my tears.

'Make up your mind about who you want to be. I am not ashamed of who I am, who I was, because it's brought me here, it gave me you. Mike was a cretin. He never knew your worth and I would give him double what he stole from you to stay away from you for life.'

'But I loved him...'

'Then you're a fool.'

My eyes widen at the insult.

'Johnny... Leave it be,' Nan exclaims.

'No, we've played your game. Now you're telling us we played along because you don't like who you are, you don't like us, that we forced you here?'

'Well, maybe I played along the whole time. All these years. Maybe I'm done pretending like this is normal, like this is how people live...'

'You two are going to say something you regret in a bit. Shut it,' Nan barks at us.

'This isn't you,' Dad mumbles.

'Then who am I?' I ask him.

'I don't know anymore, Josie. But you're not this person, that much I know.'

FIFTEEN

If you eat my fudge, I'll shank you.

New Year's Eve. What a time to be alive, going into the new year sitting in my nan's flat in Wandsworth, on my own, reading her threatening notes about what she'll do if I eat her fudge. Nan has lived in the same flat since she raised Dad. It's one of those original art deco buildings with a colourful courtyard and a set of neighbours that Nan is on first name basis with who possibly deal drugs out of one of the stairwells. But Nan likes her comforts, the fact it's near the Tube, the fact it reminds her of where she's come from. She also says she doesn't want anything bigger to clean as the dusting would be a bastard.

It's been a week since Christmas. After the fight with my parents, Nan told me to pack a bag and come and stay with her for a while. She said she needed the company, that she didn't want to be alone in the festive period, but I knew what she was doing. Harsh things were said and we all needed some space to clear the air. We're not stupid, though, we also packed leftovers and stole quite a lot of cheese to take with us. She let me sit here for a while and wallow, to lie in her dusky rose bathtub and soak away my troubles, to eat her biscuits, all of them.

That said, it's now New Year's Eve and Nan has abandoned me to go on a two-day coach trip to the coast with her bingo mates. She's spending tonight in a hotel with a three-course meal, bingo and a Tom Jones impersonator. Whereas I will be here, in my best hoodie, with a bottle of rosé, staring at her many many duck ornaments.

An incoming FaceTime call gets my attention.

'Sonny?' I answer.

'Crap, you do look rough,' my brother says.

In the call, Sonny is bedecked in a red velvet suit, hair slicked back.

'Where's Ruby?'

'She's in Berlin filming something. Back tomorrow.'

'You look super swish.'

'How many times have you chundered?' he asks, worriedly.

I shrug. The fact is, I'm throwing a sickie tonight. It's the evening of The Love Shack New Year's Eve party, the night when my parents go for broke, hire out a hotel and give all our staff a big night out with dancing and bubbles. It's something they've done since they started the business and it's a tradition that's lasted. However, I just can't tonight. There is something inside me which is too sad, too tired to show my face and pretend everything is all right. That said, I'm glad my glum, unpolished look genuinely passes for illness so I don't have to fake too much.

'Well, shout if you want me to drop anything by. Soup, chocolate, medicine...'

Sonny gazes at me from the screen. He showed up to our family home on Boxing Day to find Nan and I not there, Mum still in bed and Dad still drunk from the night before. Since then, he's tried his best to keep us all happy, mend the rift. It'll just take time, Sonny.

'You'll be missed,' he says.

'Not really.'

'Josie...' he says, tones of mild anger in his voice.

'You can't be angry at me when I'm ill.' I move a wine bottle out of view of the screen so he knows I'm not half-cut either.

'Can I come round tomorrow? At least to wish you happy New Year?'

'Maybe. Have fun tonight. There's a bloke called Derek in distribution. Make sure he goes easy on the brandy. His wife and I had to carry him to a taxi last year. I think that's why my left knee still clicks.'

He laughs. 'Love you, JoJo.'

'Have fun, kiddo.'

He hangs up. I'm serious about Derek, but also make sure the pregnant women know that there's some non-alcoholic fizz for them, that someone pays the band in cash, tell everyone there are fireworks on the roof and make that announcement by 11.40 p.m. at least because people move slowly when they're drunk. Planning the evening is always a labour of love and I think about the little green dress I have hanging in my wardrobe for it, the tag still dangling off it.

I get up off the sofa and try to navigate my drunken ass around Nan's coffee table. There will be no little green dress. There will be hoodies and leggings and much TV. It's stupid anyway. It's just another day to mark the passing of time. I think back to a New Year's I spent at university. A night where people got depressed and drunk about having no one to kiss as the clock struck twelve and so just latched on to the closest person in the room. Yes, that people was me. I snogged someone in my economics tutor group called Chris Black. His breath tasted smoky, acrid and he had hair like a kitchen sponge that needed replacing.

I sit out on Nan's balcony, which I think might be the real reason she kept this flat. It has one of the best views of the

London skyline, the sort that skyscrapers can only wish to repli-
cate, and I've spent many a lovely evening out here with a mug
of tea putting the world to rights with her, watching my beloved
city fade into shadows. Tonight, the London skyline is so ready
to see in the new year, and it almost pulses with energy. I don't
mind seeing it, I just can't be a part of it.

The doorbell suddenly goes and I take a large sigh of relief.
I will sit on this balcony with my biryani and some onion bhajis
and my stomach will be happy. It doesn't take much. I'll watch a
classic film and toast myself. I walk towards the door.

'Deliveroo for Josie,' the voice says, as I open it. 'Surprise?'

Balls. I close the door quickly. That's definitely a surprise.
Nan has a small mirror by the front door and I glance at myself.
Good lord, the horror. I try to pick the sleepy dust out of my
eyes, shake my hair out. Damn. How? Why on earth is
Cameron here?

I open the door again, peeking out. He half smiles, sparkling
eyes peeking through the gap in the door. Urgh, it's the duffel
coat that does it every time, the dimples, the beanie.

'This is for you, right? I didn't just mug a delivery man at
the end of the corridor?'

'Nah, that's me. How?'

I stand with the door half over me, knowing there is no way
in the world I can make this hoodie look sexy. I look like a sad
potato in fluffy sleep socks and I will hate whoever has directed
Cameron to this place for an eternity.

'I got a message from your nan.'

'What did it say?'

He reaches into his coat pocket and pulls out his phone.

'Cameron, this is Josie's nan. Can you do me a favour and go
check in on Josie. The sad case is all alone for New Year's –
she's housesitting my flat. Make sure the cow doesn't eat my
fudge... And then she gave me her address,' he repeats, showing
me the message.

I don't want to think how Nan got Cameron's contact details, but this is a conspiracy and, in revenge, I will eat all her fudge, take pictures of myself scoffing it and send them to her.

'Look, if you wanted to be alone, I get it. This feels like an ambush. Since I showed up on Christmas Day, I haven't really heard from you. I don't know if you're angry with me...'

I shake my head. I have given him a wide berth, but that was mostly down to the drama with my own parents. 'I'm not angry with you at all. I was just busy. And I'm not really dressed for visitors,' I whisper.

'So basically, I wore my Jon Snow T-shirt and miniskirt for nothing?' he jokes.

I laugh and the feeling is a relief. As hard as Nan has tried, she's not managed to get anything out of me since Christmas, bar grunting and tears. She called me the worst housemate she's had since Dad was a toddler and used to eat her make-up.

'I bought some beers. As long as you don't mind sharing your takeaway with me?' Cameron says, holding them up.

'You didn't have plans yourself?'

'TV and Super Noodles?'

I open the door and he steps inside, hugging me awkwardly as a takeaway bag gets in the way. I hold on for longer than needs be. I think I've missed you, I've definitely missed you.

'Hey,' he says.

'I look a state. Don't look at me.'

'Shush now. So your nan has gone on a jolly-up, has she?' Cameron asks, wandering through the flat.

'Yeah, it's her thing,' I say, scurrying beside him. 'She saves up all year.' Next to my sad potato look, I am also conscious that there is some shame in how I've let this place go since my grandmother left me. Even though I told Nan I'd be fine, I've been living off takeaways and stashes from the corner shop. Cameron is going to find out I have a serious addiction to chocolate-covered pretzels that could be deemed as embarrassing, and I also eat peanut butter out of a jar with a spoon. I run around trying to pick up packets and hide the mess with cushions.

'And I thought I slobbed it about in the week after Christmas,' he chuckles, clearing a spot on the coffee table. 'Don't fret. Here, grab some cutlery, plates.'

I step into the kitchen, realising it's best he doesn't step in here too as there's evidence that I ate a whole family tin of biscuits and drank a whole bottle of Baileys by myself. I open the cupboards to grab at glasses, napkins, and think that this might be the best moment, in the quiet and by the fragrant backdrop of a takeaway, to finally explain what is happening. We won't be having sex because I haven't shaved my legs for a week and am wearing some embarrassingly old pink knickers with a rainbow waistband. But there is no distraction here. Now I can say something and it will mend everything. It will go some way to fixing things with my parents, to making all of this right. It's not too late to make things right.

As I return to the living room, Cameron is standing by the window of the flat. 'Are you kidding me? What a view,' he says, and I smile to see the beanie and coat are off. 'Has she lived here long?'

'My dad was literally raised in that bedroom,' I say, pointing towards the corridor along the way.

'After she came back from America.'

I stop for a moment. Oh yes... Showgirl Nan. Truth was, she was living here with a man called Raymond and he left her here when she was pregnant. Never saw him again except in a local pub three years later where she tipped a full ashtray over his head.

'In other news, I think there are some things to discuss?' he says solemnly.

I take a deep breath. Now? I thought we could at least break into the poppadoms first.

'Like, how much food is in here? Were you expecting company? This feels like enough for a family of four?'

I blush as I realise I went overboard, hoping the food would at least last me into tomorrow so I wouldn't have to leave the flat. It means I ordered an embarrassingly large number of samosas.

'I like leftovers,' I say, shrugging.

'Well then, I feel less guilty for helping you out here.' He opens some of the foil containers and starts sharing out the food.

I take a quick glance in the mirror in Nan's living room, trying to sort out the state of my hair, running a tongue along my lips so they look less dry. The one thing that would help is if I turned off all the lights.

'So tell me, did you get to see your family this Christmas or did chickenpox draw a line under that?' I ask.

'Sort of. I dropped off gifts to my nieces and nephews. The company I work for is doing a tie-in with Lego, so I wanted to share the joy with them. If I can't impress the sisters, then I can at least try to get brownie points with the little people.'

I pour us two glasses of beer and I take a large sip of mine to steady my nerves. He's in a hoodie, hi-tops and jeans, keeping it casual. He leans over the table and a slice of back and underwear is visible. I want to touch it. I won't. Stop staring. Just focus. Say it, just bloody tell him everything already.

'Speaking of family, that Christmas day with your folks. Them taking me in like a stray, that was so nice.'

I pause and take another sip of beer. 'It's all good. They like you.'

'I like them. It's been such a quiet, strange Christmas and it really pepped me up.'

'Have you not been up to much then?' I say, biting into a samosa. It's slightly too hot, so I juggle it with my hands and puff out my cheeks, which makes him laugh.

'Well, I'm supposed to be at a party tonight, but I opted out.

Imogen and my ex-best mate will be there and I just don't want to bring that drama to someone else's house.'

'Oh.' I stuff some rice into my mouth, which I am aware makes me look like a goat shovelling in feed.

'I guess no one wants to bump into an ex,' I mumble.

'Oh no, I don't give two seconds' thought to Imogen, but it's Russ. I've known him since school. The lies, the betrayal. That I don't get.'

More rice, just get more rice in, Josie. Shovel it in like sand. *The lies, the betrayal.* But as I look over, I see him visibly upset, almost moved to tears. I put my fork down and place a hand on his arm. He stops and leans into me. I hug him, drawn to the sadness this obviously stirs up in him.

'Hey, don't. You didn't do anything wrong,' I tell him.

'I just feel like a bit of an idiot to be mourning him, you know? I miss him, despite everything.'

'It just makes you a nice person, a decent person, a better friend...'

'Maybe...' A tear forms in the corner of his eye. 'Now you're going to think I'm a complete wimp. It's the curry, the curry is too hot.'

I laugh. 'I'll think you more of a wimp for not being able to take this level of spice. It's sag aloo.'

He uses the palm of his hand to wipe away the solitary tear that he allowed to escape.

'Hannah McRoberts,' I say. 'Best mate at school. God, we did everything together. We stole cans of Coke from the petrol station, we had these huge nights out and I held her hair back on her eighteenth as she chucked up into the Thames...'

Cameron furrows his brow to hear that as we're eating.

'Apologies. But she went to university and I never heard from her again. The occasional Facebook like and hello, but that's it. Friendship is a very strange thing like that. Sometimes we have friends we think will last a lifetime and sometimes it just doesn't work. People grow, they move away, they change. It's OK to mourn them, to hurt.' It's an unusual moment of clarity and wisdom from me that we will put down to the fact I've been drinking solid for a week so my thoughts are not my own. 'His life will be poorer for not having you in it.'

'That's very kind.'

'You're welcome,' I mutter, trying to lick away a string of mango chutney from my chin. Cameron reaches over and wipes away the worst of it with his thumb. His hands are cold, but I hold my breath to feel his touch, that surge of magic I always feel when he does that. Damn you.

'So I do think there are some important things to discuss?' he tells me.

I nod. 'I was thinking the same...'

I break a poppadom with my hands. Do it, say it. But what does he want to talk about? Does he want to talk about where this is going and what we are? Does he want sex? I'd need a half-hour in a bathroom before that and to borrow Nan's razor that I think she uses on her face. Just come out with it.

He puts his plate down and takes off his hoodie. He really is not coping with the spice levels of this curry. He downs a few gulps of beer.

'I just don't know how to tell you...' he begins, getting more and more flustered. 'I mean, I'm sorry I've not told you before, but—'

I take his hand again. 'God, your hands are cold. Are they always so cold?' I ask him.

'No,' he says, stretching his fingers in and out. 'It is cold outside, though.'

I put a hand to his forehead. 'Cameron... you're really hot.'

'Why, thank you,' he replies, smirking.

'No, you have a fever. Let me...' I put my plate down and place a hand to his core this time, reaching inside his T-shirt. I won't lie, the physical proximity is a thrill to me, but his skin is literally burning to the touch. 'You're not well, you're boiling,' I say.

'Really? I thought it was just your nan's flat. Old people's houses are always warmer than most. This must be why I cried before. I don't usually cry. Honest.'

I smile and lift up his T-shirt to reveal his back. Again, it's nice to see, but his skin is dotted with about ten or twenty small blisters.

'Did you have chickenpox as a child?' I ask.

'My mum couldn't remember.'

Oh.

It's 11.42 p.m. on New Year's Eve and lying next to me is a very spotty gentleman wrapped in my duvet, dosed up with paracetamol and hoping his fever may break. After I pointed out that Cameron may have chickenpox, we stripped him in the flat which provided momentary enjoyment until we found spots *everywhere*, even a few perilously close to his penis (I was allowed to study those, there was some thrill involved, though it went no further). So we abandoned curry and I found tablets in Nan's medical cabinet (I also found some cough mixture with a best before date of January 1986) and hydrated him well. There was no point him going home to an empty house, so I said he could stay here with me. I had chickenpox in the summer of 2001. I got them in between my toes and used to itch them with disposable chopsticks. We then cuddled up on the sofa and put an Indiana Jones film on that he watched through bleary eyes. We snacked, we drank, we googled adult chickenpox and it scared the shit out of both of us. For the love of crap, please don't die here of haemorrhagic complications in Nan's flat before I've had the chance to tell you the truth.

I put a hand to him now and the worst of the fever seems to have subsided. He snores gently, even through the bass of the party in the flat below. I should tell Cameron now. Tell him everything. If I do it now, then he'll think it's all just a delirious, fevered dream.

Do I wake him so we can see the New Year together? That feels a little selfish, especially as he's ill. It's fine. He's here and that alone makes me so content. I think it's some milestone that even though he's unwell and spotted, I still want him close, I still think him unfathomably cute. That means something, right?

He mumbles something in his sleep and I wipe away some sweat from his brow.

'Are you OK? Cameron? Do you want another drink?' I ask him. 'It's nearly New Year.'

'I'm good. Love you,' he mumbles.

I stop for a moment. It's because he's sick. When people have fevers and are on pain meds, they love everyone. He might think I'm someone else.

'Love you too...' I can say that because I'm drunk. I'm very drunk. I've medicated with two Becks and more wine this evening.

Even though he's contagious and not well and this is not the evening that either of us had planned, I don't want to be anywhere else.

As the credits on *Indiana Jones* roll to a close, I hear my phone buzz on the table and from afar see it's my brother. I wriggle off the sofa and go out onto the balcony, wrapped in a blanket like a giant version of E.T.

'Happy New Year,' I say as I answer the phone. 'How's the party?'

But as the picture comes into focus, I see Sonny pushing Mum and Dad into view. Both of them hesitant and possibly a little too tipsy to be coherent. Mum looks glamorous in a gold sparkling cocktail dress, Dad in a dinner jacket, looking like a retirement-years Bond. We've not spoken since Christmas and the words still feel raw and barbed.

'Sonny... I... I don't know what to say?' Mum says.

'When have you ever been at a loss for words? Hey, Josie! How are you? Happy New Year! We miss you,' Sonny says, in a voice that I hope isn't supposed to be Mum's, otherwise we need to find him a new acting coach.

Instead of replying, Mum just starts crying on the screen. This, of course, makes me cry, but also sets Dad off too. Sonny just stands there watching all of us.

'Basically, I'm getting married in a month, so I need all of you to sort this out. I love you all madly and this isn't us. This isn't us at all.'

I nod, my blanket over my head making me look like a sad little orphan child. Maybe it's the moment, the alcohol or the fact that they're big sobbing messes, but my heart suddenly pangs with regret and apology. 'I'm sorry I never told you about the Mike thing. About lying. I only did it because I didn't want you to feel what I was feeling at the time.'

'I'm sorry that when we found out he got married we didn't think to tell you, to discuss it with you like adults,' Mum says, twisting her lips around.

'I'm sorry I called you cruel,' Dad says, openly crying. 'You're not. You're the kindest person I know. I've had people come up to me all night telling me what a brilliant boss you are and how you look out for everyone.'

Mum nods in agreement, trying her best to not let her mascara run down her cheeks. 'This party is just not the same without you. Everyone keeps asking where you are. I've missed having a dance with you.'

I grin broadly. Every year, we go onto the dance floor and basically hug and dance our way through The Communards' 'Don't Leave Me This Way'. It was the song we used to dance to in the kitchen at home when I was little, we even had a routine where halfway through I'd run at her and she'd spin me around. Yes, we try to recreate that when we're drunk too.

'And it kills me that you're alone tonight,' Mum adds. 'Are you OK? Come on down for a drink?'

'I'm not dressed up, Mum.'

'I don't care. I really don't. Do you hate me?'

'Never.'

'I have that TV debate thing coming up. I can't do that without you.'

'You'll have me. I wouldn't let you do that alone.'

I still cry because it pains me to see Mum so distressed. I guess she never thought about the repercussions of her career and hates that it's hurt her kids in any way. Through the window of Nan's balcony, I see Cameron reach up to scratch his neck. I'm not alone, though.

'You didn't tell me about Charlie,' Dad suddenly brings up.

'Charlie, the new lad. The trainee?' Mum says.

'Turns out Josie has paid for him to go on a management course, she's paid for it out of her own salary because he couldn't afford it,' Dad explains.

Mum's eyes widen. 'Josie?'

'Who told you?' I ask.

'Michelle is off her nut tonight. She can hardly stand. She told us you paid for Pamela's husband to get some proper blood tests too for his diabetes, and you gave that girl in marketing extra maternity leave because her baby's got colic...'

Someone take Michelle's fizz from her. 'I don't need the money. Best it gets spent on the right things.'

Mum is wailing at this point, soaking the lapels on Sonny's tuxedo jacket.

'Where are you?' Dad asks.

'On the balcony at Nan's.'

'We're on the roof of the hotel, I'll give you a wave.'

I laugh as a tear rolls down my cheek.

'I'm sorry, Josie. I really am. I love you,' Dad whispers.

'I love you too. And you were right, I need to tell Cameron everything. He's here now. I'm good.'

'You do what you need to do with Cameron. I'm just glad you're not on your own. Am I allowed to track down that shitbox Mike, though, and stove his face in?' he asks.

'Don't do that,' I tell Dad. He won't. I can't imagine him hitting anyone, ever.

'Tonight, everyone's had a story about you. You've made me so proud. Where did you learn to be that kind, eh?'

I look him straight in the eye. 'Who knows?'

In the background, I can hear a loud countdown starting from ten as the New Year nears ever closer.

'Go and join in,' I tell Dad.

'Nah...' I see him study my face in the screen as Mum, Sonny and an extremely excitable Pip from product development scream in unison. He rolls his eyes at me. Can't take this lot anywhere. I laugh.

'9-8-7-6-5-4-3-2-1... HAPPY NEW YEAR!' In the background, I see my family go a bit frenetic with movement and dancing. There's the loud banging of party poppers, possibly some fireworks, some person who is singing 'Auld Lang Syne' all on their own. But Dad's face remains constant, smiling back at me. He can't hear a thing, but he mouths *Happy New Year* to me.

I wave back. Happy New Year, Dad.

The phone goes to black and I stand there on the balcony, still wrapped in my blanket, the pulse of the downstairs neighbour's rap still vibrating off the floor, waving into the darkness. That's what this New Year needs, the solid dependency of Dr Dre. Have a drink for me, all of you. Not that I need it.

'Crap, did I miss it?' I hear a voice mumbling in the background, as the balcony doors open.

'Kinda, are you warm enough? Are you OK?' I ask, removing my blanket to slide it over Cameron's shoulders.

'It's fine, I think I still have remnants of a fever. You keep your blanket. I like the old lady villager look.'

'I've literally gone pure sex on legs for you tonight.'

He smiles and studies my face. With his puffy face and bright pink cheeks and my leisurewear, both of us are peak young twenties hot couple.

'Happy New Year, Josie. I won't kiss you because, you know, I'm viral.'

I shrug my shoulders. 'I will happily abstain. Happy New Year, Cameron. Now you'll see the real reason my nan kept this flat.'

We turn and look out of the balcony, festooned in plants, herbs and two garden gnomes engaged in a sexual position. I gave those to her. As we look out into the London skyline, the river winding its way through it, we watch as it bursts into a sea of colour, plumes of fireworks lighting the dark for as far as the eye can see. It's a sight of which I'll never tire.

Cameron places a hand over mine and we stand here for a moment, taking it in. I'd like to hold this hand for a while longer, I think. New year, new start. I'll tell you everything tomorrow.

My phone buzzes once more and I look down at it.

Happy New Year, my Gorgeous Josie! Love, Nan xx You kids don't go shagging in my flat, OK?

SIXTEEN

It turns out when you get adult chickenpox, it really is no joke. There's a reason you should get these things as a kid. For a week after New Year, Cameron really was quite ill. And itchy. Before, our messages used to be quite raunchy, about how I'd like to claw my fingers down his back. Now he was begging me to come round and do that – one message even offered payment. Literally come round and scratch me, PLEASE. I didn't, as lovely as the offer was. Instead, I sent him calamine and oatmeal, which I heard was good in baths. We had long chats on the phone and I'd attempt to distract him and make him laugh. We buddy-watched the *Loki* spin-off on Disney Plus. I sent him chicken broth and ice cream on Just Eat. When the pox really took hold, lining his throat and eyelids, that's when he stopped FaceTiming and I let him be so he could recover in peace. But yes, it meant I didn't tell him. I couldn't. It'd be like kicking him when he was down. And incredibly itchy.

So to fill the gap (not like that), I've ploughed myself into everything else in my life that needs attention. I moved back with my parents just after New Year, after our tearful, drunken apologies via Sonny's FaceTime, and we've been pretty quick to bury that hatchet, agreeing the better option would be better to bury it in Mike's head instead. Sonny also gets married in just over a month and my practical diplomacy is needed in sorting the gift list, the orders of service, the table plan. And work. I still have a job, I still run a company, I'm still the boss.

This morning, the warehouse is abuzz (not like that) because it's January and we have to work extra hard to make this month matter. After Christmas, there's always a lull in sales. People who were so excited about new toys and gimmicks under the Christmas tree realise that maybe they're not quite ready for a battery-operated nipple clamp and butt plug, so things get returned. This means Pamela has her work cut out for her. She gets through a lot of gloves. But it also means we have to think creatively about fixing that lull and ensure people still care about their orgasms in the cold light of January.

Which is why today that YouTube influencer has come into the office to chat about her Sugar Cube product launch in time for Valentine's Day. I don't know much about this girl, but I do know that her name has no vowels. She's called SGR, so I don't even know how to say that. SGR sounds like a Honda model, but to anyone under the age of twenty-one in this office, there is a lot of excitement about her pending visit. This basically means Charlie is the only one who knows who this girl is.

'Thank you for letting me be in the room, I can't believe SGR is going to be here!' Charlie says to me now, in a suit. Yes, he elevated his jeans and sweatshirt look today as he knew he was going to be in the presence of a celebrity that he might have a little crush on. He wore this suit at his prom, which doesn't make me feel old at all and I'm only twenty-six.

'Say her name again for me?' I ask him, studying his mouth.

'SGR,' he says. It sounds like sigger. Like cigarette? I am so confused. I will assume that she wasn't christened with this name.

'And she's big on the internet?' I realise this question makes me sound as old as my nan. Marketing have done all their research and supposedly this girl has a following of millions. I turned on one of her videos and it was very poppy and energetic. *YoYoYo! Big up yourselves! Welcome back to my YouTube channel, don't forget to like and subscribe, peeps. Peace out!*

'TikTok, YouTube, she's just done a song collab with KSI...' Charlie tells me. More initials.

'You're making me feel very old, Charlie.'

'You don't TikTok?'

'I do not. I dance on my own, in my kitchen, and I don't broadcast those moves to the masses.'

He laughs and there's a knock on the door.

'Come in!' I holler.

The door opens and Michelle stands there with two girls. I say girls, one is older, maybe my age, dressed in jeans and a blazer, and the other looks like teenage me in my Sailor Moon days – a tie-dye bucket hat, miniskirt, Doc Marten boots and a fluffy rucksack. I expected an entourage today, I printed out extra documents and had extra glasses on a tray waiting, so it's a surprise to see just the two of them.

'This is SGR... and her sister manager, Scarlett...' Michelle announces, able to say her name without it sounding like a hiccup.

I walk up to them and shake their hands. 'Thanks, Michelle. I'm Josie, it's good to meet you both. Can I offer you some refreshments before we start?'

'Diet Coke, if you have it?' Scarlett says.

Michelle nods. She'll have to run down to the petrol station on the corner, but we can get that for them.

I offer them both a seat. 'This is Charlie, he's on an internship here.'

'I know who you are, can I just say I'm a huge fan. I think you're legit awesome,' he says.

I smile. We need to work on your business speak, Charlie,

but SGR's shoulders relax and I'm glad he's at least broken the ice.

'Thank you,' she replies. 'This place is wild! You work here?' SGR asks me.

I nod. I guess I only see my desk and the water cooler element of my job. I forget that there are a few pop art posters around the place of phalluses and such. There's one by a famous northern artist above my desk that's a pair of boobs that look like eyes. Whilst SGR is entranced, her sister is not. She has a look about her like she's just walked into a strip club; it's focused, scared, wild-eyed. Don't worry, a dildo isn't going to jump out and slap you across the face.

'Do you mind if I take some pics along the way for my Stories?' SGR asks me, her iPhone poised in her hands.

'That's fine. Just use the good filters on me,' I joke.

Her face tells me that that was a given. She takes a selfie in my office, throwing up a peace sign, her lips pouted. How do these people know their angles so well? I need to take at least twenty selfies and move around a room three times before I find a pic I like.

'So is your name actually Sugar?' I ask. I think this is a valid question, though Charlie gives me a glare like I should know that already.

'It's Sarah, but everyone called me Sugar growing up, so it stuck.'

I won't dig about where the vowels went. 'So, I just wanted to thank you for coming in today. We thought we'd bring you in to chat about your new launch. I've arranged a fact file for you on the table that talks about the full range of merchandise, pricing and our marketing plan for the next few weeks. Samples will be sent out to the influencers and celebrities on your list.'

'Shug,' Scarlett prompts her sister, who's working out her fonts on her phone. 'Focus.'

SGR flares her nostrils at Scarlett and smiles at me.

'Charlie, can you get the box out for us?' I ask.

He reaches under the desk and gets out all the merchandise, laying it on the table carefully.

'These are the end products and packaging for your approval,' I say. 'Once you sign off on this, then we are good to go and we will start pushing advertising on all our platforms. There will be banners on the website and all social media.'

SGR leans over and picks up her multicoloured, lava lamp vibrator. Does her sister blush? I hear you ask. Well, the red of her cheeks could heat the room.

'Has the shape of this changed?' SGR asks.

'We made some alterations, we sent out samples to a testing panel we use and got some feedback. People weren't so keen about it having a face...'

'But that was the point. Then you could give them a name?' SGR tells me.

'I don't quite know who would name a vibrator?' I say.

'Then how do you differentiate your sex toys from each other?'

'By colour and size, plus I only have three. They're not easily confused,' I reply.

Charlie has a hand to his chin to try to cover his laughter. I'm not sure what he finds funnier, the fact that a girl he was crushing on names her sex toys or that his boss has three. I don't need a friendship with my dildos.

'And tell me about the shape, why is it bent? It looks wonky,' SGR tells me. She holds it and waves it around to test its endurance, which makes Charlie cross his legs.

'Shug, we spoke about this... They are the experts, so we needed to come together and follow their lead. I'm so sorry...' her sister says apologetically.

'It's to make it user-friendly. And the shape of it means it has a better fit for more intense orgasms. It'll just hit different,' I explain.

Charlie and the sisters stare at me. I talk about this stuff all the time, it's my version of business talk.

'What I'm saying is, you want it to look nice, but we have to make sure it feels nice, otherwise what's the point? These things will get returned and people will say they don't work,' I clarify, holding one to the air.

'What happens if they get returned?' SGR asks.

'We bury them. We have a graveyard for bad dildos.'

'Really?' she utters, aghast.

'No.'

The room titters and I'm relieved they get my dry sense of humour.

SGR holds the vibrator to her sister's face, who shrieks a little and bats it away like it may blind her. Naturally, this doesn't deter SGR in any way.

'So, can I ask whose idea was this? Whose brainchild?'

'Well, it certainly wasn't mine,' Scarlett utters. You don't say. 'I just manage her affairs, I make sure she doesn't hand her money over to crackpot ideas and schemes. I think this is a bit out there, but let's see.'

SGR side-eyes her sister. The relationship has shades of Sonny and myself about it: me reining in his random ideas, telling him to come down off the ceiling.

'Look,' I say, 'we have many people come to us looking to collaborate, but there was a reason we wanted to work with you. It was about the message you wanted to send to young people, to enjoy sex, to have fun sex and get in touch with their bodies. I liked that a lot.'

SGR grins at me, a bit more sincerely than she has so far, staring over at her sister. *The business person just vindicated me.* 'I guess I was thrown into the public eye quite quickly and everyone is obsessed with my relationships, my sexuality, my sex life. It's not right that I'm defined by all of that. It's not right that any girl is defined by that.'

Despite her ridiculous bobble earrings and electric blue-winged eyeliner, I like that there's a mature and measured reasoning behind it all.

'I'm all about having sex for me... Female empowerment...' she says, looking to her phone. I think she just posted herself saying that. I hope I'm not in shot.

'So let us help you make sex toys that will work but also be on brand and send out all these messages to the world,' I confirm.

'I want girls to know they don't need a man or a woman to have an orgasm, they can do that themselves,' SGR says with some confidence in her tone. Charlie can't work out if that's her saying she's not really interested in him.

'Well, this will help then,' I add, picking up the dildo. 'Good sex is about positioning. This will penetrate at an angle that hits the G-spot a little sweeter and also has an attachment which can help with clitoral stimulation.'

Charlie creases his brow at this point, mainly because I've also drawn a scrappy picture on the paper in front of me. Take notes, kid. Take notes.

Scarlett looks at me weirdly. 'But G-spots don't exist, do they?'

SGR swings her head around in disbelief, putting a hand to her forehead. 'Scar... seriously?' She looks back to me to explain things.

'Well, it depends if you've been looking for it? Our experts believe there is a spongier spot inside your upper vaginal wall that surrounds the urethra. The cells are more sensitive here and when activated properly, they can help you achieve quite an intense orgasm.'

Activated? I make it sound like it's accessible via a special code. I'm also aware that while I explain this, my fingers are making a come-hither motion that Charlie is imprinting into his mind for future reference.

'Have you never come that way?' SGR asks her sister.

Scarlett shakes her head in bemusement.

'See, this is the problem. This is the stuff girls must learn. How have you come this far in life and not had a vaginal orgasm?' SGR asks.

Her sister pushes her shoulder at that point.

Charlie looks like he'd rather be anywhere else, but I'm not sure if it's because of this sibling fight or the fact he knows he's not done that much for a woman before either.

'I have orgasms. I just get them in a different way,' Scarlett says defensively.

'I really hope Jay is giving you proper orgasms,' her sister adds.

'Can you leave my husband out of this, Shug? He does just fine.'

'Fine? If you say so. But sex should be more than just "fine". Does he still go down on you?'

Charlie and I let them rally this argument in front of us. We're only strangers they've literally just met. Where's Michelle with that Diet Coke? I mean, SGR has a point. No one should be having mediocre sex but have some sympathy for your sister too. She can take that dildo when we're done. Have a tour of this place, on the house. I've taken things home from here that I've pretty much been on hot dates with, we've shared a bath by candlelight, the orgasms could have inspired poetry.

'No, I have not done that,' Scarlett says to her sister. I totally missed what they were talking about, but I suspect that if she's unaware of her G-spot, then she definitely has never done whatever else SGR suggested. There's nothing wrong with vanilla, but sometimes it can be nice to add nuts, fruit, a little sauce.

'That's why you'd add this... so you can stimulate that, while that is happening... and then use the remote to do this...' SGR picks up the dildo and adds attachments to it. Given she's not seen this model before, I applaud how she puts it together like a soldier building a rifle from scratch. Her sister's eyes widen. 'I love the attachments, by the way,' SGR tells me.

'Yes, it just makes it easy to store and clean.'

'You're supposed to clean your sex toys?' SGR asks me.

I nod, slowly.

Scarlett picks it up, now fully accessorised, and tries to work out what goes where. She gives it a look like one would an alien, examining the shape of the bellend and the weight of it in her hands. She also smells it, which is a strange move.

'Can we make it smell less... you know, rubbery?' Scarlett asks.

'We could add a scent, that is a thing now.'

'Bubblegum?' SGR says.

It's not an ice-cream cone. 'I can look into that for you. I also would love some words from you for promo stuff. Be honest, sincere... There are very few celebrities who are sex-positive, so we can help you grow that. Actually, one of the directors here owns a charity and that's the focus of her work, so I can hook you guys up. She's going to be on a TV chat show thing next week.'

For some reason, I think Mum will get on with this girl. She'll like the attention to detail, the fluffy parts of her get-up, that excitable sweet energy.

'I want to make videos too,' SGR tells me.

Charlie's eyes widen at this point. I want to say Mum will help with that, but her days of that are long gone.

'People need to know how to use them. Maybe some animations, pictures, manuals?' she suggests.

I breathe a sigh of relief, looking down at my scrappy drawing in biro. We'd need to get someone else in to do that, but it's a good idea. 'We can work on that.'

SGR picks up some of the other merchandise on the table and holds it up to her camera to take some selfies. Those are love eggs you're posing with. I hope you know that.

'Maybe we can package some of this together?' I say. 'We can brand it as "A Girl's Night In", "Love Yourself", "Me Time"?'

'I LOVE that,' SGR exclaims, studying my face. I hope I don't seem old to her Gen Z self. 'You know your stuff, Josie. You're very cool. I'm glad we're working with you.'

Charlie nudges me a little unsubtly at this point and I chuckle under my breath. For all my reservations, this girl has surprised me today, in a good way. I don't think I'll be using her dildos with the faces, but let's just hope her three million followers will think differently.

'And what about the jewellery... Is that different?' Scarlett asks, trying to wrap something around her wrist. 'How does this work?'

SGR laughs heartily. 'They're beads, sis. They don't go there.'

'Well, where the hell do they go?'

SGR rolls her eyes and turns to me. 'Make sure the first free samples go to her.'

SEVENTEEN

I just stole someone's coffee from Starbucks, Cam's text reads.

How does one do that?

I'm not sure. It was on the counter, I took it. I only found out when I got on the bus and realised I had a drink for Carly that tastes like hazelnut.

Thief.

That makes me cool and dangerous, no?

Of course. All the cool and dangerous ones ride the number 50 bus to Battersea. How are you feeling? First day back to work. You ready?

Just glad to be out of my flat. My scars make me look like I have teenage acne though. Or leprosy. A lady on the bus keeps staring at me.

Maybe she's hot for you. It's that cool and dangerous vibe you're giving off.

She's about fifty. She looks like she'd eat me alive.

Maybe she's Carly.

You are funny. I'm scared now though. What are you up to today? Wanna hang out later?

I'm doing a work thing with my mum, but yeah, sure. We can hang out. Or more...

I'm intrigued by the more.

I'll message you later. With pictures maybe.

I just cheered out loud. Carly's just moved seats.

Look after that coffee xx

'Why are you smiling?' my mum asks as she watches me put my phone down from the mirror where she's sitting.

'Oh, just Cameron...'

Mum smiles back. 'Good to know he's feeling better. Invite him round later, for dinner?'

'Maybe,' I reply.

She narrows her eyes at me before returning to her mirror to talk into it. 'Good morning, my name is Susan Jewell. How are you?' she announces to this dressing room, practising her serious TV arms and earnest nods. 'Yes, that is very interesting. Thank you for your input. However, I do object to your line of questioning...'

I sit and cradle a cup of coffee while I watch Mum do her

thing. Today is TV debate day and I'm here as the moral support, the wardrobe advisor, the debate practice partner. Mum smooths down the dress I've put her in. It's midi, it's teal so it's calming on the eye, and she wears the earrings I got her for Christmas so looks vaguely classy. I don't doubt that she'll be amazing at this. It's hard to say that my mother has screen presence, given her former line of work, but she does. However, she's also likeable and well-spoken. As she's developed her charity, she's built amazing partnerships with schools and local health centres and it's come from a good place, from a girl who once had nothing. She's nervous as hell today, though, this is not a school assembly hall and she's not winging it in front of a room of bored fifteen-year-olds.

I get up and drape my arms around her.

'I've never heard anyone call you Susan, ever,' I tell her.

'My father used to,' she says, looking further into that mirror than needs be.

'You're Susie. You've always been Susie. Don't fake it, just be you,' I say.

The irony of my advice is not lost on my mother, who giggles, watching me in the mirror. The last week, while I've let Cameron get over his chickenpox, I've spent a lot of time making amends with my family. We chatted through the Mike situation and I showed them his wedding photos. I explained the speed in which he found a new love and I told them everything that he wrote on that note, as painful as it was to say out loud. There are still shades of anger there from all of us but mostly from Nan, who said that she had once offered him some of her special fudge. *The next time I give him fudge, it will be laced with arsenic and glass.* However, things are better now, all of that is out in the open and it's a relief to not have to hold on to it alone anymore.

'Do you think I should go with the other dress with the big collar?' Mum asks me.

'It makes you look slightly Quaker?'

'You're right. I don't want to pretend I'm all light and virtue,' she jests cheekily.

'I think we've got your vibe just right. The other option was that latex dress; we could show off a bit of bum cleavage.'

She shakes her head at me. 'Latex. Back in my day, it was PVC.'

Imagine if we brought her here, full dominatrix. We could have fully accessorised, whips and all. I laugh to myself.

'What if they use words I don't know, Josie? I left school at sixteen.'

'They won't.'

'What's that word you taught me for old-fashioned?'

'Antiquated?'

'I like that one.'

'Just use it properly. Sonny says hi, by the way. He wishes you luck,' I say, glancing at my phone.

She holds a hand to her heart and picks up a lipstick again, nervously reapplying it.

A girl with a headset, a high ponytail, dressed head to toe in black suddenly rushes in. 'Hi! OMG, I'm Becca. I am so sorry, it is mad this morning. Thank you for being so patient with us. OMG, you look amazing, like proper OMG.'

Mum smiles at her while I try to work out how many times someone can OMG in one sentence.

Becca runs a finger down a clipboard. 'We'll wire you up on set. Are you her assistant?' she asks me.

'Daughter,' I reply.

'OMG, that's super cute.' She's five thousand words a minute, but I like the energy.

'Breathe, Becca,' Mum says, putting a reassuring hand to her arm.

'I'm sorry. It's just one of the other guests is down the hall and between you and me, he's a proper dickhead. Nothing will give me greater pleasure if you give him what for today.'

Mum looks to me when Becca says that. We haven't been told about the other panellists, but already I can see the fear in the whites of her eyes. I turn and swish a finger under my neck to tell Becca she has to stop.

'I mean, he'll be no match for you, though, I'm sure. When you're ready...' Becca mumbles.

Mum pauses by the door and stares into space. 'Josie... Maybe this was a stupid idea...'

'Mum, I'll be there the whole time. Nothing bad can come of this. You'll have that doctor there too, the nice TV doctor – we like her – and the presenter will have your back.' I reach down to take her hand and she squeezes it, so hard that I can feel her rings pressing into my skin.

We start walking along a corridor lined with photos of minor TV celebrities. There's a lot of hustle and wires and people clutching clipboards for their lives. I feel mildly excited if nervous for my Mum. She'll be fine. I watch as she makes her way onto the sound stage to get mic'ed up and I wave at her, like I'm waving a child off on their first day at school. She goes to take her seat and talk to a director.

'She's so glamorous,' Becca tells me, looking me up and down. I'm the opposite of glamour, I'm reality-show realness right here. 'She'll be brilliant, I hope she takes that other bloke down,' she says, her voice trailing off.

'Who is he?'

Becca looks down her clipboard. 'He was a last-minute call-in. Umm... Henry... Henry Cox. OMG, that's a funny name! He's a proper cox-sucker,' she says, sniggering at her own joke.

O.M.CRAPPING.G. I stand there, glued to the spot. 'WHO?'

. . .

Do you have many slow-motion moments in your life? I can think of a couple. The time I nearly got run over once in a supermarket car park when someone reversed into my trolley, when Mike left me and shattered my heart into splinters of nothing, and a time on holiday when I got pushed into a pool with a tray of drinks. But this, this is rating up there as one of those moments where I want to run slowly in the direction of my mother and push her out of the way. Noooooooo. Ruuuuun. This can't be happening.

In my head, I race through the possibilities of what this means. I was hedging my bets on Cameron not watching this as he's just gone back to work so there's no way he would be stopping in his office to watch random mid-morning TV. His family dynamics are pretty fractured so there's a very slight possibility he won't see this, this will all slip through the cracks and the dots won't be connected. But there's also the very huge chance that this is all going to come out, now. Here. Without any help from me. Maybe I should message Cameron, attempt some form of damage control.

Panic sits in my soul. What do I do? Do I pull a fire alarm? Tell Mum there's an emergency? Plus, what if I bump into Henry Cox now? He was deeply unpleasant and I was mildly abusive to him in his own house, so who knows what he'll do if he sees me in the light of day. I should just steep in my terror and stay in the shadows. Maybe I should find a hat to wear. I stand behind a large man in shorts, Timberland boots, operating a large camera, waiting, watching, making him slightly nervous so I step away and find a curtain to hide behind. I think I might stay behind here forever.

'Can you leave my hair alone please?'

Crap. That's the first I hear of Henry Cox and I allow him to walk right past my curtain, not before peeking out and hissing. Look at your shiny grey suit and tie. I see him walk up to my mother and she extends her hand. Did he just totally ignore it? Slap him, Mum! Mum doesn't look too bothered and everyone takes their seats. However, she does stop for a moment to look at him. Mum is far better with faces than myself and as soon as she sees him, I see fire. She knows who it is. Not that she knows that's Cameron's dad at all; I've never told her that much. She knows him as the man who litters her letterbox with propaganda political nonsense. He recently voted in favour of the closure of two support centres in our area for new single mothers and has just started his petition to change the nature of sex education in schools. This is someone she wants to take on. This is something she's not scared of. However, it scares me. It scares me for many reasons. All these separate universes are colliding. We've crossed the streams. Please let us leave here unscathed. Please please please.

'And welcome back to the show!' The presenter has been doing these sorts of phone-in debate shows for years now, doling out his own brand of TV justice and pop psychology nuggets of wisdom. However, according to Sonny, the presenter also attends many awards shows completely coked up where he usually spends his time in backstage toilets with women who aren't his wife.

'So, the next topic we wanted to cover today is SEX! Cover your ears, Jean, if this is too much for a Thursday morning but there are some new programmes coming into schools today about sex education and here to discuss those new curriculums are Dr Sara Hafeez, MP Henry Cox, and Susie Jewell, who works for a charity called INTI-MATE which promotes sex education and body positivity in schools. Welcome, all. Let's start with you, Dr Sara...'

We like Dr Sara. She's the resident doctor in a show where she helps people with body shame and health problems they've lived with for years. She also does a nice line in kids' health shows with puppets, still works for the NHS and I think most women would agree, we'd all kill for her hair. If I could applaud her, I would.

'...which is why it's important these lessons are in place for children as young as five years of age...' she says to the host.

'Five years old?' Henry Cox says, humphing and blowing out his cheeks. 'At five years old, children should be climbing trees.'

'Yes, but they can't be climbing trees all the time,' Dr Sara intervenes. 'In the real world, it's important for children to learn about themselves, their bodies and their truth.'

'Their truth? We tell kids that a fairy comes and collects their old teeth in the middle of the night. There are some things that children do not need to know at such a young age,' Henry continues.

I was right about Henry. He likes to talk out of his backside, a backside no woman has touched for many years. He's entitled to his opinion but it's the nastiness with which he projects all his words.

'Do you have children? Can I ask when and how your children found out about sex then?' Mum asks. It's the first thing she's said and I can hear a shake in her voice. Steady on, Mum. He does have children. You spent Christmas Day with one of them.

'I do have children. I have four. That's a private matter,' Henry replies, not even looking my mother in the eye.

'It's a simple question,' my mum says. 'My children found out about sex in the last years of primary school when their bodies were changing, probably more from the school play-ground too, and I think that's where we're failing kids today.'

I found out because she bought me a book called *Why Am I Growing Hair There?* It was a pop-up book. Sonny and I used to open up the pages to the people with the pubes, roll around the carpet and laugh. Henry squirms in his seat to hear Mum talk so casually about these matters.

'Children have no idea how their bodies work and what's happening to them. We hide so much: menstruation, body change, sexuality, sexual urges,' she continues.

'For good reason,' Henry pipes in.

'For no good reason. We hide it away and then people associate shame with those things.'

YES, MUM! I hope Dad is watching this and he is crying with pride. We didn't bring him down today for that very reason.

'Tell us more about what your charity does, Mrs Jewell,' the presenter asks.

'Please call me Susie. It's INTI-MATE. I go into schools and talk about sex, consent, relationships. Important things, so young people understand more than just what's being taught through health education and biology.'

'And I do believe you also are connected to sex in other ways?' the presenter presses. Oh dear.

'Oh, I used to run a business...' I see her glance into the shadows, looking for me.

'A sex shop. And what about before that?' Henry asks condescendingly. He may be a late call-in, but he's definitely done his homework.

Mum pauses for a moment. 'Before that, I used to work in the adult film industry.'

Henry chortles under his breath and looks over to Dr Sara. 'In that case,' he says, 'I am not sure she is the right person to be sitting on a panel like this. Someone who has worked in one of the most exploitative, sordid industries preaching to us about sex education? It's laughable.'

He doesn't look my mother in the eye the whole time he says this and my heart aches.

'Well,' replies Mum, 'maybe I'm someone who has worked at the heart of an industry where I can say I've seen how messages about sex can be warped. Maybe I'm actually the most qualified person here to be talking about these things.'

You are, Mum.

'Well, no. If she has a sex business, then obviously she is here with vested interests. She wants people to know about sex so they can buy her paraphernalia,' he says, directing his words to the host of the show.

'Sex toys, Henry. They're called sex toys. Let me know if I can hook you up.'

Dr Sara is laughing, so is the cameraman next to me. I know an excellent line of cock rings I could send to his house, extra small.

Henry's nostrils are flared and I recognise this look. It's a woman, taking him down, taking him on. 'So, if we are looking at this curriculum, you think it's appropriate for children to learn about "homosexuality", "masturbation", words like "vulva"?' He spits these words out like he's allergic to them.

'Yes. I do. Because maybe then they won't have such antiquated opinions of these things as they grow up.'

'YES!' I squeal. The set stops as I step back into the shadows.

I see my mum's smug face to have used her new word. 'Basic sex education is something kids will carry for a lifetime. It's something my charity will always endorse and support.'

Henry stops to hear those words as very possibly, just before Christmas, someone said the exact same thing to him around his dining table. 'Well, not if I have anything to do with it. I've made my views known in the Commons. The reason we've lost control of the youth of today is because they are sexualised far too quickly. I mean, look at someone like you…'

He finally looks at my mother. Dr Sara freezes and I glare at the presenter to step in.

'Porn. The reason you fell into that was because you were probably sexualised far too young.'

My mother freezes, as do I. 'I... I...'

'I'm supposed to look at you and be impressed? I don't want a path like that for my daughters or granddaughters. Are your children in porn too?'

'Mr Cox, with much respect—' Dr Sara intervenes, but Henry hasn't finished.

'I have a degree, a family, I am a well-respected member of the community and I was voted in because my opinion means something. What an absolute joke that I've been called in today to share a stage with a sex worker...' he sneers, disgusted.

No. Simply, no. Is this another slow-motion moment? Because I don't know how and why I emerge from the shadows, but there seems to be some magnetic pull that makes me walk closer and closer to the lights of the studios until I'm there, standing next to the sound stage.

'So you're saying that for her opinion to be valid, she needs a degree? I have a degree.' I notice a camera turn to focus on me.

Henry Cox turns to my voice. He narrows his eyes as he recognises me.

'Umm, who are you?' the presenter asks, frantically looking through his notes.

'What on earth are you doing here?' Henry Cox says, shocked that I have re-entered his orbit.

'I'm her daughter. My name is Josie.'

I've not come dressed for today. I'm in jeans and a sweat-shirt and some Nike Air Max trainers. A shiny sheen to my face, my hair could probably do with a wash, but Henry Cox, you need to shut up now. I look over at my mother with tears in her eyes.

'I see it now. It makes perfect sense that you two would be related. Are you here to make the teas?' he asks.

Oh, I'll make the tea. I can pour it over your lap if you like? You want biscuits with that?

'Can I ask what your degree is in?' I ask him calmly.

'PPE from Cambridge,' he answers pompously.

'Oh, for a minute, I thought it was a first-class degree in being a misogynist, classist pig,' I retort.

Dr Sara gasps in shocked delight. The presenter doesn't quite know what to do, but I hear gabbled yelling in his earpiece.

'You can't talk to me like that,' Henry says. 'Who the hell are you to be coming here and interrupting this? Is there security?'

It's not *Newsnight*, Henry.

I take a deep breath. 'My name is Josie Jewell. I'm the MD of The Love Shack and last year we turned over annual profits of £8 million, all through a business that celebrates sex, that celebrates pleasure and people loving themselves and their bodies.'

He pauses, registering the fact that I lied, that I came into his house and lied to him. And his son.

'And this is my mother. Both my parents were in porn and you know what? They raised me and my brother perfectly. They raised me to work hard, respect my roots and carry no shame in anything I do. I look at you and see none of that.'

'How dare you, you hardly know me,' he barks, his face taut with anger.

'I know when I see someone who is a bully, whose opinions of the world have no bearing to what is actually happening, to how the world is evolving. Bullies like you deserve none of my respect.' I keep talking because I like how my words are turning his face a completely different colour.

'I refuse to be a part of this sort of discussion. I did not agree to this free-for-all,' he snarls, standing up, trying to disentangle himself from the set.

I shake my head. 'We're not leaving here until you apologise to my mother...'

My mother stands up and puts an arm to mine.

'When do you suddenly need to make apologies for having morals? You are all beneath me,' Henry snaps.

'Apologise to her...'

'Never.'

But I don't need to say any more, because out of nowhere, Dr Sara appears with a fist and properly lands one on Henry Cox's chin. Christ, girl.

'LET ME AT HIM!' she shrieks. 'YOU ABSOLUTE PIECE OF—'

I didn't know the respectable doctor had it in her. They won't let her back on kids' TV after this. Becca the runner holds her back. That is some punch. I think that's a tooth on the floor. Henry falls to the desk, dazed. My mum screams. The presenter throws his earpiece to the floor as more people run onto the set. Oh. Was that all on camera? I think it may have been, because the cameraman I was hiding behind before looks at me and puts his thumb to the air.

'Crap,' I mutter to Mum. 'Maybe we should leave?'

'You did that?' she says, tears in her eyes.

I nod. Oh, crappy-crap-crap.

'But Cameron,' she whispers. Yeah, that too.

EIGHTEEN

'I'm sending round some PR people, they're troubleshooters, best in the biz. Ruby used them that one time her ex put all her nudes on Snapchat. Is she OK?' Sonny asks.

I'm driving home from our rather eventful TV debut with Mum in the passenger seat. The look she has about her face is pure shock. I don't think it's shock from being abused by the turd-faced MP or even the fight that ensued after (turns out Dr Sara is also a black belt in ju-jitsu). I think it may be because I stepped onto that set. I was holding on to a lie, a charade to try to salvage a relationship with that man's son, and I threw all of it out of the window for her, to defend my mother. In the moment, as much as I knew this would out all my lies to Cameron, that this would mark the end of our relationship, standing up for what was right, my mother and her honour, was what was most important.

'She's quiet,' I reply. 'I stopped off at McDonald's and got her some nuggets and a milkshake.'

'She's a fifty-something-year-old woman, not a five-year-old child after losing a football match.'

'I couldn't think what else to do,' I explain.

'I've got Ruby here, she's on her phone, it's already trending on Twitter.'

'Is it awful?' I ask, my face scrunched up.

'Everything's mostly targeted at him. A few nice stills of you losing your shit. That'll be a meme. Oh, no they've done it already, you're a GIF, Josie.'

I don't want to know what that means, but I'm making a mental note to use some BB cream and mascara as a minimum before I leave the house from now on.

'Ruby and I have to go. Is he really Cameron's dad?' Sonny asks.

'Yep.'

'That's mad.'

'I know.'

'Look, we'll call back later. Get her home and just wait until the PR people get there. Draw the curtains. Maybe get some of the big lads from the warehouse to come down and do a bit of security for you?' he suggests.

'Maybe. I'll catch you in a bit.'

Sonny hangs up and the Bluetooth reverts to the radio.

'In other news,' says a newsreader, 'a TV debate went wild today when Dr Sara punched an MP for criticising a fellow panellist who works in porn.'

'*Worked* in porn,' my mum mutters.

I try to fiddle around with the radio stations. Boney M. She loves Boney M. This is better. I pretend to dance. There's some strange nervous energy in my bones. Cameron will know now, for sure. My presence on that set would have connected all the dots and been the final piece of the puzzle. His sisters would have watched and told him. His mother. He now knows I'm not me. It's over, it's done. And I don't know how I feel about that. There is embarrassment, sadness, but there's a glimmer of hope that maybe he'll see past it all. That what we had was enough. I keep waiting for my phone to ring, for a message to come through, but there has been nothing.

Mum sips on her milkshake. I didn't know where else to go after we left the studio, but I remembered when we were sad when we were little, Mum used to get us Happy Meals. It would always do the trick. My mum doesn't talk about her past a lot, but I know the route she took through life wasn't because she was overly sexualised. It was because she was neglected – her mother remarried someone who ousted her out of the family home. It was having to navigate her teens on her own and probably being very misinformed about sex along the way, using it to validate her young self. It's why she does what she does, so girls head down their chosen routes in life with information, with agency, with the knowledge that who they have sex with and how is not a measure of their self-worth.

As we pull into the drive, I already see Dad waiting tentatively by the front porch, and as my car rolls to a stop, he opens the door for my mum and offers a hand, looking at me strangely. You went to McDonald's? She falls into his arms straight away. I think they both might be crying. He pushes her head away to give her a kiss on the forehead.

'Excuse me?' says a voice from behind us.

The voice makes me turn quickly, adopting a strange ninja pose, hands to the air. Have the paps found out where we live already? We turn to see a mother and young child standing there at the end of the drive.

Mum wipes the tears from her face with the palm of her hand. 'Oh, hi.' She walks towards them. 'Josie, this is Leanne and Arlo. They live across the road. I remember you, you were a very good pumpkin at Halloween,' she says, bending down to greet the little boy.

Dad and I are less certain about this interaction and he

glances over to me. They may be here to borrow our hedge trimmer or tell us it's bin day, but there is also the likelihood that they saw what happened and have things to say, possibly not nice things. I edge closer towards them. I don't have Dr Sara's punch, but I will chase them back to their house if they start anything.

'We just wanted to say...' Leanne starts hesitantly. 'We saw you on television this morning and Arlo recognised you. And well, I just wanted to check you're OK. What that man said was awful... really awful...' Mum starts welling up again. 'And, well, I thought you might like to see this...'

Dad walks over as the neighbour presents them with a picture. It's a hand-drawn Mum and Dad dressed up at Halloween, holding sweets. Naturally, the proportions are all off as Dad is as big as our house, but the smiles, the bold bright colours are everything. Of course, this sets Dad off which concerns Arlo a little.

'I'm sorry. I cry at everything. Arlo, this is lovely. I'm going to put it on my fridge! Thank you,' Dad says. 'I thought you'd come round with a torch to chase us off the street,' he continues.

'God, no,' says Leanne, 'You've always been lovely neighbours. Who cares about all of that? It makes you a darned sight more interesting than most. You could be drug dealers, bonfire enthusiasts, thrash metal rock fans... Those are the sorts you don't want as neighbours,' she adds, smiling. 'Plus, I never knew you owned that company, my husband and I get the occasional bits from there...' Her face now reddens, she's possibly over-shared, but hey, that seems to be the theme of the day.

'Well, now you know... Josie can get you discounts. You could deliver right to their doorstep,' Dad chips in.

Perhaps. Like Just Eat for love gloves? Now that's a business idea.

We all stand there for a moment as little Arlo looks up at

me. 'I didn't see you at Halloween,' he says. 'Do you live here too?'

'I do.'

'Where were you at Halloween?'

'I was at a party instead.'

'What did you dress up as?' he asks, eyes full of questions.

'A Ghostbuster...'

'Like the song?' He starts to hum it and I smile, tears in my eyes.

I'm not quite sure what to say. I'm so sorry. I guess you have an idea of what happened this morning from your dad, even if you didn't watch it. Yes, that was me. And my mum. And that is what I really do. That's my name. If you wanted to chat, then I'm here. I am sorry. I'm really sorry. If there's a very small possibility you have no idea what I'm talking about, then please ignore this. I am sorry. I'm still me, really xxx

I look down at the message on my phone, sent at 2.33 p.m., three hours ago. I should have proofread it. Maybe I should have softened it with a joke or an emoji. Maybe I shouldn't have desperately ended it with so many kisses. The stinger is the double green tick to let me know it's been read but no reply.

'Which number?' my dad asks, his car slowly rolling down the road.

'It's that red block of flats there,' I say, pointing.

He pulls the car to a stop and we sit there for a moment as I watch the lamp posts flicker to life, the dark starting to settle into the streets. It's as I imagined, rows of low-rise flats, punctuated by windows lit up by the glow of their televisions.

'Sherbet?' Dad asks me, opening his glove compartment.

I nod and take a sweet.

'Take more than one.' He basically empties them into my lap.

'Have you been to his place before?'

'No. But Mum sent him some beers to say thank you for the Christmas gift. She had his address.'

'Oh.'

'Can we just sit here for a moment?' I ask him.

He nods. We have sherbets, we'll be fine.

It's been a busy afternoon today, a PR man called Pierre came round. He had a diamond earring the size of a Skittle and fist-bumped Dad when he first walked in, but he was kind and listened and made many phone calls so everything would go away. In any case, it would seem Dr Sara's fisticuffs made for far more interesting clickbait. Over the course of the day, things did escalate, the tweets became more personal, everyone suddenly had an opinion on sex education, but the small positive is that people were googling Mum's charity and donations online saw a two hundred per cent increase. People at least listened to what she had to say.

All the while, I looked at my phone. That's the problem with modern technology, you know when someone is online, when their fingers are hovering over a phone, when they last liked something or reacted to a post. I'd see him *typing...* but the messages would never reach me. I imagined him writing, stopping, deleting, starting again, but it's now the early evening and there's been nothing.

I'm sorry. I'm sorry you found out that way. I should have led with jokes. *It's Josie here! We shagged in my car? The one who humiliated your dad on live TV! Surprise! Wasn't that funny? Yep, that was Mum. The one you had Christmas dinner with. My dad's name isn't Fabio. Nan wasn't a showgirl. I'm not in catering.* But the lie would have unravelled like a big ball of wool and at the end of it would be nothing. I had no idea how to fix this or what to do next, but I thought the best thing would be to see him, to come to his flat and say sorry in person at least.

'How's Mum?' I mumble. 'Have you texted her?'

'I've put her in the bath and then she's going to watch *Bridgerton* with Dave. Nan's with her, she'll be fine.'

'That was a bad business idea of mine to let her do that debate. I'm sorry. It was naïve of me to think people wouldn't attack her like that.'

'Oh god, don't apologise. You did good by her. This was all him, not you. Your mum will be fine. You know that. She's survived me all these years,' he says, trying to joke.

A couple walk past the car and I sink into my seat. Maybe I should have dressed up for this. It was a panicked plan where, after Pierre left, I just grabbed a hat and coat and told Dad we were going out.

'You like this boy, don't you?' Dad says to me in the twilight of the car.

'Maybe. But maybe it just isn't to be, Dad. I mean, can you imagine that asshat as a father-in-law?'

'Seriously? No. I'd be the one punching him at the wedding. I'd put laxatives in his champagne.'

I laugh as he takes off his gloves and adjusts his seat, pushing it right back to get ready for this stakeout. An old man walks past the car with a greyhound, a newspaper tucked under his arm, giving us the eye. It's OK, we're here to fix my crappy love life, not for crime. I scan my eyes up Cameron's building, around cold, empty cars parked nearby, searching for his.

'The least I can offer him is an apology, though,' I explain.

'Do you want to practise what you want to say? With me?'

I shake my head.

'Well, do you think I can get pizza delivered to the car? Will we be here a while? It's just I've been running around after you girls all day, I've forgotten to eat.'

I go through my handbag and find a cereal bar.

'Since that episode during tennis, you've really got to start looking after yourself, you know?'

Dad pulls a face at being reprimanded, taking the cereal bar and breaking a bit off for me. 'That's your problem, Josie. You're always looking out for everyone else. Never you. Since you told us about that Mike stuff, this is what I worry about. Who's looking after you?'

'You do.'

'But I mean, when do you put your needs first?'

I shrug, looking down at my hands. 'Do you think Mum will be OK? Fulham kick off at 5 p.m. too, tell Nan she can watch it on the downstairs telly.'

'You're changing the subject.'

'But, seriously, it's a top-of-the-table clash.'

Dad laughs. I put a hand to his as I realise I gave him the chewy cereal bar with the sultanas; his teeth won't like that.

'The stuff with Cameron was all a bit of a mess to start with and I probably made things worse. Don't worry about me, please.'

'I will always worry.'

Our attention is suddenly taken by a figure walking towards the flats with a rucksack on his shoulders, carrying a shopping bag. It's him. Crap. The immediate reaction is to duck, but I'm here. I've got to do this. I reach for the door handle, but as I do, my dad grabs my arm. It's definitely Cameron walking, but there's a little girl who runs towards him and into his arms. 'DADDY!' He picks the girl up and spins her around. 'Erin!' He drops the shopping bag to the floor and pushes the black curls from around her face to kiss her forehead. I can't quite breathe. From a nearby car, a woman gets out carrying a bag and walks towards Cameron. They share a hug and a joke and she pokes at his face where his chickenpox used to be. I can't look at the scene any more so bow my head and let tears fall into my lap. I can't quite tell if that's pain or guilt.

'Oh, Josie,' Dad says, looking on at them. 'Shall we just go?'

But, instead, I open the door and stand next to the car. You're a daddy? How? I don't know what this is. I don't think I ever did, but now I need to at least find out.

Outside, the air is harsh and light rain paints the road in polka dots. Isn't this how they do it in the movies? People run out into inclement weather to profess something, to say everything that's in their soul. *You have a daughter? Tell me about her. Because I know I have things to say too. I know the weather is grim and I'm not wearing a suitable coat, but I think I'm in love with you. I am so so sorry. I lied. I was wrong to do that. But I'm in love with you. I really hope that's enough.*

It doesn't take Cameron long to see my figure by the car. He turns to the woman and the little girl and tells them to go inside. I notice Dad leant over the steering wheel, actually waving, the worst stakeout partner in the world.

'Hey,' I say.

'Hey...'

I try to smile, to look kindly, to break the tension, but I can't find the words. 'Look... I...'

'Josie Jewell, it's a good name.' He looks hurt, his eyes misted with an emotion I can't quite read.

'Is that your daughter?' I ask.

He stops for a moment. 'It is. That's Erin.'

'You never mentioned her.'

'We're going to have a conversation about the things we never told each other?'

We stop for a moment to let that sink in.

'I'm sorry,' I say. 'I'm sorry you found out about me in that way. It was a lie that just kept getting out of control. I'm still me, really. I just... How's your dad?'

'At the dentist, having a tooth replaced. His pride has taken the worst battering. The family hate me even more now. I didn't think that was possible,' he tells me, obviously hurt.

'I am so so sorry...'

He pauses for a moment, not allowing himself to get too close to me. It's like the reverse of all our interactions so far, this invisible wall between the both of us.

'Look, Josie... Maybe we just jumped into this too soon, too quickly...'

A lump gets forged in my throat. Tell him. Tell him all those words you have saved up.

'Was it a joke? You pretending to be someone else? Were you laughing at me the whole time?' he asks me.

'Never. I didn't know what I was thinking. I just didn't want to scare you off.'

'I just don't know what's real now. First, Imogen and now this. I feel like an idiot...'

'You're not. I'm the idiot...'

He's right. Maybe it was never real to start off with. It was two people in fancy dress playing make-believe, looking for distractions, escapism from real life.

'So, is that woman your wife? Girlfriend?' I ask, nervously.

'She's my ex. We share custody. I wouldn't have lied to you like that.'

Not like I lied to you. My shame starts to peek through and I realise we might be done here. My dad needs to eat. That cereal bar won't last him. I need to stop pretending this was anything more than it was. 'Well, I just came here to apologise. That's all. I know I've mucked up here, this was all me, and yeah... Just I'm sorry. I'm really sorry.'

I need to go now. Before this descends into really ugly crying and that's not the last memory I want him to have of me. I turn and walk towards the car. He's not following me, is he? He's not. I open the car door.

'Josie?'

I turn around swiftly. 'Yes?'

'Tell Fabio I said bye. All your family. Give them my best.'

Oh, yeah. About that... I give him one last look, before he turns around.

I think I may have been in love with him, but all those little moments meant nothing. It wasn't enough. I was not enough. I watch him as he walks into his building. Bye, Spengler. And then he's gone.

NINETEEN

I started at The Love Shack three weeks before my twenty-fourth birthday. Naturally, I wasn't enamoured with the prospect of working for the family business and having allegations of nepotism thrown at me, so I worked super hard. I was the first one in, the last out. I wore a suit to work every day even though it wasn't really required. Sometimes I'd tell Michelle I was leaving, but really I'd eat a meal deal special from the supermarket on the corner, take a disco nap on the sofa in my office and then get back on it. When my parents or Mike asked me where I was, I'd tell them I was with mates or in a spin class. I made this place my home. It was an escape when I needed an out from real life. Some would go to a spa, on a city break, on a walk. Josie goes and sleeps at the office.

Those patterns of behaviour seem to be repeating themselves at the moment. Since the TV debate and since Cameron found out the truth, work is a reprieve from having to think too hard about the mess that is my love life. It's classic Josie behaviour. I won't be able to process any ounce of that heartbreak if I just focus on work. Any time a flashback comes up of Cameron standing on Nan's balcony taking in the wonder and colour of the NYE fireworks or us walking hand-in-hand around Comic Con or dressed as Ghostbusters eating chicken wings together, I blank all of it out. I take on a spreadsheet, I write an important email, I file my personal expenses like my sanity depends on it.

'Hellloooo...'

I hear the voice inside the reception area and head out of my office.

'I have an order for Jewell.'

That's what I also do. I eat. I eat quite a bit. I replace all the lost affection with carbs.

'Yep, that's me.'

'This is all for you?'

Yes, it is.

'No, I'm expecting some colleagues to show up soon.'

The Uber Eats man looks me up and down. Yes, this is a red tracksuit. Yes, I look like an Eastern European gymnast. Yes, I am also wearing slippers and look like I've slept here in this warehouse full of sex toys but haven't touched a single one. Am I going to remedy everything with McDonald's hash browns now? Yes, I am. I don't have time to explain any of this to him, so I tip him more than I should.

When I get back inside my office, I examine my work before me. I am heartbroken, but it would seem I am also scarily hyper-efficient. Last night, I told Mum I was going to Brett and Tina's to babysit their boys when really I came here. I sorted out boxes of lube by colour, flavour and brand. I replied to thirty complaint emails. My favourite came from a lady in Fleet, Hampshire, who'd got a vibrating bullet stuck in her husband's anus and who told me it'd taken an operation and two weeks off work for him to recover from the ordeal. Her solution, she feels, is for us to emblazon the words DO NOT PUT UP YOUR BUM on the packaging. I tried on some of our new strap-on range – apparently, the harnesses need some adjusting as if you're a size 10 or under, they don't offer adequate support or appropriate fit. The person who said that is right, it needs another buckle. I also have one hundred Sugar Cube dildos to post out to celebrity influencers and such. They come with a handwritten note from SGR herself that says GOOD VIBES, ALWAYS. Did I come up with that? Yes, I did.

I sit down and bite into a hash brown from my embarrassingly large stash. If it seems like I did all this work alone, I didn't. I did it watching *Vikings*. It did help to some extent. Nothing eases heartbreak like hot bearded men killing other hot bearded men. At the moment, my computer screen is on pause as a man with no eyes is getting an axe through the face. See, Josie, any time you feel that your heart is being pulled out of your arse, then remember things could be far worse.

Did you at least get some sleep?

I spy a message glowing on my phone.

Tina has covered for me tonight, but both her and Brett have become increasingly worried about me, checking in, sending cake and links to funny things they've seen on the internet. Maybe we can fix Josie with a video of baby pandas going down a slide.

I did.

About four hours, I reckon. Successful people don't sleep. I'm sure I read that somewhere. I mean, they also wake up to someone having run them a bath, who's made them eggs Benedict, freshly brewed coffee and styled their outfits. They're not hunched in a chair in a primary-coloured tracksuit, eating a McDonald's breakfast out of a bag, licking potato crumbs from the nooks and crannies of their fingers.

I guess I'll see you later? Do you want a lift? I have the
cupcakes. We all love you, JoJo xxx

I love you all, too.

I'll see Tina later as tonight it's Sonny and Ruby's respective
hen and stag dos. My presence is sure to be a downer, but I'm
legally obliged to attend as sister of the groom and maid of
honour, so I need to plaster on a smile and tolerate this celebra-
tion of love and debauchery. I also need to go as I've supplied
the goody bags for the evening. These are the events when it
really pays to be marrying into this family because everyone is
going to leave tonight with lingerie (from our premium range),
gift-wrapped condoms, a sex toy and an edible chocolate penis
with cream filling (I've tried them and they're surprisingly deli-
cious; not too cloying). This is what I also did last night. I got out
the tissue paper, I curled ribbon, I wrote the tags. I bought a
calligraphy pen, such is my commitment to making this look
good but also putting my energy into something else other than
my feelings.

'What on earth?'

A voice behind me makes me jump and I turn around in
fright, dropping one of my sacred hash browns to the ground. I
can't pick that up and eat it, can I?

Michelle. She's dressed in skinny jeans and trainers and
stares at me. She turns on the lights in the office, which I'd like
to say were off to create mood lighting, but really it was so I
could wallow in the darkness. I flinch as the light comes on.

'Morning to you too.'

'It's 9.15 on a Saturday morning, what the hell are you
doing here? Have you been filing?' she says, looking to a pile of
files and Post-its on my desk.

'Maybe?'

'The electrical warehouse across the way called me to say

they thought there'd been a break-in, maybe a squatter had got in. Have you been here all night?'

'No? How ridiculous?' I blurt out, trying to laugh it off.

She notices a fleece blanket on the sofa, empty cans of G&T and many used tissues on the floor. She comes over and gives me a massive hug, holding it for longer than needs be.

'Oh, honey. You absolute numpty.'

'I just needed to get out of my house, do something, throw myself into work,' I mumble, my head rested on her shoulder.

'What's with the tracksuit? You look like you're about to take part in the Squid Games?' she asks.

Aaah, the red tracksuit. I step back from her and turn around. This is my Bride Squad leisurewear attire. Red for love, Sister of the Groom emblazoned across the back, sponsored by Adidas. It comes with stripes on the leg and a matching hoodie with the logo CRAZY IN LOVE. There's also a cap with hearts. I don't wear the cap, but the 'crazy' bit doesn't look half wrong. I tried it on yesterday and have kept it on as it's surprisingly comfortable. We should all be wearing tracksuits permanently.

'It's a look. And you've done the favour bags, they look awesome. What's with her?'

Michelle points to a blow-up doll in the corner of the room. Obviously, it's not a stag do without a blow-up doll. I've been asked to deliver her to a bar later. She's called Keeley, she's again from our premium range; she has actual hair like on a Barbie. I figured it was a better bet to blow her up now as opposed to on a pavement in Soho.

'She's for Sonny.'

'I like how you put a dressing gown on her.'

'Otherwise, she'll get cold.'

She looks at the giant crumpled McDonald's bag in my hands. 'I hope there's a McMuffin in here for me?' she asks.

I nod and she goes to the corner of the office to turn on the kettle, peering over at my desk at the strap-on I tried on last night. Don't worry, I didn't have an orgy here, I was literally trying on sex toys by myself. That isn't sad. At all.

'I think everyone's a little worried about you, babe,' Michelle says, smelling the milk in the fridge. 'Are you OK?' she asks.

I hand her a McMuffin and she peels back the wrapper. That one is a double. You're one of the lucky ones.

I shrug my shoulders. 'I'll be fine. I think I just need a few weeks to be like this, to overwork and not think too hard about life, watch Sonny get married and just reset.'

I make it sound so mechanical, but the truth is it hurts. And instead of feeling all that pain, I've decided to look away from the wound, to close my eyes and try to distract myself. In that time, the hurt will scab over, it will heal, and when I look back, it'll be a little scar, a sign of Josie Jewell's colourful dating history.

'You know – this was him too. He had a daughter he didn't tell you about?'

'Yeah, but I get that. You don't want to just introduce any old date to a daughter. That would just confuse her. I was obviously nothing serious.'

I swallow hard to say that out loud and Michelle takes my hand again. The fact was, I never questioned it. His social media didn't disclose much, if anything, about his personal life and the one picture he had with her, I just assumed her to be someone else, a niece, a friend's child. It turned out he just wasn't Cameron, he was also someone's father. I don't know how I feel knowing about that, but I don't think it makes me like him any less.

'Well, at least you're eating. How's your mum doing?'

'Oh, she's never been better. What happened at the TV debate has done wonders for her. People like her, I think we may see her get a second wind in her career. From porn to sex toys to a sex and relationships column in a magazine.'

'She'll be so good at that!'

'Right?'

Michelle makes the cups of tea and comes to sit down next to me on my office sofa, stepping over the box of well-organised lube.

'Your dad has asked me to keep an eye. I've had to report to him every day. They think you've been crying at your desk, blaming them for everything.'

I look over at her. 'Don't tell them you found me here. I told them I was with Tina.'

'I won't. But if you feel really sad, then you'll chat to me, yes? Tina? Your parents? Sonny? You know we all love the tits off you.'

I smile in a sleep-deprived hash-brown haze. 'I know. I think I'm just... you know... Processing? I think I was starting to fall in love with him.' I haven't said that out loud to anyone yet and it seems to hit Michelle straight in the feels. She leans over and hugs me. 'But I guess there are plenty more fish in the sea,' I say, trying to backtrack with trite cliché.

'I always hate that saying, you know?' she exclaims, chewing on her muffin. 'There's a crapload of fish in the sea, but do you know how long it can take to catch just the one? It can take a bloody age. And even then, when you've caught one, he can be a slippery old sucker. You could catch a shark and it could bite your bloody leg off. It's a terrible analogy.'

I laugh out loud, a nice feeling radiating through my bones.

'It'll come. True love always comes,' she mutters philosophically.

I giggle. 'I like that. Can we put that on a mug?'

'You filthy mare!' she says, cackling.

She glances around the room, noticing the hoover out. Yes, I also did some light cleaning last night.

'Is there anything you want me to do here?' she enquires.

I doubt she's in the mood to start going through our VAT statements. 'Do we still do penis-shaped soap?' I ask.

'You want to take a shower?' she jokes.

'I thought they'd be nice additions for the favour bags.'

'I can do you one better. We have penis bath bombs, also willy candles. Honey and vanilla, they smell gorgeous. I'll take a look at the stocklists. Has everyone got a penis lollipop too?'

I click my fingers at her. 'You're a genius.'

'I'm not just a pretty face, yeah? I'll give you a hand.'

She rises from her seat as my phone buzzes again. I look down at it.

Hi, can I check if this is the number for Josie Jewell?

I look down at the unfamiliar number. Is this another journalist? A tabloid predator? I've had a few of those emerge since the TV debate. My fingers hover over the buttons. Block or probe?

Yes, it is. Please can I know who this is?

You don't know me. My name is Laila. I think you used to go out with my husband.

I don't have the time for this. Ruby's hen party starts in five hours where I need to meet everyone in a spa. I look like death warmed up so I probably need a nap. I need to wash my hair and change my pants. In terms of time management and priorities, I should not be sitting in this café waiting for my ex-fiancé's wife. As the theme of my heartbreak is to feed it with carbs, I tear away at the cinnamon pastry on my plate. I am in no emotional place to have any of these conversations, I am sleep-deprived and still reeling from what happened with Cameron, but after having a brief conversation with this Laila, there was something in the tone of her voice that brought me here. I think she sounded how I felt, exactly how I felt.

'Josie?' a voice says from behind me.

'Laila?'

I stand, and there's a moment where we both study each other. I don't quite know what to say about the person in front of me. She's not the immaculate wedding or holiday destination Laila I saw in her photos. She's in a camel coat, hoodie and baseball cap, no make-up and visibly quite distressed. I am not such a loon that I came here in my CRAZY IN LOVE tracksuit. No, I asked my PA if I could wear her clothes instead. It's just a quick coffee, I told her. WITH WHO? YOU BLOODY MAD WOMAN! So we traded outfits, just as long as she could tag along and sit in a corner, like some covert spy with a latte and a plastic salad spork in case she needs to stab her on my behalf.

'I am so sorry to do this. Thank you for meeting with me.'

She sits down and takes off her coat. She is very pretty, a different person to me in that I know she has regular haircuts and eyebrow shapings.

'It's a strange thing. I just didn't know who else to ask?' Her tone is desperate, frantic even, and for that one moment, I think I know exactly what she is going to say next. 'It's just... You know my husband, Michael.'

'I knew him as Mike, but yes.'

'I saw you on the television with your mother. With that idiot MP fella. I saw your name and thought, that's her. That's Michael's ex-girlfriend.'

'Is that what this is about?' I ask, worried. She wants an autograph, a business loyalty account? Maybe she's a journalist after an interview.

'No. It's just Michael has... I don't quite know how to say

this. He's gone. He left me a note, two weeks ago. I don't know where he is.'

'What did the note say?' I ask, panicked on her behalf.

'He said he rushed into everything, and he didn't know how to tell me because I was "obsessed" by the wedding. He said the wedding was a "circus". He made me feel bad for it.'

I know that note. I know it word for word.

'I can't believe I'm saying it out loud. He's gone. I can't find him anywhere. Not even to talk about things. I'm devastated. Do you know where he is? Has he been in touch with you?' She starts to sob and a woman at the next table with some carrot cake looks over, giving me evils because it looks like I made her cry.

I offer Laila a napkin and put a hand to her arm. 'No. I haven't seen him since he left me.'

'He couldn't even tell me to my face. We've literally just come back from honeymoon. I am so embarrassed. I haven't been able to tell my family. My dad is going to kill me.'

'I don't think your dad would do that,' I reply, realising I don't really know her dad. 'Mine didn't. I think he wanted to kill *him* more than anything.'

She looks up from the table and takes a sip from the bottle of water in her hand. 'What do you mean?' she asks, wide-eyed. 'He told me you dumped him. That you cheated on him.'

I study her face. 'No. He left. He wrote me a note... He left it on—'

'The fridge?'

I nod. My body stiffens as I realise that his MO hasn't changed one bit. Dump her, make her feel bad for it. 'His story to me was far more dramatic. He was going travelling. He told me he went to Venezuela.'

Laila stares around the coffee shop, looking like she might pass out. 'Oh my god, I am going to be sick,' she says, over-whelmed by the emotion. She keels over and puts her head between her knees. I pat her gently on the back. 'I'm such an idiot,' she announces.

A man steaming milk looks at me. Please calm down, everyone. I am not the person making her cry.

'I believed him, every word. What's even more stupid? I gave him money for some finance start-up. Thousands gone.'

And he stole from her too. I think I want to start crying with her. 'We'd saved money together for a deposit on a house. He took it all.'

We both sit there together, wearing our joint feelings of stupidity.

'I can't believe he did it to you too?' she says, in shock.

I nod. 'His note was harsh, cruel, so I shelved it, I thought it was about him not loving me or being good enough. I feel awful he just jumped to the next person and did the same thing.'

'God, it's not your fault at all. He's a con man. I married a con man. I could kill him. Actually kill him...' she roars, slamming her bottle down. 'How bloody stupid am I to have fallen for that?' she says through gritted teeth.

I put my hand to the air. 'Don't worry. I did too. He was excellent at playing us. Or maybe he's just a king-sized wanker?' I mumble.

She laughs through her tears and the woman with the carrot cake looks less judgemental now. Michelle looks like she's bloody desperate to know what's happening, though. Put the spork down, Michelle.

'Are you OK? What are you going to do?' I ask her.

'Well, he left some stuff. I'm going to burn that. But my dad never liked him. He had a cast-iron prenup in place. I'm just in shock. Now you're telling me all this stuff? I don't know what to think. My dad will literally hunt him down, though. He'll be lucky to still have kneecaps by the end of the week,' she tells me quite calmly.

Your dad is really not like my dad. Sadness and shock are

slowly turning into anger, vengeance. At least you will never think this is because of you, Laila. I hope you never wear those emotions and let them weigh you down. I look down and she's still wearing her wedding band, a pretty hefty engagement ring that she fiddles with.

'I got a message over the weekend to go and collect my wedding dress from the dry-cleaner's. I've still got gifts stacked up in my hallway, for god's sake!'

Her tears are welling up again. I remember that pain, the feeling when I'd realised he'd taken all that money. It was an empty, stabbing feeling that he'd taken even more from me.

'I have many alternative names you can call him. My dad is keen on shitbox. But even that feels too good.'

She blows her nose noisily, half laughing, half crying.

'Never feel bad for trusting someone, Laila. For loving them. It gets better.'

I'm not sure my platitudes are going to work, but it's true, every word. Never change or feel bad for who you are. I've learnt that the hard way in the past few months.

'I'll take your word for it, Josie. I am sorry to have ambushed you like this. You seem really nice. He always made you out to be some bitch...'

'He did?'

'He said you used to steal out of charity boxes and kick cats.'

OK, now I could boil his balls in hot oil while they're still attached to him.

'Well, I don't do that, just in case you were wondering.'

'And all that stuff from the TV, do you really work in the sex toy industry?' she asks me.

'I do.'

'It's just you seem quite...'

'Normal?' I laugh. I always laugh when people say this. They assume I walk around like a grimy fella in a trench coat, flashing it open to reveal it's lined with dildos and lube.

'Are you with someone else now?' she asks me, hopeful.

'No.' I feel a jolt of sadness as I think of Cameron for a moment, fleetingly. 'But hey... one day. It'll come, true love always comes.'

I smirk a little as I say that, looking in Michelle's direction.

'I hope you know why I did this?' Laila continues. 'I just wanted answers. I needed to piece it altogether, to see if you had any information.'

'I wish I'd done the same when it happened to me,' I admit.

Maybe that's my biggest regret in all of this. I just let it happen to me.

'Can I get you another coffee? I am sorry if I ruined your weekend?'

I smile at her and shake my head. 'I'm good. I think you did the very opposite.'

TWENTY

'OMG! HAVE YOU SEEN THE WANGER ON HIM?!'

The lovely Tina is really very drunk this evening and I'm not sure whether to take the drink off her or give her more, such is the entertainment that she is providing. The wanger she refers to belongs to a man called Julius, who tonight is modelling for us, in the nude, as we try to paint him. The wanger is impressive. I hope they've given us enough paint. Around us are many gentlemen wearing thongs, aprons and bow ties, mixing cocktails and serving canapés. It's a running theme for this evening, wanger on teeny-tiny toast.

'I don't even know where to look,' Tina continues, her eyes rolling around her head. I don't know if this is alcohol or that she's trying not to look Julius' appendage in the eye. It's not the sun, Tina. You won't go blind. 'How are you not even flinching?' she asks me.

'Because I'm desensitised to it all. It's like violence and swearing on the television,' I say casually. 'I've seen them all.'

Julius raises an eyebrow to me at this point as I guess that statement could be taken in a number of ways. I've only been with eleven men, Julius. But I've seen dildos, I've seen porn, I've even been in a room with five men, all with erect penises once, stood there with a tape measure to work out whose was the best looking so that we could model our dildos on them. The best belonged to a man called Adam. It was very smooth, sturdy and the length of a healthy cucumber.

'To be fair, I've seen bigger,' Mum adds, not even hesitating. I really do not want to know where, but Julius looks slightly insulted by the comment.

I love how Mum has decided that, to take on this painting challenge, it'll need reading glasses, which she perches on the end of her nose. Her painting is careful, portraying things as accurately as possible. Tina, on the other hand, is so drunk that her painting has taken on more of an abstract Daliesque quality. I don't know if that's a leg or a penis.

I don't usually paint, but I will admit there's a wonderful creative freedom in tonight's activity. I might take this up as a hobby. Maybe landscapes, though, as opposed to trying to work out how to accurately capture the texture of a scrotum.

'Is it OK? Do you think people are having fun, Josie? I don't know if people are having fun?' Ruby suddenly appears next to me, drink in hand. She looks flawless in a scarlet minidress, her usual hair and make-up all styled to perfection.

'You're not painting,' I tell her, sitting there like Picasso. 'Chill out and get some cock on canvas.'

She giggles, cupping her hands to her mouth. Like my brother, who's just come back from Prague for a couple of days, Ruby has also drawn out her hen do celebrations. She took some mates to Barcelona, she's spent all day having afternoon tea and getting spa treatments with assorted grandmothers and aunties and, tonight, she's hired out the top floor of this swanky hotel bar. I hope she's enjoying herself, but as I see her sip nervously from her cocktail and adjust her fake veil, I see a look of panic in her eyes.

'Hey, seriously, Ruby,' I say, putting an arm around her. 'It's really good fun. Relax.'

'The girl behind us... The blonde one...'

I do a very good job of turning quite subtly to take her in. She is blonde, but it's definitely out of the bottle and I'd take bets on her collar and cuffs not matching.

'She's your co-star, isn't she? Doesn't she play your sister?' I ask.

'Yes. But I can't quite get a handle over whether we're friends or not. She's already put half of this evening on her Insta stories.' I see Ruby studying the girl's face, trying to work her out. Like Sonny, she's also twenty-four. They're in a cut-throat business and just trying to work out who to like, who to trust.

'I met two girls you went to school with before, they seem nice?' I say, trying to divert her attention.

'Oh my god, yeah. They're my bridesmaids. Known them since year eight. They were raving about your party bags by the way...'

'Oh, well... That's my pleasure for their pleasure,' I say, thinking of the very excellent sex toys I've put in. 'You know, it's the friends who've been around for years that count. Hang around with them, enjoy yourself. Tonight is about you.'

She comes in to hug me. 'You've always been really nice to me. Thank you. I'm so glad we're going to be sisters.'

It's a drunken hug, but it's welcome. I do like you, Ruby. I like how happy you make my brother and how behind that media personality there is someone who cares. She bought me a hamper at Christmas, not just some random thing ordered off a website but full of my preferred peanut butter, green tea body scrub, my favourite Prosecco, and it was even personalised. I also know it was not from my brother, who is king of the gift card. I hold her close. I especially like how she walked into our very colourful family and didn't flinch at all of the madness.

A waiter comes up to us and offers us some more canapés. I

can see your willy but you're offering me smoked salmon so I don't mind. I down some of my cocktail to go with it.

'While I'm here too, I'm so sorry it didn't work out with Cam. Sonny's been telling me bits and pieces. I never knew whether to say anything.'

As soon as she says Cameron's name, my paintbrush moves on the canvas, so it now looks like Julius has a hammer for a schlong. It's just been one yo-yo of a day from hash browns to my ex-fiancé's wife and now a very in your face hen do. I'm not sure I can process anything else but the way Ruby says Cam feels familiar.

'You knew him? Cameron?' I ask.

'Indirectly. He's good friends with my assistant. It's why he was at the Halloween party.'

I pretend to paint, holding the paintbrush up to the air and closing one eye like I've seen artists do.

'I hadn't realised you two were a thing. I heard bits and bobs off Sonny, but somehow I never worked out that it was Cam. I think I've just been too consumed by the wedding...' she says, her teeth gritted. 'I only realised after that debate thing.'

'How much do you know about him?' I ask.

'Well, he's been through it all,' Ruby continues. Do I stop her? Or do I need to know? 'Him and his girlfriend had his daughter when they were just out of university. And it just didn't work out. He was so broken. It took him a while to get to where they are now. Have you met his daughter?'

I pause for a moment to hear of his relationship trauma, my heart somersaulting with sadness.

'No. He hadn't really told me about her.'

I can't tell if this makes me feel better or worse, the fact that Ruby knew.

'His family don't see the granddaughter. They don't even acknowledge her. My assistant was ready to go to the papers when his crappy dad went on that debate, mouthing off.'

OK. So now I feel doubly worse. It makes me understand why he never said anything. He was protecting her, he didn't want me involved in a messy situation if we weren't really a thing. I think back to the dinner party at his parents' house where his sisters waxed lyrical about their kids and all their achievements and he kept quiet, sitting there like his daughter was a secret.

'So, he supports her alone?'

'In a way. He didn't get to see her on Christmas Day, which was a bit rubbish. But he balances looking after her with work and does his best. He's one of the good guys.'

I swallow as she says that. He is. Where's the naked man with the smoked salmon? I need him now so I can stress-eat through all this emotion. In the corner of my eye, I see Mum stop painting to earwig and look down to her lap. It's just the saddest of stories from all angles and it needed a happier ending, but I guess that's gone now.

'Oh god, I've upset you, haven't I?' Ruby says, worried.

I shake my head. She wasn't to know. It was all shrouded in secrets and misunderstanding. It wasn't even a thing, to be fair. In the greater scheme of things, it was a glorified fling.

'I should have told him about me too, been honest from the start. But when I first met him, I didn't know where it was going... He'd just broken up with Imogen.'

'Oh god, nasty girl. Energy vampire... The one who cheated on him with...'

'His best mate?'

'Yeah, that one. The best mate was renting a room to help with his mortgage and now's he gone...'

And I made everything just that little bit worse.

'Is he OK? He has friends, right? People looking out for him?' I ask.

'He's good. I'm sorry – this is not the conversation to be having on a night like this. I've drunk too much already.'

'No, it's good to know. Thank you, Ruby.' I look up at her very symmetrical and very smooth face. We need to talk about your skincare regime because when I'm drunk, I don't look like that. I look like I've just run a marathon in the rain. She gives me a final hug before I get back to my painting and notice Tina and Mum staring at me.

'Don't,' I tell them.

'It's very sad,' Mum says. 'He was a single dad, on his own…'

'Mum, I am at that level of drunk now that if I think any more about it, I will cry and you'll have to spend the rest of the evening consoling me and it will spoil my painting. Please. No.'

Mum nods and pretends to get back to her penis painting.

'But maybe you could chat to him. Explain…' Tina slurs.

I shake my head. Julius looks over at all three of us. The mood has changed to solemn and pensive, which makes him doubt himself and his assets. It's not you, Julius. You and your penis are great. Another half-naked man comes over with shots. I take two and down them in quick succession, burning the lining of my throat all the way down to my chest, my heart.

'It's a hen do. I don't want to talk about this.'

'But—'

'The only butt we should be talking about is that man's over there.' I signal over to the bar, trying to distract them.

They both swing their heads round. Tina drops a paint-brush. Someone needs a wax.

'Please… This evening is about Ruby and… penises, so let's not talk about that now. Let's…'

But before I can suggest what we should be talking about, some music starts up. That's Ginuwine's 'Pony'. That song is like the soundtrack to my working life. I think we used it on a TV ad once. I can't dance to this. I need me some disco. However, it turns out these waiters also have side hustles in Magic Miking. Even Julius. Hey, I wasn't done painting you yet! They all get up and there's a lot of gyration, a sound over the bass that sounds like flesh slapping flesh. There is a lot of screaming and hollering, not least from Tina, a wolf whistle from my mother. Please don't encourage that young man, Mother. Too late. He's straddling you. Another one of them is dry-humping my future sister-in-law.

'You wanna piece of me?' a man says, bending over so his crack is in my line of sight. 'You can cash in a dance?' He hands me a strange credit card. PAYS FOR ONE LAP DANCE. 'You just swipe it through my cheeks,' he explains. Oh god, no. I'd rather go contactless if that's OK. I smirk. He doesn't seem to care and twerks in my face regardless.

My mother looks over, nodding, urging me to get involved. This will make you forget. Just snog one of these naked men and let him dangle his dong in front of you. The art of distraction. This man's ass is still here. What am I supposed to do? Caress it like a melon? He is helping to an extent, though. I am laughing. A phone on the easel in front of me gets my attention and I pat the butt cheeks in my face to tell this lovely man he's relieved of duty. He shrugs and walks away, heads over to Ruby's mum, who looks like she may faint.

'Hello?' I say, answering the call from the unknown number.

'Shit, Josie – is that you? Where are you? It sounds a bit loud there.'

'Sonny? I'm at Ruby's hen. Aren't you on your stag?'

'I was. I need your help. I'm calling you from a stranger's phone.'

'Oh. Where's your phone?'

'Who bloody knows... I'm in London. I think. This kid is telling me we're in Wapping.'

'Where exactly are you?'

'I'm handcuffed to a lamp post. Can you come and get me? Don't tell Mum?'

. . .

'I think it's round the corner, mate. Nearly there.'

The London taxi driver looks at me curiously, wondering what I'm all about. I'm dressed up in a red spangly dress like Tina Turner (ruby red, it was a hen night with a theme), I'm at that point in my night where the make-up hasn't gone to pot and not that drunk that I'm off-balance but why have I made him stop off at a retail park just outside of East London so I could buy a travel rug and some bolt cutters? I look down at my phone. I persuaded Angelo, the kid whose phone Sonny borrowed, to stay with him and got him to pin his location so I could find where they are.

'I think that's them,' the cabbie says, chortling. 'I see why you made me stop at Wickes now.'

On the corner of the street is Sonny, handcuffed, chained and totally stark naked, bar a puffa and what looks like a pitbull and a blow-up doll keeping him warm.

'It's his stag, the bloody idiot. He needs better friends.'

Is he OK? The scene doesn't look great. It's Sonny surrounded by a group of teens in head-to-toe black trackies and puffa coats, all in those stages where their facial hair looks like they're growing pubes on their faces.

'I have a crowbar in the back if you want me to get it out?' the cabbie asks, but I put a hand to the air. Surely they would have killed him by now if that was their intention. Unless they're waiting for me to watch.

'I'll shout if I need reinforcements,' I say, opening the door.

'I'll keep the engine running in case I need to make a quick getaway,' he mentions, looking like this might be the most excitement he's ever had as a cabbie.

I stroll over, trying to push my shoulders back so I look reasonably confident. Yep, I'm cool.

'You Josie?' one of the lads says in East London tones.

Sonny sees me and visibly sighs with relief.

'I am... Angelo?'

Angelo cocks his head up to me, standing there in just a jumper and throwing some sort of hand signal up to me. ''Sup.'

'Is that your coat?' I ask. 'Please take it back, you must be freezing.'

Angelo pretends he's not. 'Not as cold as him, though...'

I hand the young man his coat and throw the travel rug over Sonny, tag still on, trying to shield my eyes so I don't see too much. I've seen enough wang tonight.

Sonny's teeth are chattering and I rub his arms to try to warm him up.

'Maaaaaattte... Angelo, lads. Thank you,' Sonny says. 'All you lads, you're bloody lifesavers.'

They all do their head cocking action. I know Sonny is likeable, but it would seem there is no threat here. In the way that he does, my brother seems to have talked them round, amassing a small team of hype men in the process. Even the dog likes him as he's snuggled into his lap. I get the bolt cutters out of the plastic bag and pull the cardboard packaging off it. The lads step back.

'We thought he was a right wrong 'un when we saw him there and then we realised who he was,' says one of the lads. I'm lucky that we didn't get the aggressive machete-wielding sorts walking past this lamp post, but I'm also grateful that this lot just didn't take photos, put them on Snapchat and leave. 'He's that G from the TV and my sister is mad in love with him.'

I look down at Sonny.

'I told them I'd let them have some selfies and leave his sister a message if they let me use his coat and borrow his phone,' he says to me.

I nod, just glad they didn't blackmail him out of money and bodily organs. I open and close the bolt cutters. 'Well, boys, I have it from here. You are all bloody stars. Your mothers should be very proud.'

That was maybe not the coolest thing to say, but it's a

comment that leaves them beaming as they all cock their heads to me again and fist-bump my brother before they go.

'Come on, Titus. Leave him, don't sniff him there.' Titus is the dog. He looks like he was bred in hell, so I don't attempt to pet him. Yes, Titus. Please don't sniff there. Don't eat my face.

Titus trots off with his owner as the lads all disappear into the night, waving as they go. Stay out of trouble, kids.

'You absolute plank,' I say, launching a hug at him as soon as they're out of sight.

'Thank god. I nearly crapped myself when I first saw them coming for me,' he says, jogging on the spot to try to keep warm. 'It's flipping lucky they were nice enough lads.'

'Well, we more than anyone should not be judging people on their appearances,' I say, laughing. Whoever did this used a flipping padlock. And drew boobs on his chest in what looks like Sharpie. The blow-up doll looks traumatised.

'How do you know how to work those?' he asks me as I cut the chains off him and set him free.

'We actually have a disclaimer section on our website that tells people how to free themselves from stuff if they find themselves in a tight spot. You'll be surprised the number of people who lose handcuff keys.' I unravel him and wrap the blanket around his icy cold skin.

'What happened? Where's Brett? Dad? Ruby's brother? Did they do this to you? This feels very old-school stag do. You're lucky they didn't go after your eyebrows.'

He agrees, shivering uncontrollably. 'We ended up at some mad rooftop party. I was so drunk. I lost everyone and then I got bundled in a van. I bet this was that berk from that film I worked on. I don't even know where my stuff is. My phone, they didn't tattoo my face, did they?'

I think he may be crying, but his body is too cold to actually produce the tears.

'I thought you were going axe-throwing and for teppanya-ki?' I tell him.

'Oh, we got too drunk to chuck axes, so we went to adventure golf. Then we got thrown out of that because someone tried to stick their willy in a golf hole.'

I really hope that someone wasn't our father.

'A drunken odyssey through London then...' I root around in my giant tote and find a beanie. It's not even mine; someone I once knew left it in there after a cinema date. I sigh and put it over my brother's head. 'Have you eaten?'

'Angelo and his mates were on their way back from KFC. We may have shared some hot wings.'

I laugh, my breath clouding the air. Only Sonny would get chained to a lamp post naked and be able to blag food off some kids.

'You look so nice. I'm sorry I spoiled your evening...' he cries, pouting.

'Well, I couldn't leave you here, could I? Why me, though? Why call me?' I enquire, wondering why none of his ushers, mates or his own father could have assisted.

'You're my sister. Yours is the only number I know by heart. It's the same one you've had since you were at school.'

I shake my head as I lead him into the waiting taxi, dragging Keeley the blow-up doll by her feet, remembering a time I had to collect Sonny from Reading because he fell asleep on a train, another time where I picked him up from a phone box when a melodramatic girlfriend threw him out without any shoes. The fact is I know his number too, it's one of those things imprinted into my brain.

'Well, I'm glad you called. It was starting to get messy at Ruby's.' Messy because the magic stripper men had just got out the squirty cream, but he doesn't need to know the details.

'I'm glad. Is she having fun?' he asks.

'I think so. I like her.'

'Good. I don't think I could marry someone you didn't like.'

As he sits back in the taxi, I take off my coat and wrap it around his feet. What is the stage where someone can get frostbite and lose digits? That wouldn't be a good look a few weeks before a wedding. That might lose him his magazine deal.

'Heat's on max, love,' the taxi driver shouts from the front. 'Let's get him warmed up. Is he all right? Do I need to make a hospital stop?'

I shake my head. The cabbie arches his eyebrows as he sees Sonny's face in the rear-view mirror.

'Aren't you that fella from—'

'Yep,' I say, watching him, hoping he doesn't get a phone out.

'Well, it's not a good stag if something ridiculous like this doesn't happen,' the cabbie jokes.

'True,' I say, turning to Sonny. 'But what if those lads hadn't found you? What if it had been a gang of hooligans with knives? What if no one found you? It's supposed to be -1 tonight. You could have died! Alone!'

The blow-up doll looks at me, offended. The cabbie studies the panic in my tone and face as I half shout at my younger brother, even though his face is a light shade of sky blue.

'It's good his sister found him then, eh?' the cabbie tells me.

Sonny nods, still on defrost.

'Let's get him somewhere safe... Where to, kids?'

'You all right headed down Wandsworth way?'

'Sure thing, love.'

TWENTY-ONE

'Get in, you bloody donkeys,' Nan says, as soon as she sees Sonny wrapped up in a tartan travel rug, nothing on his feet and still slightly blue around the gills. 'Whose crapping idea was that?'

'The rug or the lamp post?' I ask as I push him through the door into Nan's flat.

Sonny scampers in and heads for a sofa as our grandmother watches with some level of admiration that I'm casually just holding a pair of bolt cutters to my side like some gangland boss bitch.

'Both? And who's she?' Nan asks. In my fatigued, frozen state, I think she's talking about me. I'm your granddaughter, Nan. Josie. But then I realise she's talking about the blow-up doll. We really should deflate her, she's a faff to carry around and her hair is all matted like a wet dog.

'This is Keeley, Nan. She's Sonny's new bird.'

'I don't like the looks she's giving me,' she laughs. 'I've put the water on if you want a bath, Son? What about some tea? I don't have any clothes for you, so you'll just have to wear my house coat, wrap yourself in towels and hot-water bottles.'

Sonny doesn't talk but scampers next to Nan's portable storage heater and holds his hands out, putting on some of her woolly socks and gloves.

'I'll take a tea?' I say, following Nan into the kitchen. I like how she's still got her curlers in. 'Sorry for waking you up. It's just your place is closer. I didn't want to traipse him through the hotel I was staying at.'

'Don't be stupid.' She opens the cupboard and gets some biscuits out. Jam sandwich creams. Yes, Nan. 'Anyway, you and me need to have words.'

'About?' I ask. I'm also a tad cold so put my hands close to the warming kettle to heat them up.

'I was on Instagram. How come I didn't get an invite to this party you were at? How come I got stuck with the afternoon tea element of the hen do?'

'I don't think your heart would have taken it, Nan,' I tell her.

'I am the mother of a porn star, you silly bint. You had me at The Grosvenor with all the elderly aunties sipping Darjeeling and listing to all the medications they're on. Boring as hell.'

I dig through my handbag as she pours hot water over a couple of mugs on the counter. Did we keep Nan away to protect the strippers? Maybe.

'Here, don't be sad. You can have some treats,' I tell her, finding some favours at the bottom of my handbag. 'It's all penis-shaped, I'm afraid. These are bath bombs, smell them, they're lovely.'

Does my nan stick a penis up her nose and smell it like a Vicks inhaler? Yes, she does.

'What do you mean bomb? Does it explode? Is this going to aggravate my dermatitis?'

'When it hits the water, it foams up. I use them, they're very skin-kind. Here's some other bits. I'd mind that lollipop on your teeth, though.'

I empty my handbag onto her kitchen counter. She picks up the four-inch lollipop.

'Reminds me of someone I once dated,' she says, cackling.

'Nan!' I shriek. 'Do you want rubbers too?'

'Well, I'm not getting pregnant at my age, am I? You silly mare. I thought you worked in sex, have you not worked that out yet?'

I narrow my eyes at her. 'Do you know where the highest rising incidence of sexually transmitted diseases are these days? Older adults. I don't know who you're sharing a bed with on your bingo jollies, but I don't want you getting the clap.'

'You cheeky bird!'

She doesn't deny it, though, and I don't want to think too hard about that. I grab the mugs and bring them into the living room, stopping for a moment to see the balcony, the place I once stood with Cameron, the sofa we snoozed on. Damn it. Such is the problem with recent break-ups, everything becomes a trigger. Next time I see someone with chickenpox, I'm sure my eyes will glaze over.

'You all right, you're not going to throw up, are you?' Nan asks me, wondering if I'm a bit merry and taking pause to keep myself from vomiting.

'Nah. Just, it's been a long week, a long month.'

'Well, put your feet up, love,' she tells me.

As I put the mugs down, I notice Sonny has gone down the solid insulation route, lying on the floor rolled up in about three duvets. I hand him a hot-water bottle and some tea, trying to locate his arms.

'How's it going in there? Do I need to set up IV fluids?' Nan asks.

'No... Hello, Nan,' he says, his face poking through like a glow-worm.

'Hello, you stupid sod. Do you want me to heat up some soup? I have cream of tomato?' she tells me.

'Nah, I'm good. Just keep the tea coming.'

She bends down with a small bottle of brandy and pours him a measure too, nudging it in his direction.

'Get this down you too. I guess the positive of all of this is that you're both safe here with me. Instagram tells me your dad is making a royal tit of himself in some bar.'

She gets her phone out of her nightie pocket and adjusts her glasses, scrolling through to show me a picture Dad has posted where he's wearing stag horns and drinking a yard of ale without a top on.

'That's just poor parenting that is, Nan,' I say.

'Oh, knob off,' she says, flashing me a toothless smile.

I curl my legs up on the sofa and gaze at the television, thinking about films I saw late into the night with a spotty Cameron's head rested on my lap, running my hands through his curly hair. Double damn. Maybe this wasn't the best idea. Maybe I should go back to the hen do and run a credit card in between someone's butt cheeks.

'So, what was the goss this evening? What did I miss?' Nan asks.

'I painted a penis.'

'Why would anyone put paint on a willy?' she asks me.

'No, I painted it on canvas. I'm going to give it to you on your birthday.'

'Lovely. I'll save it for my bedroom.'

I see the covers quaking as Sonny laughs from underneath them.

'Everyone was there... It was fun,' I say, not very enthusiastically.

'Yeah, I was thinking you looked bloody ecstatic.' She studies my face. 'You still mourning over that Harry Styles lookalike from Christmas, the one who got the pox all over my flat?'

'Nan!' a voice pipes up from the sausage roll duvet.

'You were the one who invited him over!' I protest. 'Anyway, I got the place steam-cleaned for you after he stayed here. I wiped everything down.'

'And there was me thinking the worst thing you were going to do was have sex on my sofa,' she grumbles.

'How did you get Cameron's number, by the way?' I ask Nan.

'I slid into his DMs. That's what you young buggers say, isn't it?'

Sonny can't stop laughing.

'Why did you tell him to come round?' I ask her.

She takes my hand in hers. 'Because you were all sad and he made you happy. I hadn't seen anyone make you glow the way he did.' I take a big gulp of tea to let that sink in. 'I'm sorry that didn't work out, love. I liked him. Kindness in his eyes. Your Ruby has that too, Sonny. I tell you, that's where I went wrong with men, I went for the twinkle. Never go for the twinkle, it's bloody naughty and devious. Go for the kind ones, the good ones. We don't raise them people up high enough.'

I sigh because I felt that kindness shine off him too. 'Is what it is. Some things aren't meant to be. It's fine. Anyway,' I say, kicking Sonny from under my feet, 'you didn't tell me Ruby vaguely knew him.'

'Ruby knows a lot of people,' he mumbles, oblivious. 'She has like two million followers, I don't know who's real and who's not.'

'What did she know about him?' Nan asks.

'She knew he had a kid. I didn't know as much.' Nan's eyes widen to hear the news. 'She's five years old. Her name is Erin. He's a single dad.'

Nan nods her head. 'I knew I liked him, that we had something in common. And he never told you about this Erin?'

I shake my head. 'To protect her, maybe? We both hid things from each other, Nan.'

'I was never comfortable with you lying to him about who you were. Lies like that are not good.'

'She says! You were the one who told him you were a show-girl!' I exclaim.

'Because it was funny,' she says, trying to defend herself. 'Lying's never the way, though.'

'But maybe we lie for a number of reasons. Dad never told you he was in porn, for example.'

Sonny's head perks up at this point. 'Yeah, Josie told me this story. How the hell did you believe he was a plumber the whole time?' He laughs and Nan kicks him with her slippers.

'I just thought he was earning good money. Plumbing and porn, that's where the money's at apparently.'

'You never had your suspicions?' I ask her, huddling in to listen, a feeling of nostalgia to be sitting here taking in her stories. We used to do this all the time over a big tub of broken biscuits. We'd tuck in by this same storage heater and listen intently to her tales about living in this big city on her own.

'Oh, he was a good-looking lad. I thought he was getting lots of action, popular with the birds. You don't question these things.'

'So, what did you do when you found out?' Sonny asks.

She pauses for a moment to try to recollect the emotion. 'You know what hurt me the most is that he had no pride in it. There was shame, guilt attached to it. And that's not right, you know? These things go full circle, don't they? Back in my day, I was a single mum and there was stigma attached to that. That I'd failed or not done right. Back then, people pointed their fingers and spoke about you in whispers for all sorts. Your sexuality, the colour of your skin. You hid away because it wasn't the norm and for that you lose all sense of pride in yourself, in who you are. That's an awful way to live.'

I know her words are directed at me and I know she's right.

'And I will always be proud of what your dad went on to do,

I love your mum like my own. And not because they did well, you know? Because they're good sorts. And you two make me proud as bloody punch. I'll never stop talking about you two. I don't just let any old reprobates into my house at midnight and put on the kettle.'

I put an arm around her shoulder when she says that. I know she talks about us to everyone. I know because the neighbours, the man in the local corner shop and the drug dealers in the stairwell seem to know me by name. She even keeps a dodgy school photo of Sonny and I on her mantlepiece, straight out of our awkward teen years, Sonny with braces, me with a constellation of acne, standing proud in its brown faux-leather frame.

'Have you always been single, though, Nan?' Sonny asks. 'After Grandad left?'

'He's not your grandfather. He never earned that right,' she says, scolding him. 'You can call him Dick Features.'

We won't, but that's good to know that he has an official name.

'Oh, I dated all sorts. I tried, but when you're a single parent, it's hard. Your kid becomes the priority.'

I think of Cameron as she says that and look down to my lap.

'I dated some bloke who used to play jazz trumpet. Huge mouth, that one. You know that butcher's on the high street? I dated one of their sons once.'

'What was his meat like?' Sonny asks.

Nan kicks him quite hard. If he does have any frostbite, then that kick may have taken his toes off. I've always remembered Nan as single, not recalling any gentleman callers or companions, but I've never seen it get to her, I've never heard her say the word lonely. I do wonder if she was scarred by the man who was our grandfather or whether she just preferred it that way.

'There's a man at the bingo I quite like, I think he's sweet on me. His name is Wesley. I don't like his walk, though.'

'How can you not like someone's walk?' I ask curiously.

'He's bloody slow. I can't deal with dawdling walkers.'

'Do you want to bring him to the wedding as your plus-one?' Sonny asks her.

'No way. He'll get ideas. Plus, we need to talk about weddings. What's this about me having to wear black? I'll look like Queen Victoria in mourning.'

'It's Ruby's vision. Just go with it.'

'And that red tracksuit? I'm expected to wear that too?' she asks.

I nod. If I have to, then you have to. We can be ridiculous-looking twinsies together.

'Well, then, I want front-row action for the ceremony, any further back and I'll make a fuss.'

She's not wrong. I'll add that to my jobs list to keep her on a leash. Nan takes an extra loud slurp of tea given she's not got her teeth in. I glance down at Sonny and the colour is back in his cheeks. I do worry how we're going to get him out of here, though. I'll have to run out and buy him clothes or dress him in one of Nan's old nighties. Maybe he can borrow that tracksuit temporarily.

'How's all that wedding stuff going by the way?' Nan asks.

'I've been reading love poetry this week, Nan. I had to write down all the love songs I know,' he says, flaring his nostrils at me. It was an important exercise so he could get in touch with all his emotions. 'But Josie is on it.'

'Of course your sister is on it.' She looks over and winks at me. 'If she'd been at your stag, she wouldn't have let you get chained to a lamp post.'

This is true. 'Should we text Dad? Brett? Let them know you're safe?' I ask.

'Or not. Let the wankers worry for a bit. They should have

been looking out for you,' Nan says.

'I like that idea,' says Sonny. 'It also gives me a breather from all of it. It's been intense. They all just want to drink till it comes out of our eyeballs and I don't think my liver can take much more. What did you tell everyone at Ruby's do? Where do they think you are?'

'In my room with a headache.'

'So basically, you should be painting the town red with your manfriends and you should be handling some stripper's willy like a pepper grinder, but instead, you're here with your old nan. You couple of sad cases.'

We both burst into laughter. Nan doesn't look like she's too upset by this, though. Because I guess we're not little kids anymore that she can pick up at the school gate and take on the buses. We grew up, real life got in the way. I can't remember the last time we spent some time with her that wasn't a birthday or special occasion or popping by to help her move furniture. We haven't been together here for an age. There is something warming about it.

'You want to do something fun? I've got cards? We can play Shithead? Your blow-up mate can join in.'

I look over to Keeley, she's pulled a puncture and her head lolls over to one side. Sonny, however, looks ready for a card game and gathers his duvets and sits up. Now, Shithead I remember. Nan used to come on holiday with us and we used to play this after dinner. Nan always cheated, just like she does at Scrabble. I've never met someone more competitive.

'Also, if we leave the sliding door open, you can get a hit of the downstairs neighbours' weed.'

Sonny leans over, laughing, trying to get comfortable. 'Stag do of dreams.'

'Too bloody right. Now pour me some brandy, and sit with your legs together, boy. I'm your grandmother, put the jewels away for fuck's sake.'

TWENTY-TWO

There are many good things about today. It's one of those icy-cold days where spring is waiting around the corner but affording us a preview of blue skies and sunshine, a spot I developed from my post-trauma addiction to fast food has since subsided and, well, today is Valentine's Day. That is an especially good business day for The Love Shack, it's an excuse to buy cut-out lingerie and introduce new treats to the bedroom. But this wonderful day will now always have new meaning: it will forever be the day my little brother got married.

Today is all about the love. And what I am most in love with? Well, whoever decided that my bridesmaid dress should come with pockets. Hurrah to that person, these are the sorts that deserve all the awards in my opinion. The pockets are good because today I have important duties so I need to be prepared. Dog poo bags and treats in one pocket, Maoams and ceremony reading in the other. Today, I am here to wrangle, I am here to maid of honour for my life.

'Josie, come here and tell me if this girl's made me look like a raccoon?' Nan says in the make-up chair.

Speaking of wrangling. Nan is not dressed up yet. She's still in her tracksuit but accessorised to the hilt, so she looks like a Mafioso-style grandmother, who ironically would have a son called Fabio. She's the one who gives the orders and sleeps with a shotgun, live in fear of that one.

'It's a dusky eye, Nan. It's nice.'

'If I cry, will it end up halfway down my cheeks?' she asks the girl.

'All waterproof,' she tells her.

Nan doesn't look so sure.

I look to my watch. 'Nan, we've got to get a wriggle on. We need you downstairs and in position in half an hour.'

Nan nods, giving me a hint of side-eye. The reason it's taken her so long to get ready is that she's taken full advantage of a long weekend in a country house hotel. Turns out she's already done a round of aquarobics and stayed the full length of time for the buffet breakfast. That's four hours of bacon, eggs and pastries. Her dress had better still fit.

I usher the make-up girl out and go over to the dress hanging on the wardrobe. We've gone with 1950s tea dress, a suitable heel. I watch as she takes off her tracksuit to reveal some mildly exotic underwear underneath. It's a matching tangerine set, a full knicker and a very pretty full cupped bra.

'Nan, I like the knickers.'

'M&S. I thought I'd splash out.'

'Is it because Sonny invited Wesley later?'

More side-eye. He got an invite only because we're all nosy as hell. 'It's because my only grandson is getting married, you cheeky bint. I wanted to look nice. Now help me step into this.' She puts on a slip, tights, and I unzip the dress and pull it over her. It has a lovely detail to the sleeve and a jacket to go over it. 'Do I look like a president's wife?' she asks me.

'Yes, one who's engaged in all the right scandals, though,' I say, smiling as we study each other in the mirror.

'You look very very pretty by the way. Not tomatoey in any way.'

I swish about in my dress, hands in my pockets. I won't lie, there's a touch of drama to it that makes me feel elegant, though if people could look in the pockets, they'd probably feel differently.

The door suddenly opens, revealing Mum and Dad. Damn, tissues. I should have brought more tissues because they have spent most of the day just seeing things and crying. *These are the orders of service, Dad.* Crying. *Mum, this is your buttonhole.* Tears. When they see Nan and I standing there, it starts again.

'Oh my... I can't even...' Dad sobs.

'Pull yourself together, man,' Nan jokes with him. 'Don't we all scrub up well?'

Mum has gone fishtail, a lovely full-length dress with a fur stole and a pillbox hat, Dad traditional tux with velvet lapels, expertly fitted by Mr Li. Next to Mum's feet stands Dave, not really knowing what the hell is going on and why he's got a bow tie attached to his collar. But yes, we do all scrub up well, even the pooch.

The door left ajar, I spot Tina wearing the exact same dress as me. Her boys storm into the room to see us, colliding with my dad, who lifts Vinnie into the air. Oh my days, they're in little tuxedos with red Converse. My heart might just burst. Dad is still crying.

'Why are you sad, Uncle Johnny?' asks Vinnie, wiping tears from his cheeks.

'I'm not sad, I'm happy. It's all my favourite people together. And you look brilliant, Vincenzo...'

'Sometimes people cry when they're happy,' Tina explains. 'It's a strange thing.'

'I cried on the day you were born. We were relieved that you were safe and healthy,' Mum explains to Xander, straightening out his bow tie. It's a scene that brings a tear to the harshest cynic's eye. That eye would be Nan's. I really should have packed more tissues.

'Well, shall we? You OK, Josie?' Dad says, his mother and wife on each arm.

I nod. Everyone in here needs to go and take their seats and Tina is best woman so needs to go and find a groom. I salute as everyone air-kisses and leaves, the boys being given strict instructions to behave.

'I'm cacking it, Josie,' Tina whispers into my ear.

'You'll be amazing,' I tell her. 'We have dresses with pockets. Nothing can go wrong.'

She laughs and we wave them all off, leaving me in charge of twins and a dog.

'OK, troops. Let's stand to attention!' I say as the door closes. The boys listen, the dog less so. This is not a good cocktail for today, so much can go wrong and I'm wearing heels. But I have supplies. 'Have you been practising your walk?'

They nod.

'Are there a lot of people?' Xander asks me.

Only about a hundred, but just don't look them in the eye. 'A few. Just remember, your mum will be at the end of the aisle so just focus on her. Don't lose the rings. Where are the rings?'

Both boys pat at pockets in their waistcoats. I'm glad we ditched the pillows. That would have been something else to carry.

'That's good. Keep them there. I need to get my bouquet, come with me? You want to see the bride?'

They nod excitedly as I lock our room door and head down the corridor. Dave, check, room key, check, two little ring-bearers, check. I head to a door at the end and knock tentatively as the boys go in and show their faces.

'OH MY GOD, THEY'RE SO BLOOODY CUTE!' someone shrieks. That someone is Ruby's first cousin, Clara, who I think has been drunk since last night. Vinnie runs for cover by my legs. Another bridesmaid comes over and picks up Dave, who is also not sure. Please don't kiss me on the mouth, lady. I don't know where you've been.

It's a sea of red as Ruby has not just me on her squad but an actual army of bridesmaids, from cousins to schoolfriends to co-stars. I filter through the crowd of girls, going to town with the hairspray and lip gloss, to find Ruby at a window. If Ruby wanted the big fairytale wedding dress, then she's got it. It's a fitted bodice with spaghetti straps, the skirt just layers of lace, tulle and white feathers. She looks like a confection of sorts, make-up artists sprinkling icing sugar over her, a photographer snapping away in the corner. When she sees me, she comes over for a quick embrace.

'Oh my god, Vinnie and Xander – you look amazing.'

Both boys cling to me for dear life. Don't lose the dog, otherwise you'll have to crawl on the floor looking for him under people's skirts.

Ruby takes a long cleansing breath. 'Oh my god, it's so busy. Is everything OK?'

'I've just sent my parents, Nan and Tina down. Are your parents all right?' I ask.

'I think I've lost my dad. He's here somewhere. Did you hear about the swans?'

Swans were hired for the day to swim in the lake in front of the country house. The swans then realised they didn't like the lake and pissed off somewhere else.

'We found the swans.'

Dad and I found the swans. We herded them into the back of his car and got them into the lake using scraps of toast from breakfast. I hold Ruby's hand and smile. Oh my, she's so beautiful, but my nan is right. There is something that shines out of her eyes that speaks kindness.

'And all those other things were sorted. The drinks delivery threw a flat tyre, that was why it was late, but that's all sorted, your Uncle Ron isn't lost on the A34 anymore *and* we found some vegan alternatives for your little brother for the dessert.'

Ricky apparently is politically opposed to the farming of coconuts now and made a stand. I am not sure what sort of sibling would do that before his own sister's wedding, but the kitchen are making him a fruit salad later that I hope will be ninety per cent grapes with seeds. I know it's all sorted because, unlike Nan, I got up this morning with my spreadsheets and made sure this day went to plan. I don't have a headset, but I've had four coffees and Google Maps, so Uncle Ron is now downstairs, hopefully suited and booted and waiting for the ceremony to start.

'I don't know what to say, Josie... You're amazing.'

A dog barks in my general vicinity. Thank you, Dave.

'Just... Enjoy.'

The dog barks again. Oh dear. That wasn't Dave telling me he thinks I'm amazing. I know that wincing, whiny bark. Seriously, Dave? Is it a number one or two? Why have we not trained you to tell us yet?

'Ruby, I need to...' I say, wriggling my finger about.

'Yes... Do. I love you, thank you!'

I don't worry too much about Ruby as she has her red army around her, but I grab my bouquet. Dog, check. Ring-bearers. Crap, where did they go? 'Vinnie? Xander?' I find them gawping at a screen where someone has put on *Dirty Dancing*. Cover your eyes, lads. I don't think you need to watch that scene just yet and don't copy those moves later. 'Boys, come with me. Have you got your rings?' They both put a thumbs up at me. 'Right, I need one of you to hold a bouquet? Can you do that?' They nod again. I give them the flowers and we head down the corridor.

'Josie!' It's Ricky Reynolds coming out of his bedroom, in a tux and still that smug, unlikeable grin about him. You gave me extra work this morning, this means I don't like you. 'You look amazing!'

'Thank you... So do you? I sorted your coconut crisis thing...' I say, trotting along in my heels, the boys and dog by my side.

'You absolute star. Dance later, surely?'

'Of course!' I sing sweetly, not wanting to cause any friction, but if we're being honest, I'd rather spend the evening dancing with Dave. We keep moving.

'We still there, boys?' I call out.

'Yep, who was he?' Xander asks, turning to look at him.

'Ruby's brother.'

'Is he your boyfriend?'

'Yucks, no way...'

Vinnie laughs. 'Why are we running?'

'Because I think Dave needs to do a wee.'

'I think I need a wee too,' Vinnie says.

Crap. OK. Sod pockets, I need a dress with an extra pair of hands. I should have carried a phone. We head down a staircase to an empty reception as people seem to be milling around, directing guests. Brett is an usher today, he should be around, but he's nowhere to be seen.

'Right, boys... Outside.' They follow reluctantly. 'How you feeling, Vinnie? Can you hold it?'

He jiggles on the spot. I'm going to take that as a no.

Yikes. The car park outside is full and I slip in between two cars, parked at angles that hide us from view of the main house, a glorious vision in ivy and columns. The sort of place an Austen heroine would cavort with a brooding, horse-mounted suitor called Jonquil. I'm now going to taint this scene with a grumpy urinating dog. I glare down at Dave. Come on, you little muttface. Do your thing.

'Aunty Josie,' Vinnie says, swaying.

I'm not qualified to do these things. I also don't want to run into the ceremony room and announce that a kid needs a wee, or bring him in sodden. That's not a good look. Or smell.

'Vinnie... Have you ever had an adventure wee?' I ask him.

'No,' he replies, looking a little apprehensive.

'It's basically an outside wee.'

'We do those in the park sometimes.'

I do them at outdoor festivals, but I won't tell them about that now. 'Excellent.'

'Dave is doing a wee,' Xander says, giggling.

I look down and let out a sigh of relief that it wasn't near my dress or on the carpet of a posh country house. Dave looks at me nonchalantly and I toss him one of the treats in my pocket. Just don't poo during the ceremony. Do that now if you must.

'You want me to wee like that?' Vinnie asks me.

I chuckle. With your leg cocked like that? 'No. Let me help with your trousers and just pee in that hedge. I won't tell anyone. How's your aim? Don't pee on your shoes.'

'Do the shakey-shakey like Dad always tells us to do,' Xander tells his brother. He helps him with his trousers and I see them turn their backs to me. Please don't pee down your tuxedo.

'This is fun. Are you going to do an adventure wee too, Aunty Josie?'

I giggle. 'I'm good.' I notice the car we're squatted behind has a bumper sticker about the injustice of dairy farming. Oh. I think I know who this car belongs to. 'Here, lads, maybe pee more towards the car so no one sees you.'

Vinnie changes the angle of his stream over Ruby's brother's tyres. I look away, smirking.

'Are you done?'

I turn and Xander is helping him with his trousers again. I bend down, hitching up my skirt so it doesn't hang around the wee-soaked gravel. I tuck his shirt back in and help him straighten himself.

'Thank you, Aunty Josie,' he tells me and leans over to kiss my cheek.

'It's cool, shawty,' I reply, smoothing over his hair. I hope this place doesn't have CCTV.

'Do I get a treat too, like Dave?' he asks.

'Hell, why not,' I say, reaching into my pockets and getting out the sweets. 'You get one too for helping your brother. I'm going to have one as well.' Even though it will ruin my lipstick, I think we all need the sugar at this very moment. Dave, have another treat. Let's go wild.

'I think I peed because I'm nervous,' Vinnie says.

'Don't be. I got you. Let's shake it out. When I have to do an important presentation, I sometimes just shake my whole body.'

We stand there on the gravel and wriggle all that nervous energy out, the boys giggling.

'Shall we?' I say and they both jump up and down.

We jog over to the house, where we're not too late. The bridesmaids and Ruby are waiting to enter the ceremony room. We made it. It's cool. I didn't just squat between two cars so my charges could dispense their bladders and down sweets.

Ruby searches the area for me and I wave. She waves back. Let's go get you guys married. A door opens and Rick Astley starts up. There is a routine, that's heavy on a shimmy and thrusting, but I did not sign up for that. That's for her bridesmaids. I'll hold the dog.

Inside, I can see people laughing, clapping, dancing. I'm holding two little hands, a bouquet and Dave. The logistics of this have not worked in my favour, but at least we have each other. It's time for us. Xander dances to applause, his brother just waves to all. Dave still has no bloody idea. Those are some moves, Dad. Nan winks at me. At the end of the aisle is my little brother. No feathers, no kilt, just a black tuxedo where the trousers are maybe two inches too short. We smile at each other. Look at you, Sonny. My heart has never felt such pride.

I deliver the boys to their parents, hand over the dog to my mother and stand, waiting for the bride to enter. It is a magical moment to see her appear, gliding down that aisle. Everyone holds their breath as she gets to Sonny, a look in his eyes that he is enraptured, blissfully happy.

'Ladies and gentlemen, welcome,' says the celebrant. 'We are here today to celebrate this wonderful day, a day to bring these two magnificent people, Sonny and Ruby, together in matrimony. But before we start, I believe the maid of honour and the groom's sister, Josie, will be reading out a poem. Josie?'

I leave my bouquet on a chair and reach into my pocket. That's not a poem. That's a poo bag. Don't pull that out. I pull out a piece of paper and head towards the lectern and microphone. Vinnie had a point. I should have had a wee. This is a lot of people. But people I love. Friends, family, colleagues. It's also not a poem, it's Ed Sheeran lyrics. But before I reach the lectern, Sonny intervenes.

'Umm, don't read that out. Here, I wrote something for you...'

I react with a huge open mouth. Sonny, I practised Ed Sheeran in the mirror and printed it out in a font size that I knew would lend itself to public speaking. You are killing me here. What is this? I hope you haven't given me a limerick. I'm not reading out Nicki Minaj either.

'Please... I'm sorry...' he says, smiling at me.

I will have to get my revenge later, find a naked baby picture to project onto a wall. I walk up to the lectern and open the folded piece of paper, hoping he's spellchecked this.

'This poem is by Sonny.'

I clear my throat. All I taste are Maoams and panic. I smile at the first line.

> *'One day, I asked my sister about love songs,*
> *So we started to compile quite the list.*

We managed to get to seventy-five,
I am sure there are some we'll have missed.

Love can be endless, bleeding and burning,
"You Can't Hurry Love"... that's true.
You can be "Crazy in Love", "Addicted to Love",
And "I... Will Always Love You".

"Will You Still Love Me Tomorrow?"
"Can You Feel the Love Tonight?"
"Where is the Love?"
"Who Do You Love?"
"My Love",
"Love at First Sight".

It's a "Crazy Little Thing Called Love",
"Love On Top",
"Love is in the Air",
"All You Need is Love",
"Love Me Tender",
"All in Love is Fair"...'

I take a deep breath and the crowd laugh.

'"How Deep is Your Love?"
"Make Me Feel Your Love",
"Baby, I Love Your Way",
"I Want to Know What Love Is",
"As Long As You Love Me",
I'd better stop or we'll be here all day.

Maybe love is just a song looping,
Where you know all the words, every beat,
A melody as sweet as the sun itself,

That'll make you dance, make you fly, down the
    street.
A magic rhythm, a pulse that flows and soars,
That makes all other sounds melt far away,
It really is everything. It is enough.
A love song to keep, to repeat, to play.'

I sigh as I say the last line, a tear rolls down my cheek. Don't, Josie. Mum and Dad look over at me and are gone. We are all gone. I scoop the tears up with my fingers. I really should have brought extra tissues. Sonny looks up at me and beams. You idiot.

'You forgot "Love Shack". Amateur.'

The whole room roars with laughter. Let's get this wedding started.

TWENTY-THREE

'That is a snazzy suit,' I say, a green crayon in my hand as I help Vinnie colour in the book he has at his table. I made all the kids little party bags and they've gone down a treat. Even with my limited knowledge of children, I know that they go batshit crazy for bubbles, stickers and colouring. We've gone for broke with this colouring page, the groom to the centre has a patchwork suit of about five different colours and the bride is a wonderful shade of cyan, which means she might be part-Smurf.

I know you shouldn't wallflower at a wedding, but this current situation suits me to the ground. Thank god lovely Vinnie is here to act as my date for the evening, to allow me to sit down and not dance all night. I'll leave that to Mum, who's taken off her shoes and lost her fur stole. On the dance floor now, Xander steps on her feet and they rotate adorably. Dad is by the bar. He's on the shots and buying tequila for many people, so there will be Cossack dancing tonight and I am taking bets that he will have to wear a knee brace tomorrow. Don't talk to me about Nan because she had some personality change when Wesley arrived and went slightly googly-eyed at the sight of him in a very fetching tweed suit. They danced and now I can't see them. In my head, I hope this means they went on a moonlit promenade around this nice country house. In reality, I think she bought that tangerine lingerie set for different reasons.

However, it is a joy to see Sonny and Ruby enjoying themselves. After we sampled some of Sonny's poetry and I ugly-cried in front of the group, the ceremony had us all under its spell. It was always going to be emotional, but the words never fail to cement it for me. *To have and to hold.* It just makes me picture two people intertwined together, in an embrace. Like a love pretzel. That's a nice cosy way to be for an eternity at least.

Since then, it's been a whirlwind of food, speeches, tears and one of Ruby's bridesmaid's boobs falling out of her dress. This is why God invented tit tape and this is why I had a ruck-sack under my table at the wedding breakfast for such occasions. She can now twerk the night away without fear of boob spillage.

Sonny and Ruby are on the dance floor now, arms around each other and singing to one another under the pastel flashing lights. Did they change outfits? Of course they did. Is there a strong Baz Luhrmann *Romeo + Juliet* vibe with feathers and a breastplate? Yes, but look how bloody happy they are. I haven't seen much of them today, but I didn't anticipate I would, it's their day. I only hugged Sonny the once when he was doing the rounds at the breakfast. I got a chance to tell him he sucked at poetry, he told me the blade of beef was an inspired choice.

'What are those two people doing?' Vinnie asks, as I scan the room.

I look over to the dance floor and there is a couple who are getting slightly over-amorous. I guess it is a wedding and the sparkling beverages have been flowing since early afternoon. It's one of Ruby's bridesmaids and Ruby's brother, which takes a weight off my shoulders as it means I've been relieved of that duty. He is very handsy, though, and he needs to remember there are children in the room.

'They're dancing.'

'Is that how you dance? It's not how Aunty Susie and Xander are dancing, or Mummy and Daddy.'

I catch sight of Vinnie's parents and toss my head back in laughter. Tonight, Brett and Tina have officially clocked off. Their duties are over, the childcare is in healthy supply and all they have to do is crawl upstairs at the end of the night. It's time to throw it down and from the looks of it, sing along to ABBA's 'Voulez-Vous' quite vocally, hanging off each other and baying to the ceiling. Super Troupers, the both of them.

'Dance is whatever you want it to be. You not keen?'

'No, I went on there before and that lady over there nearly fell on me.'

He points over to Michelle. Gorgeous Michelle, who's maybe in a dress that's two inches too short for a wedding but, by god, she's going for it. Keep the legs down, girl, or I'll be able to see your wedding breakfast. She sees me looking and waves with both hands, beckoning me onto the dance floor. I signal that I'm otherwise committed. Colouring is my bag at the moment.

I feel something bumping into my ankles and see Dave at the foot of my chair. I have to dog-sit too. I let him sit on my lap and Vinnie gives him a pat on the head. Thank you, lads, for looking after me tonight. I break a bit of wedding cake icing off and let Dave have a nibble.

'Don't tell Aunty Susie,' I say, winking at Vinnie.

He smiles. 'Aunty JoJo, why aren't you married?' he asks me.

To be fair, he's not the first person who's asked me this evening. I've had the odd person come up and ask if I have a boyfriend. Some have gestured that it's my turn next. Others have looked at me a little pitifully, like Sonny getting married first broke some unwritten rule. These are the people who I've made sure got their food last.

'Oh, I'm just waiting for the right person, Vinnie. I haven't found anyone who wants to marry me.'

He colours in the groom's shoes pink. 'Well, you should want to marry them too,' he says casually. 'When I'm older and you haven't found anyone yet, I'll marry you.'

I'm not sure how legal that will be, but I lean over and kiss him on the forehead.

'Who would you like to marry? If you could marry someone famous?' he asks me.

'I don't know what you mean.'

'Like out of all the Avengers, who would you marry? All of them are very hunky. Mum says she likes Thor.'

'Don't we all, Vinnie. I guess Hulk is cute. Bit angry, though. And the same colour of broccoli.' This makes Vinnie giggle uncontrollably. Please don't pee yourself. God, that sound is a tonic.

We keep colouring as the music suddenly changes. Is it sad that I know the playlist tonight? I told the DJ to keep it to disco classics and I vetoed the list. No modern dance anthems that will make us feel like we're in Ibiza. The Bee Gees for days. I now watch as the crowd of people wait to hear for the bass change to see if it's time to scream in joy and keep dancing or return to their drinks. There's a roll of drums as a synth kicks in. Someone yells and breaks into a strange dance like they need an exorcism. Really? This is not a wedding song nor was it on the authorised playlist. I guess Sonny and Ruby did get engaged on Halloween, but it feels a little cruel. It's the *Ghostbusters* theme song. Vinnie's ears prick up.

'What is this song? It's funny,' he says.

'It's from a film. A very good film. I'll watch it with you when you're older. It's a bit scary. But there's a character called Slimer that I think you'll like.'

He starts to move his shoulders and I chair dance with him, Dave jumping down from my lap, scared by the motion.

'There used to be a special dance to this song,' I say, jumping up. 'It from the credits of the cartoon. You shoot up your fingers like this and then put your heel out.'

I may lose my cool points for this, but the giggles continue so I keep doing it. It's not co-ordinated and I pull faces as I do it, but I guess it beats bursting into tears.

'I saw that cartoon too.'

As soon as I hear those words, that voice, I stop dancing and freeze.

No.

You're here. You're here? Did he see that? I can't quite breathe. I turn around. Yep, you're here. *Cameron.* You're at my brother's wedding? You're in a suit. Beside him, a little girl holds his hand and hides behind his arm. He looks at me and I feel every bit of breath leave me, feeling completely weightless, shocked. Say something.

'Hey.'

'Hey.'

He stands there smiling. I don't know what else to say.

'Are you Josie?' the little girl asks.

I snap out of my spell and smile, bending down to her level.

'I am. It's good to meet you.' I put my hand out and she shakes it. 'You must be Erin?'

She nods her head, she's dressed in a sparkly rose tulle dress, little ballet shoes on her feet. A big mass of curly black hair and her father's blue eyes. Hey, Erin. I can imagine an event like this is a lot to take in, but fear not, I have crayons.

'I like your dress,' she tells me.

'I like yours. You don't think I look like a tomato?'

She giggles. 'Is that your dog?'

Dave goes and sniffs her ankles. 'He's my mum's. His name is Dave.' She bends down to pet him. I can't look up. I can't believe he's here.

From behind them, I see my mum and dad approaching.

'Cameron, you made it,' Mum says, going into air-kiss him.

What? You. You did this. He's here. He's not supposed to be here. But he is. Next to me. Maybe where he's always supposed to have been.

Dad shakes his hand but pulls him in for a hug.

'Good to see you, Johnny!' he tells Dad, who smiles widely in response. He knows his name isn't Fabio at least.

Mum bends down to say hello to Erin.

'Well, kiddies,' she says. 'You never heard this from me, but I hear there's going to be candyfloss in a minute, shall we go and find it?'

Mum puts a hand out to Erin whilst Vinnie takes a piggy-back off Dad. Cameron looks shocked as Erin just leaves his side so easily. That's what my mum does. She blows me a kiss and they all walk away.

'There's candyfloss?' he asks.

'There is. And a retro sweet bar and ice cream and a fish and chip van outside.'

You're here, you're here, you're here. I need to be cool. Don't list the wedding extras. I also don't need to be pulling a face like I'm trying to work out algebra.

'Just saying... You're the prettiest tomato I've ever seen,' Cameron says, his face rising to a blush. 'I also see that they're playing our song, I may have made a request.' His fingers point into the air.

I laugh but still can't seem to find the words, the breath, to even think straight. He's here. He's in a suit with his white

Converse, the lights of the room bouncing off his messy hair. Standing here. With me.

'You also look very... dapper,' I say. 'Bit disappointed you didn't come in your Ghostbusters costume, though. The one thing this wedding is missing is a proton pack.'

His face lights up, the way he does when he's really happy. 'I'll take dapper.'

'Did my parents invite you?' I ask.

He smiles broadly. 'Oh, I've had about fifty invites to this thing. Your PA Michelle, your nan, your mum, your dad, your brother, your new sister, the best woman. I've been bombarded with messages about you. Begging me to give you another chance.'

If Sonny's dodgy poetry didn't set me off before, this certainly does, because the once very busy dance floor has stopped and a crowd of people look over, trying not to stare but all looking hopeful, the bride and groom included. It's a conspiracy. What did you all do?

'You have quite the fan club, Josie Jewell. And I'll be frank, I'm a little scared of your nan.' He looks over and waves at them. Everyone pretends to go back to their disco side steps. Is that Nan? She's back? How does she know the *Ghostbusters* song dance?

'They did that?' My lip trembling.

'If ever you need a reference, you have the best people in your life. You are so loved. It blew me away. I think so many people just want you to be happy, they feel you put so much into other people and never yourself.'

I look down to the floor as he says that, almost unable to accept the compliment.

'And then your mum and dad invited Erin and I out for lunch, to explain, to chat.' I jolt to hear it, they had lunch?

Looking across, I see Mum has sat Erin up on a bar area and together they share a massive stick of candyfloss, some secret joke. I think back to a hen do where she heard Cameron's story and how heavy that would have made her heart. Even he looks over now and there's emotion to see his daughter treated so sweetly by an almost stranger.

'Your parents told me everything. About Mike? They explained that was why you weren't straight with me.'

I intervene immediately. 'I am so sorry if I hurt you by lying to you. That was never my intention,' I say, twisting my lips around.

'I think I get that now. You were just scared I wouldn't get it. It's a unique thing.'

'It's kinda weird.'

'No, what's weird is that you thought it would make me like you any less.'

His blue eyes smile at me, hopeful.

'You liked me?'

'Very much so. You're pretty cool. Scrap that, you're really fucking cool.' A smile creeps across my face as he digs his trainer into the floor. 'Maybe we need to start again. My name is Cameron. It's really nice to meet you. I design video games, I have a five-year-old daughter and my dad's a bit of a dick.'

I don't disagree with him.

'Josie Jewell. My brother is Sonny, that bloke over there,' I say, pointing over to the groom. He waves. There is a herd of people there, all waving, all watching. Josie is in the ring. The next move is crucial. No more side-stepping. 'My parents used to be in the adult film industry and I now work for The Love Shack, which means I'm very good at selling vibrators.'

He can't quite keep his smirks to himself. 'Now you've said it like that, I think I understand why you didn't tell me. Do you have that on business cards?' he jokes.

'I should.'

'Are they good vibrators?'

'Award-winning and in many different colours, shapes and

sizes, depending on what the young gentleman may be in the market for.'

'You're very good. Well, Miss Josie Jewell. It's a pleasure to meet you.'

'The pleasure is all mine.'

He puts a hand out and as soon as our fingers touch, he wraps his fingers around mine, a thumb lightly stroking the circle of my palm. This was all I ever wanted, really. To have him close to me and have that feeling, that magic spark, just skipping down my veins forever.

'Can I kiss you?' he asks.

I stop for a moment, his face looking panicked to have asked first, to have got in the way of the spontaneity of the moment. Yes. Please.

'I mean, I want to. I like you. I've always liked you, but I also feel like if I don't, then the dancefloor will start booing me—'

I don't give him a chance to talk anymore. I go in, cupping his chin, and kiss him. He beams. It is everything. The way his lip catches mine, the feeling of our bodies entwined, together. I'd like to say it makes all other sound melt away, but there's a collective cheer from the dance floor, like someone has just won a fight. The killer shot, the knockout, the crowd go wild. Cameron backs away from me and rests his forehead against mine. You're here. I just stay there in his arms, to let him hold me for a moment. Maybe longer.

Over his shoulder, I sense the protective gaze of everyone just looking on. The newlywed couple hold drinks to the air like trophies, Brett and Tina embrace, Nan fist-pumping, what feels like the whole working staff at The Love Shack in a collective shimmy, Dad's tears, Mum carrying her new little best friend. It's a moment of love in every sense of the word, and I couldn't be prouder to have them as a part of my life. That has always been everything.

'Can I ask a favour?' Cameron whispers.

'Uh-huh.'

'Please can this really be our song?'

I knock my head back in laughter as the disco lights catch his face. I have a dance to teach you. You'd better be ready.

'Sure thing, Spengler. Sure thing.'

A LETTER FROM KRISTEN

Dear lovely reader,

Hello, there! You're bloody marvellous! Thank you from the bottom of my heart for reading my book. And if you're new – where the hell have you been all my life? It's a pleasure to meet you. I'm Kristen!

If you want to keep up to date with all my latest releases, you can sign up at the following link. Your email address will never be shared and you can unsubscribe at any time.

www.bookouture.com/kristen-bailey

I hope *Great Sexpectations* lived up to expectation? If you came here looking for a sexy Dickens rewrite then I apologise, but I hope what you read instead provided plenty of escape and giggles, and that you've fallen in love with Josie, Cameron and her family. I hope it also made you log on to your sex toy website/shop of choice and treat yourself. If not, why not? Go for it. If you are a long-time reader and, dare I say it, fan, I also hope you enjoyed the references to the Callaghan Sisters series. Did you spot them? It's a Kristen Bailey literary universe where everyone knows each other, and I'll keep that going for as long as people are reading. Captain Mintcake forever!

I never thought I'd write a proper romantic comedy. I'm far too cynical for all of that, but I must say, it was a joy to write this, to introduce you all to Josie and Cameron and put a bit of joy, hope and spark into the world. I think I said it in my last letter to my readers, but I also believe in lots of different types of love too, not just romance. So I hope what you also got from this story was how much love there was in the Jewell family, how Josie was loved by so many different people, how much she loved them, how she deserved love. I hope, good reader, you have love in your life in many different forms.

For a book with only one sex scene, I also hope the subject matter made you laugh rather than blush. Did I do my research? Of course I did! Vegan condoms are a thing, in case you thought I made it up. And there are some BIG dildos out there. Ones that made me gasp (just from looking at them, I should add...). But there were other subjects in this book that I hope made you think: sex education, sex positivity, about having pride in who you are and what you do. I have four kids and I like how the landscape is changing in this way: that I can have honest conversations with them about their bodies, their sexuality, their responsibilities. I remember it being very different when I was little. I think for years I believed in the stork story and then later believed I could get pregnant from kissing. I hope we can keep pushing things in the right way so words like sex stop people blushing because, to quote the lovely Josie Jewell, sex should also be about pleasure, self-love, connection. I also hope, good reader, that you have all of that in your life too. If not, seriously... sex toys. I've done the research like any good author. Let me know if you need any recommendations.

I'd be thrilled to hear from any of my readers, whether it be with reviews, questions or just to say hello. If you like retweets from Fesshole, then follow me on Twitter. Have a gander at Instagram, my Facebook author page and website too for updates, ramblings and to learn more about me. Like, share and follow away – it'd be much appreciated.

And if you enjoyed *Great Sexpectations* then I would be overjoyed if you could leave me a review on either Amazon or

GoodReads to let people know. It's a brilliant way to reach out to new readers. And don't just stop there, tell everyone you know on social media, gift the book to your mates, send to all on your contacts list. I mean it, even your nan...

With much love and gratitude,

Kristen xx

www.kristenbaileywrites.com

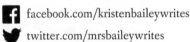 facebook.com/kristenbaileywrites

twitter.com/mrsbaileywrites

instagram.com/kristenbaileywrites

ACKNOWLEDGEMENTS

Christina Demosthenous. For as long as I write, I will keep shouting that name from the rooftops because you're just the bestest editor there is. We went in a different direction with this book and I wasn't sure I was going to be able to write it – I thought I was too jaded, too old, too married, but you convinced me otherwise. You make me believe in the process, you've almost let me believe I'm funny. Thank you for that magic thing you do that allows me to grow and flourish as a writer.

That said, Bookouture is full of magic people like you. Sarah Hardy, Jade Craddock, Becca Allen, Mandy Kullar, Iulia Teodorescu, Abigail Hardiman and all the team who work their book wizardry, turning my scrappy manuscripts into books. My eternal thanks for your energy, enthusiasm and hard work.

My acknowledgements for this one are going to be semi-brief because at the time of writing, I kept my circle small, I just got on with it. Sometimes I write with a crowd and draw inspiration from everyone, sometimes I lock myself in a cave and write like a mofo. This was one of those times. So this is me acknowledging me, well done you for getting on with it and not getting distracted by box sets and biscuits. Thank you to anyone who also provided the soundtrack to the writing of this book, but it was mostly Tom Misch. I don't know you, Tom, but *Geography* is just perfection.

As I've said before, I wasn't sure I had a romcom in me. I've been married for nearly fifteen years. Not to take anything away from my wonderful husband, but we don't do long protracted snogs anymore. We're too tired a lot of the time. So, my research involved watching every romantic comedy from the nineties and beyond. Thank you the nineties for your sterling efforts in this film genre. Thank you for reminding me about sparks and meet-cutes and Kate Hudson's yellow dress from *How To Lose A Guy In Ten Days*. Yeah, it's all a bit convenient and corny, but don't those films just make you glow? In a time when we all could do with more feel-good, love and happy endings, it was the best research I've ever done. I recommend it. I also watched box sets for days. We'll thank three weeks of COVID for that. Thanks to *Sex and the City* for the title inspo. Thank you *New Girl* for the hottest first kiss I've ever seen (Jess & Nick > Ross & Rachel... don't fight me on this...) and Joey and Pacey for reminding me why I was in love with Joshua Jackson for a decade. Whatever, I'm still in love with him.

I also did some research on Lovehoney and watched a hella lot of documentaries on porn, sex toys, etc. I learned a lot, too much sometimes, but if my hours of viewing taught me anything, it's that behind these industries are people and we really are sometimes too quick to judge those who work within them. Thank you for reminding me that behind the sex and the comedy that I'm trying to write there are human people there who deserve our respect.

There are spades of film references in this book and that is mostly down to my teen years where I did spend a lot of time in front of the television, buying *Empire* magazine and sneaking into the Cineworld in Feltham. I shared this passion with my brother and sister, Jon and Leanne, so thank you to them for all the shared laughs along the way. I love how we still quote things decades later, and that if I told you to do the *Ghostbusters* cartoon dance, you would jump up, we would do it together and all our kids would die of the shame.

I've mentioned the husband and I'll mention him again. Thank you for loving me and letting me write and when I say that, I mean thank you for letting me run into the next room, allowing the dinner to burn because I've thought of a way to resolve chapter eleven. In the evenings, thank you for bringing me tea and joking about my tippy-tappies. We are more Susie and Johnny than Josie and Cameron, but I like that very much.

Kids, kids, kids. Thank you for making me laugh every single day. You are the reason I don't lose my mind which is strange for a mother of four to say, but you ground me, you calm me, you allow me to wear many hats. My mum hat will always be my favourite, though.

Sara Hafeez. You are now in my book, you are a TV doctor, and in my mind, you have Sesame Street-style puppets and ALL the children love you. Think of the merch! I'd buy that merch! Thank you for all your friendship and love over the years.

To all the book bloggers and Insta book people who show me such wonderful support. You are at the heart of the writing community and thank you for all the tremendous work you do for us authors.

And here are all the other random people who just are there and have inspired, supported, liked and recommended. You know what you do, I owe you all a pint: Will Simpson, Graham Price, Drew Davies, Elizabeth Neep, Jo Lovett-Turner, Javier Fernandez Perez, the Lovedays, Luke Travis, James Burgon, Adam Bogdan, Nikki Clayton, Helen Williams, Barry Paul and Mum, who told me about sex when I was eleven years old. I still have that book you gave me. I still haven't read it all.

CPSIA information can be obtained
at www.ICGtesting.com
Printed in the USA
BVHW070909250722
642935BV00009B/160

9 781803 144788